WEDDED CHAOS

TINA SAXON

Cover design by: Y'all That Graphic
Edited by: My Brother's Editor
Proofreading by: From Beginning To The End

CHAPTER 1

GRACYN

"Gray, stop!"

I hold my fist in the air, flicking my middle finger straight up. He probably thinks I'm saying he's number one. *Number one asshole.* I'm so over this. I don't need this bullshit. Especially from that joker.

"Oh, that's professional," he shouts over the music behind me.

That's rich coming from him, considering his hand was just squeezing my ass, offering a quickie in his office. I turn but keep walking backward. "It only needs to be professional if I'm actually working here. And I'm not, since I quit."

"You can't quit." His eyes plead with me as fear sobers him up enough to realize the colossal mistake he made. He starts to panic. "I'm sorry. I fucked up."

"That we can agree on. And yes, I can. I just did." I glance around the bar one last time, irritated it's come down to this. Four years, a million drinks served, enough tips to put me through college on my own, and memories that'll last my life-time, all coming to an abrupt halt because of this schmuck.

Talk about a buzzkill.

The time I had left here was short-lived, anyway. I'd already cut back to working weekends since this semester was entirely student teaching, and graduation is a few weeks away. And as my mother reminds me daily, *I'll need to get a real job.* Which was always the plan. Waitress to elementary school teacher. I've had a lot of practice dealing with juvenile people. Those single-digit kids should be a breeze.

But this is not how I wanted to go.

"Where you goin', Gray?" Rory asks from behind the bar, his gaze jumping from me to Justin, who's following me like a puppy, begging me to stay.

A sly grin plays on my features, savoring the panic in Justin's voice. It's that vindictive streak I inherited from my Italian heritage, one that I owe to my dad's side of the family. A trait that only comes out when my temper flares, which is rare. Were it not for my light olive skin and dark brown locks, nobody would accept I'm half Italian. With my green eyes, freckles, and a mismatch of European ancestry on the other half, it's obvious I take more after my mom.

"I'm going out to celebrate my retirement."

His bushy black brows furrow. My friend knows I would never quit like this. "What happened?" he barks at Justin, readying himself to jump over the bar.

"Nothing," he clips, holding his hands up. Minutes ago, Justin assumed nobody could touch him, and he would've made sure Rory knew that. *Not now.* Not when I've yanked his power-hungry tongue out of his mouth.

I stare at him and blink.

"It was a misunderstanding. I thought you were Lissa."

What the actual hell?

I take a step forward, getting close to his face, my smile disappearing. "Is that right? So, you're saying that would've been appropriate if it had been Lissa?" Total scumbag.

"Oh, um..." He stumbles through his response. *Careful, Justin, you're about to make things worse.* He rakes his hand over his jaw. "Please, Gray, don't make this something it's not." His voice loses all its steam as he hangs his head.

"But it is *something.*"

Power.

I have it.

I don't like it, but I'll use it if I have to.

I have the voice that hangs between a life and death sentence. I'm not proud of it. Actually, I've run from it my entire life. But right now, at this moment, it's making me feel invincible.

"I'll do anything," he continues to plead.

I'm sure you will.

"Quit."

"But—"

"No. That's the only option." I straighten his black tie and pat it down over his heaving chest. "Or I'll tell the boss you sexually assaulted me."

He cracks his neck and then yanks out a phone from his pocket. "Fine! I'll quit."

A delicious sense of satisfaction warms my heart. I suppose enduring the unwanted advances and shameless propositions was all worth it, considering how much I hate the guy. It was a mistake to hire him from the start, with his crooked smile and those piercing, beady orbs that sent chills down my spine whenever they fixated on me. I watch him storm off to his office, the walls quivering as he slams the door shut behind him. This is probably the highlight of my career, right here.

How things have quickly changed.

"I guess that means you're back?" Rory leans back against the bar, his thick, tattooed arms folded over his chest with amusement in his blue eyes.

Twisting my lips, I seriously think about it. It would be nice to be free the last few weeks of my college days and do whatever floats my boat without any responsibility.

"Nope." I blow him a kiss and wink. "Tell Ray he's welcome. And he should give you the manager's job."

"DAUGHTER OF MINE, what happened this afternoon?" Ray barks out on the other end of the line. Shit. Why didn't I have the forethought to come up with a story *before* I answered his call? "Why on the same day did my club manager *and* daughter quit?"

"Coincidence?" I squeak out, tugging Charli to stop while I worm my way out of this mess without creating a bloodbath. We move to the side of a building, letting by the rush of tourists walking the Strip.

"Not likely," he deadpans.

If he wasn't already aware of my disdain for Justin, this would be an easier sell.

"Listen, all you need to know is I did you a favor. I took out the trash, and while doing so, I quit. We both win. You and Mom have wanted me to quit since the day I started."

My father owns four hotels on the Vegas Strip, but you'd be

hard pressed to find a place around here that he doesn't control, one way or another. Even some of the metro cops are on his payroll. All except one person, *my stepfather.* Chief Judge Bart Carmichael. My mom went out of her way to find the exact opposite of Ray when she married Bart. She single-handedly started a war with me smack in the middle. My name is fitting. The area between black and white. Good and evil.

Gray.

Then they made it more complicated. As if it wasn't bad enough.

Bart adopted me when I was three. It was my mom's way of cutting Ray out completely. I grew up calling Bart "Dad" and Ray by his name. Even though I found out he was my real dad when I was eight, it's stayed that way. I'm like the worst-kept secret of Vegas. Everyone knows.

"I don't like being kept in the dark, Gracyn. You know I'll find out."

I recall the dark corner table Justin had settled into. No witnesses. I should have known he was up to something when he called me over there. The club was still prepping to open for the night. It was early.

"Ray, please let it go. Nothing happened I couldn't handle myself."

He sighs. "I don't like letting things go unresolved. They always find a way back."

I squeeze my eyelids shut. This is why I should leave the power trips to him.

"But I'll let it be. *This time.*"

Not giving him a chance to change his mind, I say bye with a quick "love you" and hang up. We jump in between two large groups, and I let out a long sigh.

"That was intense. I need coffee," Charli says, yanking me into the café as we almost pass it.

As if *she* needs a reason.

"How was that intense for you?"

"Oh, I felt every syllable that man said. He's scary."

I don't argue with her. He is quite intimidating. "You should look into caffeine addiction. Maybe you need an intervention," I joke, following her to the line. I'm pretty sure brown sludge from coffee fills her veins.

As we wait for her drink, she purrs next to me. "Wow. He looks like a delicious cup of ice cream. Rocky road with a sinful drizzle of caramel."

I giggle and glance up from my phone, and my attention lands on a gorgeous male specimen, and I hum in agreement.

"Wonder if he works somewhere like Chippendales? I'd pay to see him undress," she boasts.

I nod. He fits the part. Dressed in an expensive pair of dark jeans with a snug-fitted black T-shirt that beautifully contours his broad shoulders and strains against his powerful biceps, he's a man who prioritizes personal fitness. He leans casually against the wall, engrossed in his phone, ignoring the admiring stares from every woman in the room.

The barista calls out Charli's name, and she grabs her coffee and moans while taking her first sip. I shake my head. If I had coffee at eight at night, I'd still be awake at eight in the morning.

"Ready?" she asks.

My attention is drawn back to the guy, and I find myself studying him. No ring, brown hair, square jaw that's accentuated by his perfectly trimmed short beard. Definitely older than me. He glances at the counter to see if his order is up. I catch his light brown eyes right before they return to his phone.

"Brooks," the barista calls out.

He looks up again and pushes off the wall, heading toward us. Well, to his drink, but we're standing a foot away from it. I don't know what comes over me. What comes over my hand as I reach out and wrap my fingers around his hot drink. Immediately, I pull the lid to my lips and take a drink as if I'm going to get a taste of him. Charli's eyes are wide in shock when I wink at her, swallowing the bitter black coffee.

"Um, excuse me..." the man's deep and rich voice says behind me. "I think you have my drink."

Holy hell, his voice is even more manly than he is, and hearing it takes the edge off choosing to drink plain black coffee.

I whip around, and our eyes lock in a moment that makes me forget how to speak. Which never happens. His warm, piercing gaze is almost too much to handle, with the most striking green outline surrounding his hazel eyes—*not brown*. As he stands next to me, I realize that he's taller than I expected, an entire head length, at least. He looks down at me with a lifted brow in amusement, as if he's already figured out that I'm playing some kind of game.

"Do I? I'm sorry." *Definitely not sorry*. I bite my lip as I hold the drink out for him.

His eyes drop to my lips, subtle yet unmistakable. He shakes his head. "You can have it. I'll just wait for yours. What's your name?"

Charli snickers to my right, and I elbow her, keeping my attention on him.

"Gray."

One side of his lips rises, forming a crooked smile in amusement.

I playfully grin. "Yeah, yeah. I've already heard it all. I bet you're about to ask me which shade of gray?"

"That's not at all what I was going to say." He leans in close to my ear, and the mixture of soap and woodsy scent invades my senses. "I was going to say gray is my favorite color."

Goose bumps prickle my skin. He takes a step back with a wicked grin as I swallow hard.

Oh dear. I didn't expect that.

I clear my throat and hold up his drink. "Well, thanks."

"My pleasure."

If he's offering pleasures, I could think of a better one than bitter coffee.

Charli taps my hip and nods toward the door. It figures, the one time I want to stay and continue flirting with a stranger, I have somewhere to be. I let out a resigned sigh and flash him one last lingering smile before heading toward the door. There's something about him that has piqued my curiosity, and I'm tempted to change my plans for the night. But it's *my* party.

As I reach to push the door open and before I can walk out, he asks, "So what kind of girly drink am I getting?"

A devilish chuckle escapes as I push on the door. Just before stepping out, I say over my shoulder with a wide smile, "I didn't order one."

His laugh follows me out.

I fan my face as we step out into the busy Strip, heading toward Planet Hollywood. I've flirted with a million guys, but that was an adrenaline rush that I can't explain. My heart beats fast against my chest, and my cheeks hurt from smiling.

"Girl. I can't believe you stole that guy's drink."

I can't either.

"You should've invited him to go out with us."

"He made it hard for me to think. Damn, he was gorgeous."

"Thanks. The feeling is mutual."

My heart stops full tilt at the voice behind us. I slowly spin around. Heat washes over me as he overheard us talking about him. The Vegas heat isn't helping either. And it's only May 3rd. He looks at the drink in my hand. The one sip of black coffee was enough to give me a buzz. Definitely could attribute to the racing heart.

"Is that it? *That* was your play? Stealing my coffee and leaving?" he asks.

I gesture between us. "Nope. This is my play," I say, quick thinking. I didn't expect him to come after me, so this is turning out better than I imagined.

He nods with an amused grin. "Ah. Hook, line, and sinker. In that case, come to a party tonight with me." He pulls out a black leather wallet.

"Where's it at?"

I don't have to party *all night* with my girlfriends, right?

"Apex." Reaching into his wallet, he pulls out his business card and hands it to me. It's then I notice how big his hands are. Jesus. The things he could do with those. Some girls need muscles. I need large hands. Granted, he has both, so it's a win-win for me. "Text me when you get there. We're in VIP, so I can come and get you."

I press my lips together at his assumption that I'm for sure going or that I can't get in without his help. Nevertheless, I'm intrigued. VIP at Apex is hard to get into. It's the playground of the rich and famous, where the paparazzi congregate outside and wait to snap pictures. So, the burning question is, who is this guy?

Rich or famous?

With a nod, I reply, "Thanks." I glance down at his card to read his name and notice he's the CEO of a marketing company in New York. *Nice.* "Brooks Handley, maybe I'll see you later."

He walks backward. "Well, *one shade of Gray*, you owe me a drink." He flashes a panty-soaking smile and turns, disappearing into the crowded sidewalk. My day keeps getting better and better.

"Happy retirement to you," Charli teases.

CHAPTER 2

BROOKS

I'm lost in thought, still preoccupied with the fiery brunette from earlier, when the server stares expectantly at me, waiting for my order. I glance down at the menu, realizing that I've been holding onto it for a good five minutes without even reading it. All I can think about is her perfume still lingering in my nose. Trying to refocus, I quickly blurt out the first thing that comes to mind. *A hamburger.*

The server leaves, and Jared tents his fingers in front of him, his expression curious. "A hamburger? Since when do you order a hamburger at a steak restaurant? Where's your head at?"

That's a good question. The coffee-stealing thief has hijacked my thoughts since I walked away from her, and I can't seem to focus on anything else other than that intoxicating scent and the image of her luscious lips.

"Gray."

His brows furrow. "What's Gray?"

More like, *who* is Gray?

I've had women pull all kinds of stunts to get my attention, so her little tactic wasn't as surprising as she might have thought. Original, I'll give her that. One thing is for sure, the green-eyed, brunette beauty definitely grabbed hold of my attention.

And still hasn't let go.

"Some woman I met tonight at the coffee shop. Invited her to the party."

His head jerks in my direction. "Asshole, it's my bachelor party. Unless she's a stripper, why are you inviting a woman?"

"What the hell does it matter? We'll be at a nightclub, not a fucking poker game. And I'm sure there'll be plenty of women around us. Who cares if it's one I invited?"

I'm in Vegas for one weekend.

No responsibilities.

No judgments.

No rules.

What happens in Vegas stays in Vegas.

And I hope Gray happens.

DINNER WAS ONLY a couple of floors below the club. As we pass the long line of people waiting to get in, I scan it, searching. Hoping. But when we make it to the front, I swallow my disappointment. I flick my wrist to glance at the time. Eleven.

It's still early, Brooks. Calm down, killer.

She'll be here. Especially when she sees I'm CEO of one of the largest marketing firms in North America. A quick internet search and she'll find out that I'm worth a lot of money. Handing her my business card, attached with an invite, is like winning the lottery. Let's get real, my ego's not that large, it's just been proven women see me as their meal ticket. Which is why I'm thirty-two and not married. But that's not to say I don't use it to my advantage sometimes.

Like tonight.

As the night moves on, my mood sours. Midnight and no text or call. I keep an eye on things from the sidelines as the guys dance with many women, counting the minutes until I can leave. I can't figure out why I'm so pissed, which pisses me off even more. A two-minute interaction with a woman shouldn't have this effect on me. But I've taken on the job to make sure Jared keeps his dick in his pants. Not that he wouldn't, but just in case, I'm keeping his hands busy with drinks rather than women. Anabel would castrate us both if Jared cheated on her.

Somehow, it would be my fault.

Chase plops down across from me, wiping the sweat from his forehead. "They need to pump the air up in this place." He turns in his chair to see Jared dancing with four women. "Our boy is having a hell of a time. Should we worry?"

"Pshh." I whistle. "If he was dancing on one girl, maybe. Four, he wouldn't have a clue how to handle all of them. He's just having fun." Chase laughs and nods because he knows I'm right. Jared's the straight and narrow one out of all of us.

Hands cover my eyes from behind, startling me. "What's your poison?" the woman murmurs into my ear, sending a spark to my dick, instantly cheering me up. "Seems I owe you something."

Gray.

Despite wanting to tell her she might very well be my poison, I settle for a whiskey.

As soon as she lifts her hands, I turn in my chair and watch her stroll toward the bar. A simple, tight black dress outlines her slim body and her heart-shaped ass. Long, chocolate-curled locks hang down her back, and my fingers itch to run through them.

"Is that the chick you invited?" Chase asks, leaning forward on his elbows.

I nod, watching her interact with the bartender. He leans over the bar and gives her a hug, and I realize she got into the VIP area without me.

"She got a sister?"

I shrug, more excited that she's here than I should be. "She was with another woman when I met her." Truthfully, I don't remember what she looked like. My focus was on Gray the entire time, like right now.

When she turns around with a drink in each hand, I pull in a quick breath at the sight. Her backside is definitely a marvelous sight, but from the front … *damn.* And it's not because her top is so low-cut it reveals her perfectly round tits, or the four-inch black heels she's wearing that show off her toned calves and long legs. Don't get me wrong, she's downright gorgeous.

But it's the way she's looking at me.

There's no ulterior motive behind her playful smile, unlike the fake women I deal with daily. The ones that will do anything to get a ring on their finger and a high-dollar bank account with their name on it. No, she's only here for a good time.

To which I can oblige.

Gray takes a sip of my drink before handing it to me, and I lift a brow. She bites her lip and innocently shrugs one shoulder. "Habit." I want to bite that lip for punishment.

Our fingers brush for a moment, and my pulse picks up speed. Damn, one touch. Just think what'll happen when I'm inside her.

She sits down in the chair between Chase and me. "Hey, I'm Gray."

She stretches her hand out, and Chase slips his into it with a goofy smile plastered on his face. She seems to have that effect on everyone. Thankfully, she turns back to me because I was already concocting a plan to kill Chase if he didn't stop touching her.

She crosses her legs and sits back like she's sitting on a throne, her confidence palpable and sexy as hell. "So, Brooks Handley, what brings you to Las Vegas?"

I point to the dance floor. "Bachelor party."

"And I bet he's the groom?" I nod when she looks back at me. "I'm surprised you're not at a strip club."

"That's what I said," Chase barks.

"We promised the fiancée we wouldn't."

"Wow. Guys with morals. Why come to Sin City?"

"There's obviously more than strippers in Vegas," I say with a pointed grin.

She laughs. "But you didn't come here to meet me."

That I didn't.

But who am I to argue about unexpected surprises?

"Wanna dance?" she asks after finishing her drink. Pushing off the chair, she walks over to stand in between my legs and looks down at me with her petite hand stretched out.

My hand swallows hers, and she stares at our joined hands for a beat before she tugs, helping me up. At full stance, her head barely hits my chin even with her wearing fuck-me heels.

"Ready for me to show off my dance skills?" I rotate my hips, making her laugh.

"Should I be afraid?"

Still holding her hand, I lead her out to the floor, and say over my shoulder, "Very."

I pull her close, our bodies moving to the beat of the song. As my fingers grace the edge of her dress, skimming the exposed skin of her lower back, a shiver runs up her spine, and I feel it reverberate through me. Her eyes, a bright green that glows like the northern lights, meet mine and there's a stillness in the air, a magnetic pull I wasn't expecting.

She wrinkles her cute button nose, and I notice the freckles dusted lightly across it. Innocence is hidden by the sexual vibes the rest of her body is radiating. And I'm here for the ride.

As she twists her hips against me, I mimic the motion. "You've got some moves," she says, lifting on her toes, closer to my ear so I can hear her over the music.

I casually shrug. "It pays the bills."

"Who knew I'd need dollar bills tonight?"

I let out a throaty chuckle. *I'll strip for you, for free.* "Show starts at two."

I don't miss the heat in her eyes, and I wonder how far she'll take this. Hopefully, all the way to the bedroom.

"The CEO gig didn't work out, huh?" she teases, running her fingers down my chest and then wrapping her arms around my waist.

I shake my head as I feel the heat between our bodies rise. Her leg rubs against my hard cock, and it takes effort to remain in control. "Chippendales was my calling. What can I say?"

She buries her face into my chest, laughing.

"What? You don't believe me?"

"Oh, I do. That is one show I won't miss."

Damn straight.

Show's in an hour.

CHAPTER 3

GRACYN

Hangover headaches are downright agonizing. I groan from the relentless pounding behind my eyeballs. The sound of unforgiving sheets clings to my legs, and it takes a moment to gather my thoughts.

These aren't my soft T-shirt sheets.

And where are the voices and beeping coming from?

I widen my eyes and jerk to a sitting position in a hospital bed, but the sudden rush makes me dizzy, forcing me to lie back. A surge of nausea hits, and I frantically search for something to throw up in.

"Gracyn," Mom says, jumping to her feet from the corner chair.

"Trash can," I snap with my hand over my mouth, pointing with my other hand. She rushes and grabs it, holding it up just in time for me to empty my stomach. I take back what I said earlier. *Throwing up* with a hangover headache is the worst.

Why does my head hurt so badly?

It's not until I touch my forehead that I realize it's bandaged.

"What ... what the heck happened to me?" I search my memories, but there's an unexplained void of blackness. Like someone took an eraser to my brain, leaving behind a dust of black confusion.

My mom's brows cinch. "What do you mean?"

Did I stutter?

"Why am I in the hospital, Mom?" I swallow back panic, slowly lifting the sheet and taking stock of all my body parts. Dressed in an ugly blue hospital gown with paisleys, all my limbs seem to be in working order.

"Honey," she says, lifting the back of my bed so I'm in a sitting position. "A car hit you when you were walking in the middle of the street. *With just a hotel robe on.*" I don't miss the hint of disapproval in her tone toward the end.

Say what? Again, I search for any recollection. Met up with a guy named Brooks. Drank. Danced. Gambled, I think. Drank. A lot. I remember a hotel room. A taxi ride. The memories are sporadic, and I don't know if they're in the right order. But I definitely don't remember a car hitting me.

"I don't..." I pause, all the unanswered questions clouding my mind. "When?"

"This morning around five."

Rubbing my temple, I think about being with Brooks last night. I just don't remember him leaving. Or myself, for that matter. "Was I by myself?"

"Witnesses said you were. Do you not remember anything? You told the paramedics your name and gave them all your information."

I shake my head, leaning back into the pillows and stare up at the ceiling. Was I drugged? Oh god. Did Brooks drug me?

The door swings open, and a middle-aged doctor with a

head full of gray hair walks in, taking long strides. His youthful face doesn't match his hair. He smiles at me. "Look who's awake. How are you feeling?"

"Like a bus hit me."

The doctor looks at his chart. "Nope, not a bus. A four-door sedan," he deadpans. Mom scowls at the man. She doesn't find his dry humor amusing, but it gets a smirk out of me. Shining his penlight in my eyes, he instructs me to follow it. "Can you tell me your name?"

"Gracyn Rae Carmichael."

"What day is it?"

I glance at my mom. We didn't go over this. "Um. *Sunday*?"

"You're not sure?" he questions, angling his head, and I nod. "Do you remember coming to the hospital this morning?"

"No. The last thing I remember is being in a hotel room. At least, I believe that was the last thing. My thoughts are jumbled, and not being able to remember is making me question if they're even real."

He hums and nods before he starts questioning me. "When's your birthday? Who's the president? What's your grandmother's name?" By the time he's done, he knows more about me than my best friend. It's a relief when I can answer all of them. "Let's get an MRI done. You landed on your head pretty hard. Definitely have a concussion and have a wicked gash that needed ten stitches in your forehead, but let's make sure nothing else is going on."

When the doctor leaves, my mom's eyes fill with tears. "Don't cry, Mom. At least I still remember you." Humor always breaks up tension, right?

She wipes her tears away and softly slaps me on the

shoulder as she sits by my side, grabbing my hand. "That's not even funny."

No, but I can see she's relieved that I do.

Later that morning, I'm rolled around the hospital, stuck in a tube and tortured with knocking sounds. Nerves shot and exhausted, I'm passed out before I reach my room.

———

"I CAN'T BELIEVE your blood alcohol level was that high," Mom scolds as we're driving home.

Seems it accounts for some of the memory loss. Not all of it, though. That's been ruled amnesia due to the head injury. The doctor rattled off a long description of what was happening, but the only part I focused on was there was no brain damage. I just lost a few hours of memories that I might never get back. Fun times.

"I wasn't driving. What's the big deal?"

"Gracyn. You could've died."

She's scared, and she's trying her hardest to deal with the emotional turmoil eating at her. So, I get it, and now is not the time to argue that I'm an adult and not a kid anymore, that I'm allowed to drink.

Letting out a winded sigh, I lean my head back and close my eyes. Exhaustion stops me from fighting. "I'm sorry, Mom."

She leaves me to my clouded and muddled thoughts. I keep trying to piece the night together, but I can't even remember what hotel I was at to find my stuff. My mom said she'd call the Aria, because that's where the accident happened.

Sleep is the only thing I want to do when I get back to her

house. Hopefully when I wake, the cloud of black in my head won't be there.

I'M LYING IN BED, dreading getting up when I hear, "Someone needs to tell her." My stepdad's voice is hushed, but he couldn't ever be quiet enough for it not to carry. He has one of those voices. Deep and authoritarian. The perfect judge's voice.

"She's been through so much already. I just don't want to tell her today."

For a few minutes, they go back and forth before I roll out of bed. It sounds important. When I stroll into the kitchen, both their mouths snap shut, and they just stare at me.

"This house isn't that big. And you guys can never be quiet." When I was younger, I always knew my punishment before they entered my room because they would debate it for an hour before they would give it to me.

My mom chews on her inner cheek.

"Have you remembered anything?" Dad asks.

I shake my head. I've tried. But zilch on the memory front. "So, what should I know?" I ask, heading to the fridge to grab water. When I glance back at them, they both stare at each other. "Spit it out, already. How much worse could it be than me getting hit by a car, losing my memory, and not being able to remember what hotel I was at—"

"You're married," Dad blurts out.

The water bottle slips out of my hand, falling to the kitchen floor. My mouth falls open, and I lean in, bewildered. "I'm sorry? I have temporary brain fog and I don't think I understood you because there's absolutely no way in hell that I'm married."

My dad plays with his wedding ring, twirling it around and around, something he does when he has to do something he doesn't want to do. "Someone gave me a copy of your marriage license this morning. The court clerk suspected a mistake and feared someone was pretending to be you."

Panic raises my voice an octave. "That must be what happened."

"I had the same idea. But we pulled security tapes." He lets out a long-winded sigh. "It was you."

Oh. My. God.

It mortifies me to ask this. "To who?" I can assume, but at this point, it could be Ronald McDonald, and I wouldn't be certain. But holy hell, I don't freaking remember a wedding.

"Brooks Handley."

I bury my face in my hands to shield myself from the disappointment in their faces. I've always been a headstrong, stubborn individual, earning every gray hair my mom has. But I've always argued that I was in control of every situation. I can't argue that now.

"Did I look like I was being coerced or held at gunpoint? Or drugged. I must've been drugged."

The times I remember with Brooks, holy smokes, it was addictively hot. But how it got from having mind-blowing sex to getting married is a black hole of mystery. My body fights the exhaustion, wanting me to go back to bed.

"Darling, who is Brooks Handley?" Mom murmurs.

Good question. I wonder how she would take it if I said she knows as much as I do.

His name.

Flushed with embarrassment, I hang my head. "We met in a coffee shop. Yesterday." When they say nothing, I lift my head to see if they've both passed out. My dad's eyes are wide as saucers, and shame fills my chest. Being a judge, he deals with this stupidity daily. I've heard it all, and I always wondered how people could be so irresponsible.

Now, I'm *that* person.

"I met up with him last night, and I guess we had a really good time." I let out a sarcastic laugh with tears threatening because I don't know what else to do. What else is there to say? "I'll take care of it. Please don't tell anyone. Especially Ray." I'll go from being a bride to a widow if my real dad finds out what happened.

A chuckle escapes my dad. "You hit your head harder than I thought if you expect Ray not to find out."

My motto is living up to expectations—*go big or go home.*

CHAPTER 4

GRACYN

If there's anything worse than getting hitched to a guy you can't remember, it's figuring out how to become unhitched to a guy that lives out of state and is ignoring you.

Seriously, he is being rude.

It's been a week of calling. Seven days straight of phone calls. Thanks to the business card he gave me, I know where the asshole works. His secretary, undoubtedly under strict orders to not put me through, is making me rage.

"Listen, if I don't talk to him, my attorney will. And she won't be as nice."

"Ms. Carmichael, Mr. Handley is a very busy man. I can't help that he's in meetings every time you call."

I shake the phone in the air in aggravation. Lies!

Pulling in my anger, I respond, "Can you please give him *another* message?"

She hums, clearly not intending to write anything down. But I'm done being nice.

"Tell him *his wife* needs to talk to him as soon as possible." I hear her gasp. That's right. His wife. Not that I'd tell anyone else that, but I'm desperate. Maybe this time, I'll have his attention.

"I don't know what game you're playing, but—"

If only this was a game.

I hang up on her. She'll give him *that* message. Flinging my phone onto the dashboard, I press my palms into my eye sockets. I groan out loud and stare at Charli. She's driving me to the doctor's office to have my stitches removed. "Remind me not to pilfer any more drinks from cute guys. It's not worth it. This is a disaster."

"Remember, it's not your phone's fault." She snickers.

I narrow my eyes at her, not at all amused. It's not like I *always* take it out on my phone.

"Any more memories?"

I shake my head, my mind a jumble of fragmented memories that don't seem to piece together anything solid. Nothing that leads me to understand what in the hell I was thinking by getting married. The strangest part, I constantly hear "Can't Help Falling in Love" by Elvis Presley in my dreams. I can only imagine there was an impersonator at the wedding chapel that sang to us.

Talk about romantic.

My phone vibrates from the dashboard. "That's what I thought." I should've thrown the wife card around days ago. I sigh when I see it's a Vegas number. "Hello?"

"Hi, is this Gracyn Carmichael?"

"It is."

"This is Tammy Durst from the Bellagio Hotel. I'm the customer relations manager. We have a box of your belongings.

I'm sorry it's taken this long to reach you. The box was placed on my desk while I was on vacation."

The Bellagio? I thought we were in a room at the Aria? Despite having called every hotel on the Strip, including the Bellagio, they all gave me the runaround about privacy laws because the room wasn't in my name. This is the best news I've had all week. Even though I've already bought a new phone and canceled all my credit cards, it's a relief to get my stuff back. And a piece to the puzzle.

With a nice shiny red scar at the base of my hairline, Charli and I head to the Bellagio after the doctor visit. Within minutes, I'm carrying a small box of my personal items out the main doors. I didn't bother to search my purse. I'd be more surprised if everything was still there.

I slide into the car, idling to the side of the entrance. "Got it."

"It's weird that you stayed here and don't even remember. Are you sure no drugs were involved?"

"Positive. The doctor's toxicology report was negative. Which, thank God. But, yeah, it's weird."

I dig through the contents, shuffling my heels around. What possessed me to leave the room without my shoes? A folded piece of paper is at the very bottom, and I pick it up and wave it around to grab Charli's attention. She watches me unfold it.

Written on a paper with the hotel logo at the top is a note from Brooks.

In a different life, you would be the one.
This life is too complicated.
Thanks for stealing my coffee.
Brooks.

"Aww. That's sweet," she coos.

A flashback strikes. I'm reading the note in the hotel room. Without thinking, I throw on the white terry robe and run after him, knowing he just left. The last part of the memory is me dashing out the front doors of the hotel. The same ones I just left.

And that's it.

Dammit, *don't stop there!* I knock on my head with the edge of my palm. Wake up!

I relay the brief memory to Charli. "How did I get from here to the Aria? Did I really run after him all that way? What the hell is wrong with me?" The mere image of walking the filthy, urine-soaked Vegas Strip without shoes makes me nauseous. Thank God I was drunk. Remembering all the specifics might not be necessary.

———

ONE WEEK LATER.

No new memories.

No Brooks.

Still married.

I curse while stuffing the duffel bag with enough clothes for the weekend. It shouldn't have come down to this, but I can't sit back and wait for him to pull his head out of his ass. Since I lack control over when my memories return, I have to take control where I can. When Mom's special knock echoes throughout the small apartment, I take a quick break to let her in.

She follows me to my room. "Going somewhere?" she asks, eyeing the black overnight bag on my bed.

"Yes. That's why I wanted you to come over. I'm going to see Brooks."

"As your mom and your attorney, I'm advising you that's not a good idea."

I peek my head out of the bathroom, wrapping the cord around my curling iron. "My life right now is a basket full of bad ideas. What's another one?"

She drops her head and shakes it. I'm pretty sure I see another brown strand of hair turn gray.

"He can't keep ignoring me."

"I can take care of all of this. If you would let me."

"No. I got myself into this mess. I'm going to get myself out."

"You can't just waltz into his business and talk to him."

My smile widens. That's already occurred to me, and I have a plan. I'm going this weekend because I know where he'll be. And he can't hide or run.

"Don't worry, Mom, I got this."

"Mm-hmm. That's what worries me."

I stuff the bag with toiletries and zip it up. "I'll be home in a couple of days." Graduation is next weekend, so this is going to be an in-and-out trip.

Just enough time to crash a wedding.

BILLBOARDS FLASH with ads as I stare below from my room, highlighting the bustling sidewalks. A bright green glow from the Green Giant ad floods my room, and I gawk at the enormous size. And I considered Las Vegas the ultimate example of excess. Having never been to New York, I get the same vibe that Vegas has to attract people with lights and relentless action.

I'm not a fan already.

After a quick text to everyone that I made it, I fall onto the double-sized bed. I wish Charli had come so we could explore the city. A perk of being jobless: being able to leave at the drop of a dime.

I rub the newly minted scar, a reminder of the main reason I'm here. Let's just hope I don't end up arrested. *Can you be arrested for crashing a wedding?*

I mean, I bought a gift.

My mind drifts to Brooks. The coffee shop. Dancing. Absently, I wonder if he thinks about me. It infuriates me he probably remembers our wedding. I'm still wrestling with the idea that I'm married while trying to undo something I find difficult to accept, as it didn't register in my memory. The only memories I have of him are intense, insatiable lust. And lots of sex. Great, mind-altering sex. Like, he set the bar really high.

THE THREE-HOUR TIME change works in my favor. Nerves mixed with a brief panic didn't let me go back to sleep when I woke at five a.m. my time. Which is eight here.

I shake my hands as I jump around the room, expending

some of the anxiety filling my chest, and instead replacing it with encouragement. "You don't get to marry me, leave me, and then ignore me. I'm freaking Gracyn Carmichael with two powerful fathers who have instilled in me to be fearless, relentless, and impossible to ignore. I will not be walked on."

I flip through the hotel guide, searching for the gym. Daily yoga sessions. Perfect. Meditation, here I come.

With only an hour left till the wedding, I stand in front of the bathroom mirror. Yoga wasn't as relaxing as I had hoped. It was hot and harder than my normal classes, but it helped take my mind off Brooks as I pushed through balancing and breathing and not dying.

One last swipe of the mascara wand, and I smile at myself. If he thought I looked amazing the night we got married, wait till he gets an eyeful of me now. The red lace dress fits like a glove. The midi length is sexy and elegant. When I saw it on a mannequin at one of Ray's hotels, I knew it'd be perfect for the occasion.

Vengeance red.

It's showtime.

The town car glides to a halt in front of a grand cathedral church, and I crane my neck to take in the entire building from inside the car. This is where the wedding is? I stare up at the spectacular architecture of the stone building. Wow. A nervous knot tightens in my throat. Between limos arriving, paparazzi stationed on the sidewalks, and the elegant dresses, this isn't your average wedding. But then again, I should have known, given the wedding was a feature article on *Page Six*.

The driver opens my door and extends his hand to help me. I grab my purse and take his hand, stepping out of the car.

I clear my throat and take a deep breath. "The guy getting married. Is he royalty or something?"

The driver's eyebrows pinch, but he smiles in amusement. "Not royalty. Just your average billionaire. You sure you're in the right place, ma'am?"

I square my shoulders and smile. "Oh, I'm positive."

He chuckles and murmurs in his heavy New Yorker accent as he walks around the car. "Good luck with that."

I don't need luck.

I need an annulment.

The marble stairs leading into the church are as grand as the building, but they're incredibly daunting as I glance around at the couples entering alongside me. Nothing quite like standing out when you're alone, especially in a bright red dress. I should have considered this more carefully. A few people glance curiously at me, and I offer a small smile, trying to blend into the crowd.

Brooks, being the best man, is a detail I remember from that night. A gentleman in a tux and white gloves escorts me down the aisle. When he asks which side, I tell him the groom's side. He gives me a sidelong glance, as if trying to figure out who I am. Was he in Vegas? It occurs to me that someone could recognize me before I have time to speak to Brooks. Let's hope not.

Fresh flowers adorn each pew, and I can't help but marvel at their blush pink hues and gold ribbons. I maneuver past five people before finding an empty seat. My nerves intensify, so I reach for my phone and send a text to Charli, hoping for something to occupy my racing thoughts.

Me: This wedding is insane.

Charli: Oh, yeah? How**?**

Me: Remember when Prince William and Kate got married?

Charli: SHUT UP! Really?

I giggle to myself, and the guy next to me gives me a side-eye. I ignore him and text her back.

Me: lol. Kinda like that. There are no king's guards, but I have no doubt there'll be a horse-drawn carriage.

Charli: TAKE PICTURES

And then the wedding begins.

I shift to hide myself behind the tall guy sitting in front of me and lean back as the wedding party passes by. It works until the groomsmen fan out on the stairs, Brooks at the very top. Taking my breath away, he's strikingly handsome in his tux. It's tailored to fit his muscular arms, narrow waist, and long legs. Obviously, it was custom made. At least I found the hottest guy in Vegas to marry. My thighs let out a quiver involuntarily, reminding me that the yearning for his touch wasn't one of the forgotten memories. He smiles at the groom, offering a pat on the back, while the groom himself looks like he's on the verge of passing out.

I feel the same as I blow out a shaky breath.

The bridesmaids walk slowly down the aisle, one by one, and I keep my focus on them. And then the cute flower girl comes down. She whisper-yells behind a fake smile to the boy she's holding hands with to keep up. I can't help but laugh when he looks at her with such apprehension and terror in his expression. But she looks forward and marches them both down with no bailouts.

The bride unites with her groom, and we all sit. That's when it happens. That's when I'm not hidden anymore. Green eyes meet hazel. The war begins. I sit up taller despite wanting to crawl under a pew and hide. I tilt my head in defiance as if I'm saying *yes, it's me, asshole*, to his questioning expression. *You made me do this.* Except now we're stuck in a battle where neither one of us can move. We can only assume what each other is thinking. His stoic expression gives nothing away. Is he furious I'm here? Does he have the same unwanted sexual feelings I'm feeling at the moment? My gaze drifts to his hip area, wondering if his dick is hard.

Seriously, Gray, stop!

I glance around the room to distract myself from his penis and its current status, but when our eyes meet again, he flashes a knowing grin. My cheeks flush with warmth as I drop my head, picking at a few beads on my dress. Okay, that was a little obvious.

God, please don't let this be a long wedding.

I attempt to focus on anything and everything except him for the rest of the ceremony. The quick ceremony seems to last for hours. Between counting the shapes on the patterned floor to studying the windowpane right behind the priest and checking my emails, I accomplished my goal—avoiding Brooks.

After the wedding party exits the church and our row is released, I make a beeline for the bathroom to regain my composure before facing him. My fingers grip the porcelain sink, and I lean forward, dropping my head between my shoulders. "Stop it, body. Stop it right now," I demand as everything feels like it's on fire. This was a mistake.

A faint sobbing comes from a closed stall. It was so quiet I assumed the restroom was empty. I pivot around and listen. Sure enough, a small cry comes from the last stall, and it sounds like a child.

I tap on the door with a knuckle. "Are you okay in there?"

"No," she cries louder. I observe the other stalls, all open, and wonder where her mom is.

"If you want to come out here, I can try to help."

I wait a couple moments, debating what I should do if she doesn't come out, but then the lock clicks. The door swings open, and the flower girl stands there with her arms draped at her sides as tears cascade down her chunky red cheeks. Bright turquoise eyes stare up at me. She doesn't appear older than six or seven.

"How can you be this sad at a wedding? You did an amazing job out there."

Her breath shakes as she exhales. "I … I lost my dog. My dad told me not to bring it, and I still did. And I lost it. He's going to be sooo mad."

Who could ever stay mad at those eyes?

I hope she means a stuffed animal. "Hmm. Let's see if I can help you. When I can't remember things, I focus on something else, and then it just pops into my head." Except for my lapse in memory. Nothing has worked so far. "What's your name?"

"Presley." She sniffles, blinking back tears.

"Well, hi, Presley, my name is Gracyn." I hold out my hand.

She slips her small hand, adorned with neatly painted white fingernails, into mine, and her lips form a toothless smile. "I like your name."

"I think yours is much cooler. Didn't you love being a flower girl?" It's the best job a little girl can have and the most memorable.

She nods, giving me a sad smile. "Except for Rafe. He made me put down my dog 'cause he had to hold my hand, and then I had the basket in the other hand." She pulls in a sharp breath, her troubled expression doing a one-eighty, with so much excitement she squeals and jumps up and down. "I know where it is. It's at the bottom of the flower basket because I was not going to put him down anywhere."

She runs out of the bathroom before I can stop her. Hope her parents are close by.

All right, Gray, back to your problem. He's already seen you. Go out there and deal with this. The quicker this is over, the better.

Rolling my shoulders, I stand tall and stride out of the bathroom, offering polite, yet curt smiles at people I squeeze past. A few curious stares linger longer than I'm comfortable with, probably wondering who I am. All the more reason to hurry and get this over, considering I might be trespassing.

My gaze sweeps around the large room, scanning the packed foyer. Before I can find him, a pair of tiny arms wraps around my waist.

"Look, Gracyn, I found Puffers." Presley releases me to show me the ragged, old pink doggy. This thing has seen a few dirty floors and certainly carries a few diseases.

I squat down and inspect the dog. It needs a good washing and a leg sewn back on. Maybe her mom is waiting for it to disintegrate so it can go in the trash, where it belongs.

I clap my hands once. "Awesome! You better hold on to him this time."

She stuffs it into her hidden dress pocket, nodding. Her expression brightens, looking behind me. "Daddy, this is Gracyn. She helped me find…" She pauses and then sighs, pulling out her dog. "Puffers. I'm sorry I brought it, but I found it."

I spin a smidgen on my heels, still squatting, and glance up.

Oh damn.

I blush, stupidly.

Now, I understand complicated.

CHAPTER 5

BROOKS

If she was trying to hide, she shouldn't have worn red.

I couldn't help but focus on the red siren in a sea of black and muted colors. Imagine my surprise when I saw the woman who has invaded my thoughts for the last couple of weeks seated between a row of people in the church.

A thief.

And now, *a wedding crasher*.

I can't help but feel intrigued and slightly frightened by her boldness. Does she have any boundaries? I spot her in the foyer before she finds me, and I'm able to study the delicious lines of her body from a distance. I questioned whether my memories of her beauty were exaggerated, but as I take her in, they were on point. She's even more stunning than I remember. Her silky brown waves tumble over her shoulders as she glances around, searching.

For her husband.

I curse under my breath as I realize my mistake. Why didn't I answer her call? I've never been one to shy away from a challenge, but dealing with an annulment from a woman I don't know has me feeling like a coward. I haven't even confided in my attorney yet. Admitting that I made a mistake this big and acted recklessly is a bitter pill to swallow.

So, I've ignored her.

Not the smartest of plans.

Unwanted desire twists my insides, and two things run through my mind. One, if she wasn't my wife, I'd drag her into one of the confession booths and fuck the sins out of her. We know she has them. And two, how do I get out of this mess? It's not lost on me that both situations end with me being fucked. The latter is the one going to hurt. She's here because she wants something from me.

Like money. *Typical woman.* Can you tell I have trust issues?

I let out a frustrated groan under my breath. This could have been avoided had I dealt with this immediately, or even after the *wife* message debacle.

She wanted my attention; she got it, all right.

The wrong kind. I had to talk my secretary down from contacting legal, convinced that I had a stalker on my hands. That little stunt could've turned catastrophic. I didn't pick up any crazy vibes from Gray when we were together, so that surprised me. *You drove her to it.* Yeah, I get it. The nagging voice in my head likes to remind me. Which is why it's in my calendar to fix this problem on Monday.

But here she is.

Now it's become an immediate problem. One I didn't want to deal with at a wedding. Who does she think she is? *Your wife.* I roll my eyes at the voice.

"Who is she?" Jade, one of my friends, murmurs, staring at Gray.

I sigh, running my hand over my beard. "Just a girl I know." Jade waits for more, and I shrug. It's not like I'm going to tell her who she is.

"Looks like she's made a new friend."

Rage prickles throughout my chest.

Fuck. Me.

I storm toward her as she bends at the knees, talking to *my* daughter. Touching her sacred toy like she has a right to it. Like she belongs in our world.

Like hell she does.

It takes everything in me not to rip my daughter away. When I clear my throat, Presley looks up, jumping with joy. "Daddy, this is Gracyn." She continues blabbering about something, but my mind is stuck on the woman, *on her knees*, looking up at me with flushed cheeks.

It's like déjà vu at the most inappropriate time. "That's great," I say with a tight-lipped smile. "Hey, Pres, where's Judith?" I ignore Gray as she stands and straightens her dress with her hands running down her hips. Okay, *ignore* is not the right word, but I jerk away when she raises her head. "Oh, look, there she is. Can you go tell her we'll be leaving soon?"

Presley looks at Gray. "Will you be at the reception?"

Gray's laugh is awkward as her gaze bounces from her to me. "Probably not."

That's an absolute no.

"But you have—"

"Presley," I snap, interrupting her nonsense. "Do as I say, please." The excitement in her face falls at my harsh tone, but my patience is on the verge of bursting. Her shoulders droop as she nods and ambles over to Judith. I'll deal with the guilt of being a mean dad later.

As soon as Presley is out of sight, I grip Gray's arm and escort her toward the front doors.

"You seem to have a problem communicating." She twists out of my grasp. "All you had to do was ask me to talk outside."

Who said I wanted to talk? I just need to get her away from *my people*.

The second we exit the church, I stop walking. "Stealing my coffee was cute … *this* is another level," I say through gritted teeth.

"You thought it was cute, huh?" she replies with a sly smile, as if I'm *flirting* with her. "I mean, I guess it was cute enough to get you to marry me."

I glance around, afraid of people within earshot. She steps in closer, her body brushing up against mine. When I pull in a quick breath, her familiar sweet scent fills my nostrils. I shake out of the momentary draw, irritated with myself.

"What. Do. You. Want?" I spit through clenched teeth. "If you think you're going to come here and use my daughter to get to me, you have no idea who I am."

Her shoulders square as her face hardens. *Ignore her sexy, pouty, red lips.* "You have no idea who I am, either. Brooks Handley, you've been served." She shoves an envelope into my chest, and it catches me off guard, causing me to lose my balance and take a step backward. "And I do have an idea who you really are. You're an irresponsible playboy who has a daughter, who I'm sure only sees her every other weekend because it's court mandated, and gets drunk in Vegas and reck-lessly ends up getting married. And then is afraid to pull his big boy pants on and deal with the mess we found ourselves in. *Am I close?*"

Her nostrils flare as she gets in my face, and I want nothing more than to throw her inaccurate accusation back at her, but I can't because it's *almost* correct. She looks at me like she has more to say, but she shakes her head and says, "Goodbye, Brooks. I'd love to say it's been great knowing you, but it hasn't."

She storms down the stairs, her heels clicking, echoing in my ears, and I tear open the envelope to see what she's demanding in the annulment. My mind races with worst-case scenarios as I brace myself for the financial hit that's coming my way. However, as I skim through the document, a wave of relief washes over me. Gray isn't trying to bleed me dry or tarnish my reputation. She just wants to sever ties with me.

No payout for her silence.

No stipulations.

Just an annulment.

A fleeting memory of us saying I do flashes through my thoughts, and then a heavy pang of regret follows. That was one of the best nights of my life. And that's saying a lot. I pace for a few beats, staring down, the shine of my shoes catching a glare off the setting sun. How can I feel the loss of something that was a mistake? Over someone I despised seconds ago? It's a perplexing emotion I can't make sense of.

There was a connection.

It doesn't matter, I argue with myself. My responsibilities don't involve an impromptu wife.

Then let her go.

"I'm trying, dammit!" A few people look over at me, probably wondering who I'm talking to.

I can't resist stealing one last glimpse of her as she weaves through the crowded sidewalk, wishing her a silent farewell. Passersby crane their necks to peek at the stunning woman in red. She demands attention even when she's not trying.

With a hasty decision I might regret later, I run down the stairs, two at a time. "Wait, Gray."

She glances over her shoulder and rolls her eyes in exasperation. Her hand shoots up in the air, hailing a cab, and one appears within seconds.

Frustrated, I step in front of her, blocking her from getting in, and lean in the window to say she's not going. Her brows shoot up in surprise as the taxi pulls forward. A vengeful expression takes hold of her face as she waves her hand in the air again, and again, a fucking cab appears. Why does it take *me* ages to get a cab in this place?

"Would you stop that?" I wave him off with a sharp, angry jerk of my thumb. "I think we should talk about this."

She blinks in confusion as I hold up the envelope.

"What's there to talk about, Brooks? It's pretty straightforward. Despite what you thought about me, I want nothing from you, *as you can see.* Your only task is to send your *attorney* in your place on the court date. It's rather simple."

Unfortunately, I never do things simple.

"I was wrong," I admit.

But so were you.

Her red, pouty lips quirk up on one side. "I bet that stung coming out of your mouth."

"You have no idea." The air thins around us, and I blow out a ragged breath through puffed-out cheeks and scratch my head, not sure what the hell I'm doing. "How long are you in town for? Can we meet for lunch tomorrow?"

"I leave tomorrow."

"You came here for a day?"

"I came here to do one thing, and I did it."

A woman wanting nothing from me is a foreign concept. In fact, that's never ever happened. Which has to be the reason I can't stop the words that come out of my mouth. "Come to the reception."

She looks away, biting her bottom lip, and shakes her head. "Brooks. I don't think that's a good idea. You have a daughter. Remember, *complicated*?"

I wondered if she'd bring up the note. When I woke to an alarm I don't remember setting, I was lying next to her. It took everything in me to not wake her and be with her one last time, but I knew I had to leave. Instead, I wrote that note as I watched her sleep, her naked body on top of the sheets. I almost took a picture so I'd never forget how beautiful she was. But that was a line I wasn't willing to cross, so I stared at her for half an hour, memorizing every curve, every freckle, every detail that made her … *her*. With a plane to catch and still drunk, I left a lucky man.

Little did I know, I left as a *married* man.

What a life lesson to teach Presley someday. You can get drunk enough to get married and not remember it the next morning. It didn't take long for the blur from a hangover to move our night of debauchery into focus. I haven't slept one night without remembering it since.

The wind whips her hair across her face, and she pulls it back behind her ear. *What is that?* I trace a deep red line across her forehead that wasn't there a couple of weeks ago. I vividly memorized her face that night, and I would've remembered that.

"What happened?"

She takes a step back from my touch. "You happened."

What the hell does that mean?

CHAPTER 6

GRACYN

W*hy did I say yes?*
Curiosity. Plain and simple.

We'll ignore the fact that I can't say no to Brooks Handley, *drunk or sober*. But why did he stop me? Why was there a hint of desperation for me to stay? What does he want to talk about? Reminisce how stupid our decision-making skills are when we're drunk? Can't wait to tell him I don't remember most of it.

But curiosity got the best of me.

The moment I sat down at a table with strangers, the regret set in. My name was handwritten on the placard, putting on display that I was a last-minute add-on. It's not the strangers that scare me, it's the man who looks at me like he hates me one minute but wants to devour me the next.

Soft pink hues flood the reception with tiny white lights flickering above. I'm smack in the midst of a fairy tale. This is the picture-perfect wedding all little girls dream of from the day they watch their first princess movie.

The emcee announces the wedding party, and Brooks enters,

Presley in one arm, his partner on the other. A split second of jealousy has me reaching for my drink and downing it.

"He's a sight to see, isn't he?" the woman sitting next to me leans in and whispers. "Makes my ovaries dance."

I quietly laugh and nod, because look at him ... he's a walking sex ad. I don't know if it's my ovaries or my vagina dancing, but things down south are acting like they had an energy drink. His eyes skip over the room, and they meet mine for a brief second, and my lips quirk up before he continues on. As if confirming I came.

Yep, party of one, right here, *not looking desperate at all*.

"Work is never a dull moment when he enters the building," she continues, oblivious to our quick exchange. "You can practically feel the smiles on the womens' faces as he walks by. It's that obvious. Like Brooks Handley is going to notice the peons that work for him." When I arch a brow at the chatty blond, she points to herself and says with amusement, "Peon number four hundred forty-eight. I eventually settled when I knew there wasn't a chance in hell."

"Hello. I'm sitting right here. And I can hear you," the guy to her right bellows.

She laughs, waving him off. "You know I love you, Pete."

He leans over so he's in my sight and waves. "I'm totally kidding. I'm not Brooks Handley, and she ain't no Taylor Swift. I'd call us even."

I love this couple.

We all break out in a fit of laughter, and I squeeze my lips shut after a few guests glance in our direction. My laughs always seem to carry, usually embarrassing the hell out of Charli. He wraps his hand around her neck, pulling her toward him, and kisses her, heat and all. They're so cute.

She fans her face and takes a sip of her drink and then turns her attention to me. "Anyway." She beams, blushing.

"Is that the girl's mom?" I prod.

"Nooo." She inches closer, her voice more hushed. "You haven't heard *the* story?"

I shake my head because this sounds like one story I want to hear. A juicy one. And who can walk away from one of those, especially if it involves your *current husband*?

"Back in the day, Brooks was the bad boy of New York City, especially when New York crowned him its hottest bachelor. And when I mean bad, I mean a freak in the sheets, bad."

I can confirm he's still a freak in the sheets.

"There was a different woman on his arm every night, and the media ate it up. Millionaire, *at the time*, and sex, no better story than that." Her eyes skirt around our area. I'm assuming to make sure no one is listening, which is ironic since she doesn't know who I am. "One day, out of the blue, baby Presley shows up." Ouch. I bet that put a huge kink in his plans. "Here's the juicy part. Rumor is the girl's mom tried to kill Brooks's sister and then killed herself."

I gasp with my hand over my mouth, searching for Brooks. He's at the head table, laughing at Presley with a slice of orange between her teeth. My heart hammers against my chest. *You're an idiot.* I'm a fool for assuming he's a part-time dad and then telling him what I thought when in fact, he's the total opposite. He's all she has.

Why didn't he say anything?

"He needs to find that baby a mama, but he's shut that part of his life down, focusing on work and Presley." She seems to know a lot about Brooks, and when I twist toward her with a questioning expression, she waves me off. "Well, that's what they say, anyway. Working in the mailroom, you hear it all."

Wow. He's a man who has his priorities straight, his life in order, and then I storm into the picture and disrupt his world. Even though our marriage is an inconvenience on my part, I assume it's a bigger deal for Brooks. So the question remains: Why did he want me to stay?

She takes a drink, licks her lips, and leans back. "I can see why he's guarded, considering the hell he went through."

The rage in his face when I was talking with Presley, it's understandable now.

"That little girl is everything to him. But enough about him." She lifts a curious brow. "So, what's your reason for being stuck in the back forty? Piss off the bride?"

Nope, just a wedding crasher.

"Jared and I are old college friends." I shrug while lying and hold up the handwritten placard. "Late RSVP, and it seems she was hoping I wouldn't come."

"That'll do it." She laughs.

For the next half hour, we're served an appetizer, salad, and then dinner. Not surprisingly, everything runs to perfection. My new best friend keeps talking to me throughout dinner, which I'm thankful for.

When the music starts and people take to the dance floor, I grab my empty wineglass. "I guess we're not a top priority back here to get refills. If you'll excuse me, I'm off to find the bar."

Waiting in line, I spot Brooks on the dance floor, an older woman in his arms. They laugh as he guides her across the floor in a fluid two-step. A man who can dance always catches my attention. My thoughts go to the night I was in his arms. His hips in sync with mine as we danced to a slow, heavy beat. The music matching our movement, fingers digging into my hips as we got lost in each other.

No wonder we ended up in bed. I remember the sex so clearly. It still baffles me I can't remember anything else. Talk about leaving a lasting impression. The memory sparks a new memory. We're in a taxi, and Brooks is ravaging my mouth. He left me breathless. When the car comes to a stop, Brooks asks why he stopped. The driver swore we told him Bellagio. But I don't remember where exactly we were supposed to be.

"Bellagio, it is," Brooks rasped, grabbing my hand and leading me to the front desk before carrying me to our room.

Wait. Were we already married?

My pulse races, and I spin away from his direction before someone catches me staring. I'm sure I look like a complete loony tune as I struggle to piece together our night. I glance over at the limited menu on the bar.

"You're not from around here."

A guy to my right leans his elbow on the bar and grins in my direction. He's an attractive guy, but nothing stands out that would make me want to steal *his* coffee.

"What gave it away?"

"Your smile. Your red dress and your accent."

I respond with a quick chuckle before ordering a glass of chardonnay. "I'll give you the dress because that's pretty obvious, considering I stand out like a sore thumb and, of course, the accent is a dead giveaway. But the smile?"

"I'm at the table next to you, and I haven't seen you once not smile. That is definitely not a New Yorker trait. And there's nothing *painful* about the dress you're wearing."

Oh, this guy is laying it on thick. I have to work hard to not roll my eyes.

"I'm Cooper," he says, offering his hand. To be polite, I shake his hand.

"Gray."

He looks past me for a millisecond. "Here by yourself?" I nod, and he adds, "I had a plus one, but they canceled at the last minute."

"They're missing out. I'm in town just for the wedding, heading home tomorrow."

"Where are you fr—"

"Gracyn!" Startled by the sound of my name, I spin around to find Presley, barefoot, red-faced and wearing a cheeky grin, running toward me. "I thought you weren't coming." She stops in front of me and cocks her head like a confused dog.

"Last-minute change of plans." Her expression brightens, and her turquoise eyes glimmer with mischief. "I saw you dancing like a professional," I say, pointing to the dance floor. She hasn't stopped dancing to even eat dinner yet.

"Thank you. You want to dance with me?"

"Ah…" My gaze skips around the crowded room over her head. A flutter of panic tickles my belly. "I actually just got my drink." I hold up my wineglass.

"But you have to." She pouts, dropping her arms to her side.

"I don't think you're getting out of this," Cooper quips. "How about I take your drink to the table? I'll drop it off on the way back to mine."

"I think you're right, but I'll just drop it off at the table first. Thank you for offering, though," I say and turn toward Presley. "Be right back."

When I place my drink down, my new friends are deep into their people-watching game. "Looks like I'm going to go dance. I'll definitely be back for that." I point to my wine.

"Have fun," she says.

Presley waits for me at the edge of the floor, jumping up and down, grabbing my hand.

"All right, Presley, show me what you've got."

Her dimples deepen, and I wonder if Brooks has them hiding under his beard. She pulls me to the dance floor, right as "The Chicken Song" comes on. Figures, the worst wedding song ever comes on.

"Stay right here, I'll be back," she demands after a minute of the annoying song, holding up her tiny finger, before darting off through the crowd.

Nope, this isn't awkward at all dancing by myself.

My heart seizes when I see her dragging Brooks by the hand on to the floor. Our eyes meet, and his expression falls flat. "I swear I had nothing to do with this," I snap, with my palms up. *Remember, this was your idea.* "I'll let you guys dance." I turn, but Presley grabs me, stopping me.

"No. Stay and dance."

"But the song ended." I laugh nervously, needing that drink right now.

"We're taking it back with an oldie but a goodie. And we're slowing it down," the DJ announces. The song plays, and I let out a gargled chuckle, dropping my head. How in the world?

"Daddy, dance with Gracyn."

Shock flanks his face as "The Lady In Red" by Chris de Burgh bellows out of the speakers. Then a lopsided grin creeps up under his beard as he holds his hand out for me.

This isn't a good idea.

I slip my hand into his large one, and he pulls me into his chest, his other hand pressing into my lower back.

Yep, bad idea.

One touch, and I'm gasping as his scent floods my senses, especially my common sense.

"Sorry. I didn't think I was raising such a sneaky lil' shit," he murmurs.

"She's very calculating."

"That's what scares me the most." He spins with me, holding tight around my waist.

"Brooks, what are we doing?" Unwanted and not welcome feelings creep into my chest. For all that I can remember, he's a one-night stand, so where is this need to be close to him coming from?

"I guess fierce confidence and boldness in a woman is my weakness."

I chuckle. "I'm sure you deal with those types of women every day."

He pulls back, giving me a view of his chiseled face. "None that I'm dangerously attracted to."

Exactly. Dangerous.

Glancing around, I notice several eyes focused on us. "It's bad enough your daughter is trying to set us up. Now everyone is watching. What if our news gets out? I would hate myself if I hurt Presley."

His hand tightens around my waist. "Dammit, Gray. You are not helping me hate you."

"Are you trying to? Because it doesn't seem like it." Instead of answering, he spins me out, pulling me back into his arms in the next beat, and we dance for a few quiet moments.

This is not how this trip was supposed to go.

It was a drop-and-run type mission.

Until the point he asked me to come to the reception. That came as a surprise. Hostility, I expected. I knew I'd catch him off guard, and men like him don't like losing control of situations. Which is why I'm surprised I'm here. In his arms. He could've had his team of lawyers on it at the snap of a finger. His silence has me thinking.

"You're more reserved than I remember," I murmur.

He laughs once. "In my real life, I have an image to withhold. Drunk, sloppy, and stupid isn't it." After my simple hum, he stares at me. "Don't get me wrong, I wasn't pretending to be someone else. That *was* me. There's too much at risk for me to act like I did in my early twenties."

"Right. Like getting drunk and married to a total stranger." I sigh. "Brooks, why didn't you take my calls?"

"I like *Gracyn*," he says, avoiding the question. "I don't remember that being your real name. It fits you. *Sweet mixed with a little dirty.*"

My cheeks flush with heat, and I shift my attention to the bride and groom dancing next to us to avoid the amusement in his eyes. I've always loved my name, but when I was in kindergarten, a little jackass boy decided it would be hilarious to call me Sin. Soon enough, all the boys joined in with the teasing. I hated my name after that, so I called myself Gray, unfazed by the taunts that I was a boring color. At least I wasn't the devil. By the time I didn't care about the sin part, Gray had stuck. To this day, my mom still refuses to call me that, so I go by both.

But the way Brooks says it, how he lingers on the last consonant, his *definition*, I like it. A lot. But not enough to make me lose my train of thought. "Don't change the subject. Why didn't you take my calls?"

"I..." His words trail off with the final notes of the song. He leans down and whispers, "Let me send Presley home. Meet me on the next level's terrace in fifteen minutes. You'll see it when you get off the elevators."

With a quick nod, I turn to walk away, grateful for the glass of wine waiting for me.

The table is empty when I make it back. I grab my wine and let out a sigh, my heart still beating fast from the way he looked at me, the weight of his hand on my back. Everything lingers, refusing to let me breathe normally.

Out of the corner of my eye, I spot Cooper standing at the next table talking to a group of guys. Sipping my wine would have been more appropriate, but still disoriented from my dance with Brooks, I down half the glass. Cooper glances over, catching my eye, and I muster a polite smile. He waves with an eager smirk. Again, I have to control my rolling eyes.

Moments later the couple returns to the table, and she stops at her chair, staring at me with a curious expression. "Did I just make a fool of myself by telling you all the gossip? Because by the looks of that dance, you're not strangers."

Actually, we are.

Married strangers, but strangers.

Her husband is already sitting down, so we pull our chairs out and sit. "I've only met Brooks one other time." Her lips twist in disbelief, and I hold up my right hand. *Habit of a judge's daughter.* "I swear."

"Well, you two have a solid connection for only meeting once. Only one man has ever looked at me like that." Her head rocks to the side. "And he's sitting right next to me."

I sigh because no matter how I resist, Brooks makes me feel differently. I dismiss her with a wave of my hand, finishing the last of my drink. My nerves are already buzzing with anticipation, and her comment only makes it worse.

CHAPTER 7

GRACYN

I step outside the double doors, and I'm immediately swallowed by a warm, humid embrace. It's as if someone is hugging me too long. It's suffocating. But the city's lights twinkle, providing a magnificent backdrop that makes up for the sticky air. The terrace is empty, and I wonder if I'm on the right floor. I pull out my phone to check the time. Exactly fifteen minutes have passed.

As I make my way across the pavement, the loud clicking of my heels resounds, a distinct *clip, clip, clip*. When I reach the edge of the building, I'm captivated by the mesmerizing view of the city below. I press my forehead against the cool thick glass that blocks the edge of the skyscraper. Muffled sounds of music and laughter drift up from the terrace just outside the reception hall below. Definitely on the right floor.

The moment I hear the doors opening, I twist around and sigh in disappointment when I find Cooper. Oh boy.

"There you are," he says as if he'd been looking for me. I look past him, hoping Brooks is right behind.

But nope, it's just the two of us.

I wave my phone in explanation. "I had to make a phone call. It's quiet up here." He bares his white teeth in a predatory smile, and my creep meter dings off the charts as he ignores my reason and continues toward me. I've dealt with plenty of guys like him over the years. He reminds me a little of Justin. Not wanting to be trapped up here by him, I head toward the doors.

"Did you know that around midnight, all the billboards in Times Square display a digital show in perfect synchronization?"

I politely smile, slowing my pace, but continue to move toward the door. "I didn't. I'll have to check that out later."

He grabs my bicep with a possessive squeeze as I try to move past him. What is with the men here thinking it's okay to put their hands on me?

"I have a suite here. How about we go to my room and check it out now?"

How about no? My mouth opens, ready to tell him he's about to lose his dick if he doesn't let me go, but I'm stopped mid-breath.

"I suggest you remove your hand. Now," a stern voice demands from the terrace door. I turn my head to see Brooks holding two glasses of wine. Fury casts a dark shadow over his face as he sends a warning glare at Cooper's hand.

Cooper releases me, and I step back, rubbing the red handprint.

"We were just getting some fresh air, weren't we?" Cooper's icy gaze flicks at me, and my brows shoot up.

"It seems the lady doesn't feel the same way."

Cooper's nostrils flare. "This doesn't concern you, Handley."

A wicked grin stretches across Brooks's face as he moves closer to Cooper. This should not turn me on, but I can't help it. He's dangerously gorgeous right now. He's my black knight. And it's a good thing for Cooper that Brooks's hands are busy holding glasses. Maybe I should grab them. "I would love a reason to have you kicked out of the party, Rossman." Both men puff out their chests, clearly revealing there's some history between the two. "I'm not even sure who invited you to begin with."

Cooper regards me once more, surprising me as if he's debating if I'm worth the fight, but then relents and storms through the same door he came through moments ago. *Yeah, that would've been the wrong move, buddy, because I would've bet on Brooks.*

"Wow," I say, stunned.

Brooks releases a low, throaty growl. "He's a grade-A asshole. He blames us for his company failing, which I'm certain is more about him than us. And he has a couple of restraining orders against him. I have no idea how he received an invitation," he murmurs as he hands me a glass. "I saw you leave without a drink." His tone softens.

He's lost the jacket and tie and looks good enough to eat right now. "Are you trying to get me drunk?"

"Definitely not. Been there, done that. It didn't end well."

That's an understatement. At least you remember it.

My body heats under his slow perusal of my body.

"I really like this dress," he says.

I knew you would.

"I didn't think I'd stand out as much as I did. Don't you people wear color here?" He chuckles as he leads me back to the edge of the terrace. "I mean, look down there. People walk around half naked. What is that about and how is that legal? But that's not my point." I throw my hand up. "People are very eccentric down there, yet everyone up here wants to blend in together."

Where the hell is this rambling coming from?

And why can't I stop?

"I'm not a fan of how bright New York City is." The notion falls out of my mouth as I stare down below at the hustling city that never sleeps. "I mean, yeah, Vegas is bright, but most people don't live on the Strip. I like my sleep. Pitch dark. And don't get me started on the glow of the cable box."

He laughs to my side, running his finger up my forearm, and I shiver.

"Noted."

I twist my body to face him. The shadows of the night against the sharp edges of his face make him look dangerous. *A good dangerous.* Like the guys on motorcycles where you fantasize about having passionate sex on the bike.

As I trace the pads of my fingertips along his jaw, a tingling sensation courses through me. "You're very handsome," I murmur, mesmerized by his masculinity.

"And you are gorgeous," he returns the sentiment, snaking his arm around me, pulling me into his chest. He places both our drinks on the edge, by the glass.

My breath catches in my throat, misplacing all my thoughts. "We're supposed to be talking about something, right?"

"Can I kiss you first?"

His heartbeat is like a hammer to my chest. Whoa. That's intense.

I don't even finish nodding before his lips connect with mine, drowning out my soft moans. His hand squeezes, getting a handful of my ass, pressing me into him, my back against the cool glass. When he pulls back, my breaths are rapid and my lips swollen and … numb?

I touch them, my thoughts blurring together. "You kissed the feeling out of my lips." My voice is almost unrecognizable, like it's dragging down a long tunnel. I widen my eyes and blink. My face feels like it's drooping.

I feel drunk.

"Gracyn?"

"I guess you did get me drunk." I giggle. He scowls as he hooks my chin with his thumb and finger, angling my head up, studying my eyes. The intensity in his face makes me giggle again. "Don't be mad. You can't marry me again. But we can do other things." The words come out slurred as I wiggle my hips.

"How much did you drink?"

I hold up one finger. "One." And then another. "Two." And another. "Three. I think."

"Fuck," he grates out. When he swoops me up in his arms, everything spins. Wheeeee!

"That's a great idea," I giggle again. "Let's go fuck." My body heaves in his arms as he storms across the terrace. "Brooks, should I take your last name?" I slur the words right before darkness pulls me under.

CHAPTER 8

GRACYN

"I don't care if you take your whole fucking life to search the security feed. I need proof! You told me you were the best when I hired you. Prove it!"

I'm awakened by loud yelling, the sound exacerbating the pounding in my head. I dig my fingers into my eye sockets and pull in a deep whiff of … *bacon?*

Wait. Whose voice was that?

I shoot up and listen for them to talk again. *And whose bed is this?* Panic sinks deep inside my belly as my gaze darts around the unknown room. I jerk the comforter away, wearing only a white oversized T-shirt. Where the hell am I? Who took off my dress? Squeezing my eyes shut and tapping my forehead with my fingers. *Think, Gray, think.* Except, the last thing I can remember is Brooks coming out on the terrace.

Just as I'm about to leap out of bed in search of my phone, the door swings open, and I let out a startled yelp, yanking the blanket up to my chest. Brooks offers a shy smile as he strolls in wearing only blue plaid pajama bottoms. *Tattoos.* I totally forgot he had tattoos hiding under his shirt. I shake out of the thought and tilt my head in confusion.

"Does your head hurt?"

Seriously? *Again?*

This is getting out of control.

"Why is it I always lose a part of my memory when I'm with you?" His brows pinch in confusion. I throw my hands up, irritated this keeps happening, and blurt out, "First, it was our wedding, and now last night. Do you know how out of control it feels to not—"

"Hold up," he clips, and I send him a scowl for interrupting me. "You don't remember us getting married?"

Oh yeah. About that…

My nod is slow and steady as I sigh. "I chased you." I roll my eyes at how pathetic that sounds but keep going. "After you left. Those memories are hazy, so I'm not exactly sure what I was thinking. Let's just blame the ridiculous amount of alcohol we consumed. But I ran into the street and a car hit me." I lift my hair off my forehead, showing off the fresh red scar. "I woke up in the hospital not remembering anything. Kind of like *right now.*"

He paces at the foot of the bed, his hand clutching the back of his neck. "I don't even know where to begin," he mutters, coming to a halt and fixing his hazel eyes on me. "Shit, Gracyn. You ran after me?"

I sit up straight in the bed, tucking my feet under me. "Looks like it," I mutter.

He leans against the gray dresser, his arms crossed and concern etched into his features.

"I'm fine. It wasn't a bad accident. Just a little amnesia and a scar to remind me that every poor decision comes with consequences." As I sense his guilt, I quickly add, "It's not your fault."

"Isn't it?" He pushes off the dresser, taking long strides to sit by me on the bed. He drags his finger through my hair and runs his thumb over the scar. "I shouldn't have left like that. I could've said goodbye."

I lay my hand on top of his and pull it away. "I don't blame you. I blame *drunk Gray*. She's irresponsible and impulsive." I lean in closer and whisper, "Hopefully, we never see her again."

He chuckles once, but I can still see the worry in his eyes.

"But I have *some* questions about that night. But first, let's talk about last night. What in the world? How did I end up here? There is no way I was too drunk to not remember this time, so what the hell happened?"

He pulls in a ragged breath and lets out a throaty growl as his eyes darken with the switched topic. I hit a nerve.

He stands again, pacing. Note to self: he can't sit still when he's angry. "Did you put your drink down at all last night?"

I pause, recalling my drinks. "I don't … think so. I remember only having three. The one at the table when I first sat down, the one I got at the bar, and then the one you gave me. But I left my drink at the table because Presley wanted me to dance." Things fall into place. I slap my hands down on the bed. "Did someone put something in my drink?"

"Yes."

"That guy … what's his name…" I snap my fingers a couple of times, trying to remember. "*Cooper*. It had to be him. Is that why he followed me up to the terrace?"

Realization strikes me like a punch to the stomach. How could I have been so stupid? For years, while working in the bar, I was always on the lookout for women who had been drugged and made sure they didn't leave unless it was safe. The number one rule: never let your drink out of your sight. *But I was at a wedding.* Bile rises in my throat as the memories of last night return. That's why he was so insistent on me going to his room.

I swallow hard, fighting back the rising nausea.

The prick put a date rape drug in my drink.

Oh, he messed with the wrong woman.

With force, I throw the covers off and scoot to the side, planting my feet on the hardwood floors. I spot my purse on the chair in the room's corner, and within a couple of seconds, I have my phone in my hand. "What's his last name?" I demand. I'm sure Ray has a few acquaintances here in New York that would be glad to give Cooper a visit. Past being rational, I glance up when Brooks stays quiet. "Well? And don't tell me you don't know because you do. Barking each other's last names at each other like a pissing match. Roscoe? Roman? I know it starts with an R."

He blinks with a tilt of his head. "You seem like a woman on a mission, and as hot as that is right now, what exact mission is that?"

My lip quirks up. "Not one that you should worry about."

Brooks's tongue darts out and wets his bottom lip. I want to yell at him to stop flirting while I'm trying to manage the situation. "Oh, but you are my wife, sweet Gracyn. Anything you do concerns me," he replies without a hint of humor.

Ignore the wife comment.

Ignore the wife comment.

It's a mere technicality that doesn't carry any significance to me. After all, I don't even remember getting married, so truthfully, it holds zero weight on my end. "Exactly. I can't go to the police because the last thing I want is for this"—I gesture between us—"to become public. But I have other means that I intend to use because that asshole drugged me. He can't get away with it. Had you not been there, who knows what would've happened? I will find out his name with or without you." I toss my phone on the bed and cross my arms tightly across my chest.

"I don't doubt that." He chuckles in amusement. "I'll give you his name when we can confirm it's him. Security is working on that right now."

"This isn't a laughing matter, Brooks."

"You're right, it's not. Despite me being entertained by your *five-foot-and-a-little-more* of badass, I take this situation very seriously." His body hardens, muscles tense, as he walks over and stops, shoving his hands in his pockets. "If you want to go to the police, I'd understand and be behind you one hundred percent. But if not, let me handle it. I have plenty of connections that can make his life hell."

So do I.

"I'm sorry this happened to you. At a wedding, no less."

As he passes me, a masculine, woodsy soap scent fills my senses. Damn, why does he have to smell amazing this early in the morning? I turn to see what he's doing, and he reaches for something right outside the bedroom door. *What the heck?* He rolls in my bright blue suitcase.

"How did you get that?"

"Your key card was in your purse. And before you ask how I knew what room, it was still in the key card sleeve with the number written on the outside. I hope you don't mind."

I'm not sure how I feel. If it were anyone else, I would feel that they violated my privacy. "You packed all my stuff up?"

He hesitates for a beat. "I had my assistant do it. I didn't know how long you'd be out, and with your flight today, I thought you might be on a time restraint." He shifts his weight from side to side, as if he's second-guessing this plan. It's sweet and cute.

My flight doesn't leave until this evening, and truthfully, I am grateful to have my stuff. "You're so confusing," I finally say.

"Why is that?"

"You're this take-charge kind of guy. I watched you at the wedding. You made sure things got done and the same at the reception. There was a plan in place, and you took the job of making sure it was executed. Even if that meant dancing with the bride's mom cause you could see that the bride was becoming overwhelmed by her."

He lifts an amused brow. *Way to admit you were watching him, Gray.*

"And now this." I point to the suitcase.

"What can I say? I like being efficient."

"You like being in control," I counter.

He doesn't miss a beat. "Always."

"Yet, you couldn't deal with our marriage," I deadpan.

He swallows hard, nodding. "I also don't like to admit when I fail." Apparently. "There's an appointment scheduled with my attorney on Monday," he slips in, as if he needs to prove to me he was taking care of it so it doesn't cloud his *efficient* persona.

"Better late than never," I joke, stepping over to take the suitcase. When I turn to walk toward the bathroom, I catch a glimpse of myself in a floor-length mirror and do a double take. Oh my god. I'm a cross between a person who went swimming with their mascara running down their face and a person who used a whole can of Aqua Net in the eighties. My hair is matted down in one spot and teased everywhere else. I'm a train wreck.

Choo choo, all aboard.

"You could've told me I looked like this," I say, attempting to pat down the crazy hair.

I glance at him through the mirror, and he shrugs. "Oh, please tell me how I'm supposed to tell a woman that her hair looks like she got cum in it after a night of being drugged."

I can't help but burst out laughing. I was not expecting that. "And how do you know what that looks like?"

He rolls his lips, shaking his head. "Conversation for another day."

I give up trying to make it look decent. The only thing that will help at this point is a shower.

"How much of that night do you remember? In Vegas," he clarifies.

Which is embarrassing because there is more than one of those nights.

The lie slips off my lips. "None of it."

"Really?" he says, surprised. There's that pointed brow. "Nothing?" he prods.

"I mean, I remember you giving me your coffee."

He laughs out loud once, sliding his hands in his pajama pockets. I watch them move a little lower and force my attention up to his face.

"And then meeting you at the club. That's about it." I don't need him to know that I remember every detail, every second his hands were on me, every inch of skin that his lips grazed. That it's the only thing I remember so clearly. What does that say about me? And his pants hanging dangerously low on his hips are not helping clear those images. He clears his throat, and I shift my attention back to him.

"You sure? You're looking a little flush right now," he muses.

I fan myself. "It's just an aftereffect of the drugs," I jest, pulling my bag to the bathroom so I can hide behind a closed door. I blow out a heated breath and lean against the door, thankful for the separation.

His voice on the other side makes me jump. "There's a clean towel and washrag on the sink. I'd appreciate it if you didn't steal anything."

I cover my mouth so he can't hear me laughing. But I hear his chuckle.

"I'm taking a shower," I say back.

"Lock the door," he replies, his voice trailing off as I can only guess he's walking away. That's a weird response. Whatever.

I click the lock on the door and then turn on all five shower heads. It's like a car wash for people.

As water sprays every inch of my body, instead of enjoying the water massage, the thought about what might have happened last night gets the best of me. I can't stop the tears from forming in the corners of my eyes. I'm in a city by myself. Nobody would've missed me for who knows how long. Cooper could have done whatever to me. He knew I was in town for the wedding alone. Ugh! That was a stupid confession. Could I have made myself any more of a target?

So far, nothing is going to plan.

The worst part? I like my husband.

CHAPTER 9

GRACYN

I don't bother with much makeup. Powder, blush, and mascara with some gloss, and I'm a new person. At least I don't look like a thrown-out rag doll next to the ungodly attractive man in the other room.

Or a woman with a guy who aimed his load poorly.

My lips twitch when I find him in the kitchen, a hand towel draped over his broad, bare shoulder, cooking something on the stove. The living room boasts a wall of windows, with a sprawling view of the Hudson River. It's obvious he hired a six-year-old decorator, stuffed animals adorning almost every surface. In one corner, there's an artwork station, filled with crayons, paints, chalks, and every shade of rainbow paper. I wonder how he keeps his light-gray couch so clean.

That reminds me. I clear my throat, and he turns around. "Where's Presley?"

"She stayed at her friend's house last night," he replies, taking a sip out of a mug. "Coffee?"

"No, thank you, not a fan."

The corners of his lips curl up. "Is *that* right?"

I press mine together, attempting to hide my smile and walk back to the windows. Holy shit. The terrace is amazing. I kind of want to go outside and check it out.

His sweeping footsteps from bare feet on wood floors draw closer.

"This is a crazy view," I say.

"Let's not change the subject."

I turn to tell him I saved him from the bitter coffee but then freeze. "Don't you dare," I warn, holding up my hands, as he has the towel that was on his shoulder in his grip.

He rolls his wrist to twist it up.

"I mean it."

He laughs, still stalking me. "I can't believe you're a coffee thief who doesn't even like coffee."

I fumble over a pink dinosaur as I'm backing up, but I catch myself. Reaching down, I pick up the dinosaur and throw it, hitting him in the chest, and then run around his couch. "I'm pretty sure I'm not supposed to have any physical activity after being drugged last night."

He halts his advance, lifts a brow as if he's really wondering if that might be true. I have no clue. I'll say anything to avoid the sting of the end of the towel. "The doctor didn't say anything about that."

Doctor? I stand up straight, all joking aside, and my brows pinch together. "You took me to a hospital?"

He shakes his head, tossing the towel back over his shoulder. "I have a good friend in the building that's an ER doc that came and checked you out. I debated taking you, and if Greg would've told me to, I would've," he adds, reading my unease.

Truthfully, the whole thing is a little unnerving. "Thanks.

You saved me thousands of dollars. I need to stop drinking." It's done nothing but get me in trouble this month. "Thank you for taking care of me."

"My pleasure."

Every time those words come out of his mouth, dirty, dirty thoughts come to mind. This time, I have memories to back up the pleasures he can provide. Specifically with his fingers and tongue. And his…

"Okay," I say, flustered, heading to the kitchen to get his cock out of my head. *Again.* Why do I keep focusing on that? Because *it was one of a kind.* Not that my subconscious needs to remind me, but it was *scream out loud* extraordinary.

I clear the knot of lust from my throat, peeking under a lid on the stove. "What'd you cook?"

"Your typical breakfast. Eggs, bacon, potatoes, and I just have to finish the pancakes."

Does this man have any flaws?

"I'm impressed," I say, looking at the crisp hash browns. "You did not have to do this all for me."

He picks up the spatula. "Who said it was for you? I'm hungry," he teases, bumping me out of the way with his hips.

I step to the side and watch him turn on the griddle and stir the batter. A man that cooks is second on my list, after dancing.

"Truthfully, the doctor said you needed to eat this morning. So, I figured I'd make you some of everything, and you could pick whatever you like."

"I like it all."

"My kind of woman," he says.

"I'd hope so, you married her," I joke, walking to the kitchen table and sitting down. I watch him until he finishes with the pancakes.

"How'd you figure out we were married? If you couldn't remember anything?" How he says the last part, he suspects I'm lying. Well, to his credit, *I am.*

"All right," I say, caving. "I remember the sex. Or at least *some of it?*"

"It's good to know I'm unforgettable, even with *drunk Gray.* It sucks you don't want to bring her back. I really liked her." He places two plates full of eggs, bacon, and potatoes down on the table, grabs the plateful of pancakes, and sits down in the chair next to me.

I scoff. "Of course you did. She did anything you asked, obviously."

A wicked smile plays across his lips. "Yes, she did."

I kick him under the table. "This is so not fair. It's like you cheated on me with me. Tell me what she did." I regret the words as soon as they fall from my lips. "No, wait, don't tell me." What if there's a sex demon living inside me and it came out with *her*? I'm not vanilla, but I'm not a sexual deviant either.

"Don't worry, I don't have a golden-shower fetish," he jokes.

I slap the palm of my hand to my forehead. "Please tell me *she* doesn't either."

His boisterous laugh echoes throughout the room of windows. Charli would love this conversation. She always talks about her sexcapades, none of which include peeing on each other, but it's always a lot more adventurous than me.

Sounds like she'd be proud of *drunk Gray.*

"She did not," he says with a laugh. Thank God. I almost needed another shower imagining it. "Tell me what else you remember."

"Things are spotty and out of order, I think. We were at the Aria, but then remember going to the Bellagio. Next thing I know, I'm waking up in the hospital. I've since got a snippet of a memory running after you, but that's it." He chews a big bite of food, so I continue. "Oh, yeah ... how I learned we were married. This is a good story."

He swallows, sits back, and gives me his full attention.

"My dad is the chief judge at the courthouse, and *he* told me."

"Your dad's a judge?"

I nod, picking up a piece of bacon. "I made him proud that day."

Whatever's on his mind, he keeps it to himself and shovels a forkful of eggs into his mouth. Everything about this feels wrong, sitting and having a casual breakfast in the home of a man that I barely know after a night of being drugged, yet could legally share a last name with.

A blanket of embarrassment engulfs me. "I'm so sorry, Brooks. I should've left in that taxi."

He wipes his mouth with a napkin. "I'm glad you didn't."

"You say that, but our *complicated* situation got more complicated."

He has a nonchalant attitude about all of this. "Just call it our wedded chaos."

Confidence has always been my forte, and I've prided myself on being a woman who is in control of her life. Growing up with a judge, an attorney, and a dangerous power-house in Vegas as parents, I had to maintain a sense of control. Everyone watched me, with huge expectations weighing me down. There was an invisible line, a boundary that I could never cross.

But that line went poof when I met Brooks. Gone. Disappeared. As if it was never there.

Now, my life is in *wedded chaos*.

Awesome.

I lift a brow and cross my arms. "For a man who has a lot to lose in this game, you're being very blasé about it." After a quick internet search, I found out he was worth a billion dollars —and after picking myself off the floor—I expected a lot more pushback. I expected an attorney pounding on my door the next day screaming for me to sign an NDA. Neither happened. What I didn't expect was to find out he had a daughter. I'm kind of surprised that info wasn't anywhere I looked. Like I said, it was a quick search, but nothing ever mentioned his daughter.

He stuffs another forkful of pancakes into his mouth.

"You want this annulment, right?"

He doesn't answer right away, and my eyes bug out in surprise. We *can't* stay married.

"Yes. But there's this weird feeling of ownership of a woman that I never imagined I'd like as much as I do."

I blink. How caveman of him. I puff out a scoff, holding a hand over my heart. "That's the most romantic thing you've *ever* said to me," I reply with the most sarcasm I can muster. Because, wow. "Just so you know, you do not own me, *by the way*."

"Would you take my last name?"

"Brooks!" I exclaim. Is he serious?

His laugh is lighthearted. It's a cute, boyish laugh behind a rugged man. "I mean, *when* you marry a man, would you take his last name?"

I nod. "I would. But not because I'm giving him ownership of me," I add quickly.

He twists his lips. "You know that's what it means, traditionally."

"Well, times have changed, and traditions have evolved. Taking a last name doesn't mean the same to everyone these days."

"What's it mean to you?"

"It means I'm entering a partnership where *we're both equals*, commitment, and unity. It's about sharing a life together, not me giving up my identity or independence." I doubt he can grasp my perspective, given his wealth. How could a woman ever be his equal? He'd probably hold his financial power over her head like a carrot, giving her an allowance, or something else degrading like having someone else dress her. The mere idea enrages me. "Thank you for everything, Brooks. But I should head out." I place my napkin on the table, and he grabs my hand.

"Hold up. Why are you mad all of a sudden?"

I move my hand out from under his, irritation getting the best of me. "You wouldn't understand. We live different lives."

"You don't think I want those same things?"

I scoff. "Clearly, you want to *own* a woman."

He lets out a chuckle. "Geez, woman. I was kidding. I want those things. Everything you said. Which is probably why I'm not married, because all the women I meet *want* to be owned."

In fairness, I'd second-guess everyone's intentions if I were in his position. I know plenty of women who would jump at the chance to be with Brooks, not out of a genuine connection but for his status. It's rather disturbing.

"Yeah, women can be vicious."

"I've learned," he says, and I can't help but wonder what

type of women Brooks has fallen for. Has he ever been in love? "But Presley is my number one, and always will be, so it adds another layer of difficulty finding someone who will accept that. They think they're competing with her."

First of all, *swoon*. I keep expecting something about him will come to light that I'll hate, and I thought I figured it out. I was wrong! Second, competing? What women is he dating? It's not a race for his love. What woman wouldn't want her man to be an incredible father? That's a character trait I'd love to figure out *before* marrying someone.

I contemplate asking about Presley's mom, but after hearing about her tragic fate, I decide against it. It's none of my business. We're getting too personal as it is.

Hazel orbs stare at me over the rim of his coffee cup as an awkward silence falls between us.

"I really should get going."

"What time is your flight?"

"Five."

He twists his wrist to glance at his watch. "It's only ten."

I stand up and collect both our plates. "I've never been to New York, so I planned to be a tourist for a couple of hours."

He follows me to the kitchen, taking the plates out of my hand, and puts them in the sink. "Care for company?"

"I'm slightly afraid of what part of my brain you'll erase next if I stay with you." I move around him, grabbing the rest of the stuff left on the table. "I swear you have one of those memory zappers from *Men in Black*."

"Pshh," he says, washing the plates off. "None of the lapses in memories has been caused by me."

I narrow my eyes in disagreement.

"I did not push you in front of that car."

"No. Instead, you married me and then left me," I joke, poking him in the side. "I had no other choice than to chase down my husband." I gasp, realizing this is turning into a habit.

Chasing Brooks.

CHAPTER 10

GRACYN

"That is not a boat," I say, staring at the sleek white and black monstrosity moored at the dock. "That's a yacht."

When he asked if I wanted to take a boat ride out to the Statue of Liberty, my mind imagined a crowded charter, crammed to the brim with tourists, all packed like sardines.

"Disappointed?"

"Well, hell, had I known I could've owned half of this thing, I might have fought a little harder," I retort with a playful snicker.

"You were this close," he quips, pinching his thumb and index finger close together, "to being a billionaire."

I let out an unbelievable laugh as he assists me on board. "I have no doubts that any woman you marry won't be getting a dime of your money, not with a solid prenup in place."

"That's where you're mistaken, *dear wife*." I arch a brow at the sarcastic endearment. "If I deserve the woman I marry, then she deserves all I can give her."

His unexpected words linger in the air. That is possibly the sexiest thing a man's ever said.

But he's in his thirties and single, which screams he's not in any hurry to share his fortune. It's one thing to say, it's another to do it. I snap out of the *Brooks is deliciously amazing* daze and venture further into the boat.

"Have you ever been on a boat?" he asks from behind.

"For my eighteenth birthday, my parents rented a boat, not as fancy as this one, for a week, and we sailed around the British Virgin Islands. Ended up docking at an island called Peter Island."

Brooks's smile lights up, and I fix him with a deadpan look.

"Don't tell me you own the island." It's a tiny island with only one resort, so it wouldn't surprise me.

He chuckles. "Did you hear it had significant damage from a hurricane? It's closed for renovations."

I raise an eyebrow, noting he sidestepped the question.

"The island isn't mine," he finally clarifies.

"But you've been there."

Nodding, he replies, "A few times." His attention shifts over my shoulder, and his smile falls flat. "Let me give you a tour."

Confused at the sudden edge of annoyance in his voice as I follow him inside the cabin, I glance over my shoulder. A group of onlookers has gathered, watching us.

That's creepy.

And a little unsettling.

I pick up my pace, stepping out of sight from nosy people. As we step into pure luxury, I freeze, taking in the bright, airy room with expansive windows framing both sides. A U-shaped cream-colored couch, with countless pillows, centers the room. Behind it, a small half wall that separates the dining room, complete with a full-size table and eight chairs. I can picture myself curled up taking an afternoon nap or reading a book on the oversized couch, all the while listening to the gentle lull of the ocean waves and feeling the subtle sway of the boat.

"Let's go, Paul," Brooks calls out.

I glance around, confused. *Who's Paul?*

A response echoes down from above. "Yes, sir." The boat hums to life beneath our feet.

"Oh. We're not alone." Why am I surprised he has a driver for this monster? Of course he does.

He points up to the ceiling. "That's Paul."

"I gathered." I chuckle. "Not a fan of driving the sea mansion?"

"Not when I have company." The mention of company has me wondering how often he entertains guests. Does he bring all the women out on his yacht, trying to impress them? He walks over to the bar and asks, "Drink?"

"I'll take a water."

Water is safe. I need safe right now.

He grabs two bottles and hands one to me. Our fingers brush against each other in the exchange. A simple touch, yet it sends my heart into a flutter. I turn away to avoid his amused smirk, as though he's fully aware of the effect he has on the entire female population.

Hell, he probably revels in it.

As the boat eases away from the dock, I peek out the window, watching.

"Ready for the tour?" he asks at the base of the staircase.

"Of course."

He leads me up to another sitting area, this one smaller and more casual. It opens up to a spacious deck with a table and lounging area beneath a shaded cover.

I peek up the continuing staircase. "How many levels are there?"

"Three and a half."

I blink. "Your boat is bigger than my apartment." And here I am, not even employed at the moment. "I'm in college," I blurt out, as if I need to provide him a reason that I'm not working.

His eyes widen, followed by a sigh as he drops his head. "You're still in college? Holy shit." He lifts his gaze. "Please tell me you're at least twenty-one."

"Sorry." I wince. "Nineteen."

He practically leaps away, putting a significant distance between us as if mere proximity to me is illegal. I laugh at his exaggerated response, enjoying him squirm a little too much. "You act like I'm jailbait."

"I thought…" he starts, running his hand through his hair and then taking a long chug of water. He wipes the wetness off his lips with the back of his hand. "You don't act nineteen. Jesus Christ, I'm married to a teenager. Jared is never going to let me live this down," he mutters the last part to himself.

He's shown more distress about my age than us getting married.

"Brooks, I'm twenty-four," I add, so he stops freaking out.

He collapses back on the couch, stretching out his legs and taking a moment to collect himself.

"Good to know you have some hard passes with women," I jest, walking around the couch and sitting on the opposite side, tucking my legs under me.

With his hands linked behind his neck, he asks, "Are you close to graduating?"

So close I can taste it. "Next week."

"And then what?"

I open my mouth and then snap it shut. While I've never been shy about sharing my passion for becoming a teacher, it feels almost inconsequential in Brooks's world. Our lifestyles couldn't be further apart.

"I don't know yet," I mumble, and his eyes narrow in disbelief. "What's with that look?"

"I have no doubt Gracyn Carmichael always has a plan. Why the secrecy?"

I hate that this man can read me already. But he's right, I'm a planner. When things don't go my way, I tend to break things. Usually my poor phone. Charli and my mom even place bets on how long until I'm shopping for a new one.

"The less you know about me, the easier this will be?"

"This?" he prods.

"You know"—I throw my hands up—"whatever this is. A somewhat of a date with my soon-to-be *ex-husband*?"

"Is that what this is? A date?"

I blink twice, irritated that he enjoys pushing my buttons. "What would you call it?"

"A tour of the Hudson," he nonchalantly replies.

A slow, wicked grin creeps up when I shoot a glare his way. Liar. He did not bring me on this boat to be my tour guide. Yesterday, he begged me to stay, kissed me last night, and I'm pretty sure it would've been a Vegas repeat minus the marriage. Because you can't do that twice. I'm okay with that. Casual sex between two consenting adults is perfectly acceptable. But let's call a spade a spade and not lie to ourselves calling it a heart.

Whatever this is, knowing what I'm going to do with the rest of my life is irrelevant.

"All right, Captain Brooks." I push off the couch, saunter toward him, and stop between his legs, meeting his gaze with a daring smirk. "*Guide me.*"

His Adam's apple bobs, and his eyes fall to my chest before he catches himself and brings them back up. He clears his throat, and I can see his control slipping. I take a step back as he rises to his feet, his body brushing against mine. The moment is brief and electric, heat crackling between us.

A low, playful groan rumbles from his throat as he shakes his head. "We should head upstairs. It won't take us long to get to the Statue of Liberty."

I'd continue poking his control until he lost it, but I really want to see the iconic statue. For now.

I spin around in excitement and follow him up the stairs. Stepping onto the boat's highest deck, the brisk wind tousles my hair, and I struggle to pull it back in a ponytail. The famous skyline I've seen so many times in pictures is nothing like it is in real life.

"Wow. It's gorgeous." The cityscape sprawls out, framed by sparse, giant, white fluffy clouds that seem as if someone pasted cotton balls in the sky for added effect.

"It's treated me well," he says, fixated on the city.

"Have you ever lived anywhere else?"

He turns his head and lifts a playful brow. "I thought we were on the *don't ask, don't tell* cruise."

I wrinkle my nose as he calls me out. "You're just so much more interesting than me."

"I suspect you are more interesting than you let on."

Yes, a normal person might think of my life as anything but boring. But Brooks isn't normal. He's lived his life, while I've lived my parents' life. There's a difference.

I sidestep his attempt to lure out information from me. "Do you come out on the boat often? I'm sorry, I meant *yacht*."

"It's just a boat," he retorts, not happy with my correction.

I don't know why, though. If I owned this monstrous thing, I'd incorporate "yacht" into my everyday vocabulary.

He stares down at the wake. "Not as much as we used to. Not since my daughter got a social schedule on par with a Kardashian."

It strikes me as amusing that he won't admit to owning a yacht, but has no problem dropping the Kardashians' name. He probably knows them personally.

"Well, she is the daughter of the infamous *Bachelor of the Year*."

He tsks, shaking his head. "You had to go and ruin that."

"I'm pretty sure our marriage was your idea," I clip out. My attention shifts as the boat veers to the right, and she comes into sight. The Statue of Liberty. I've only seen the quarter-sized replica in Paris, but ever since seeing that one, I've wanted to see this one. "Huh. She's a lot smaller than I imagined."

"That is one disappointment that I'm happy to say I'll never receive."

Figures. He's all about boasting about his large cock, but not his large boat. Not that either is less impressive, but I've got to go with him on this one. It's at a level of *I don't think that'll fit*. It does, perfectly, I might add.

His smile widens. "It's nice that *my wife* doesn't disagree."

Bemused, I choose to ignore the wife comment. He's not technically wrong. "I mean, you got me to marry you *somehow*. Truthfully, that's the only logical explanation."

In fact, I've never thought about marrying a man for the size of his cock, but it's going to be hard to find someone who can compare to Brooks. Not that I'd ever admit that out loud to him. He already has two large heads.

Instead, I stare at the statue as the boat circles her. I take a few pictures and then notice the time. I calculate in my head the time it'll take us to get back and me to the airport. Looks like there won't be a Vegas repeat. I twist my lips in disappointment. "I need to go if I'm going to make my flight."

He flicks his wrist to see the time. "Can you take a later flight?"

I wish I could stay in this fairy tale longer, but I sigh. The clock is about to turn midnight. "I booked the last flight out."

He steps in front of me, encasing me with his arms as he holds onto the rail behind me. "What if I could get you another flight?" His expression mirrors the one he wore when he asked me to go to the reception. A subtle hint of desperation. The warm breeze carries his scent around me as if tempting me.

"I might be persuaded."

He licks his lips, focusing on mine. "You were just talking about my magical dick. Isn't that persuasive enough?"

"It depends." I lift a brow.

"On?"

"If you plan on using it."

CHAPTER 11

GRACYN

"Your flight leaves at eleven tonight." Brooks slides his phone into his pocket, resuming his position in front of me with his arms, caging me in on either side.

I'm not going to even question how he made that happen. I already know money talks.

Tilting his head, he asks, "What next?"

I smirk, amused that he tries to make me think I'm the one in charge. Something tells me he rarely gives up control. "You're the captain of this boat."

He lifts his sunglasses, sliding them on top of his head. "Tell me what you're doing after college."

"That again?"

"Why won't you tell me?"

"Why do you need to know?"

"I didn't. Until you made it a *thing*." He chuckles. I'm surprised when his head falls to my neck and he gently kisses it. I roll my head to the side to give him better access. "What"—

kiss—"is"—kiss—"it?" The trail of kisses tingles against my skin as he moves up to my jawbone.

I drag my hands down his back until they reach the hem of his shirt. His breath hitches a beat when I snake them under his shirt, pressing into his hot, bare skin. "You're going to be disappointed," I breathe out, losing myself in his touch, making it almost impossible to focus on the conversation he's trying to have.

Suddenly, he stops and steps back. "Fuck." His breaths are heavy, his chest rising and falling. "I was going to coerce you, but that's not a strategy I'll win. Once I start, I'm not sure I'll be able to stop myself."

"Then don't stop," I reply, biting my swollen lip.

With a slow, deliberate motion, he reaches behind him, grabs the back of his shirt, and pulls it over his head. Tossing it aside, he leans against the bar. "Tell me."

My eyes flick to the bridge behind him we're about to go under. I huff, knowing he's never going to let this go. "I hate you."

He lifts a wicked brow. "Are you embarrassed?"

"Absolutely not," I say defensively and then grunt. He's as stubborn as I am. "I'm going to be a teacher."

He stares at me, his body motionless. "Huh," he finally says. And then he turns and walks away.

Walks. Away.

I blink, staring at the space where he stood, my jaw hanging open. What the hell just happened? When he strolls back out, taking a long pull from a water bottle, his sunglasses back over his eyes, anger takes hold. I press my lips together in a tight line. Unbelievable.

"For the record, teaching is one of the most important jobs out there. You wouldn't be where—"

"I agree," he fires back, cutting me off.

I throw my hands up, confused. "Then what's the problem?"

"My mom's a teacher," he explains, his voice softer. He pauses and runs his hand through his hair. "She would love you."

"Oh." That's surprising to me. It's hard to imagine a billionaire being the son of a teacher. "What does your dad do?" *Stop asking him personal questions.* "Wait, don't answer that."

He laughs to himself, then jerks his chin toward the chaise lounge. He walks over to it and stretches out on the king-sized lounger, his arms resting behind his head. The sun beats down on him, but the breeze keeps it bearable.

I crawl across it to join him, but when I lay back, the space between us clearly isn't to his liking. With a playful tug on my legs, he pulls them over his thighs. He sighs and leans back, his thumb circling my knee, and he closes his eyes as he relaxes.

I look around, knowing I'm in over my head, but damn, how freaking amazing is this? The boat glides along the Hudson River, the city skyline glinting in the sunlight.

"An accountant," he replies.

I hum, surprised that his wealth doesn't come from family money.

"You're wondering how I got here?"

"Well, yeah? You're only thirty-two, and there are a lot of zeros behind your name."

He chuckles once, gaze shifting to the water. "Luck."

I tilt my head, surprised by his answer.

"Don't get me wrong, I worked my ass off to get our company where it is today. We landed some big deals early on that catapulted us forward. But Jared and I built an app in college to track prospects and a bunch of other features. We sold it to a software company a couple years later for a pretty penny. I invested the money into startups, stocks, real estate. Some flopped, but the ones that didn't? They paid off. Big time."

"So, one lucky break turned into an empire?"

He shrugs a shoulder. "Luck opened the door. Hard work made sure it stayed open."

I stare at him, amazed. But then, inwardly, I cringe. I refuse to be more impressed by him, dammit. "We should get back to the *don't ask, don't tell* cruise," I tease, nudging his side.

A lazy grin forms on his face, and I hate that I can't see his eyes. "So, a teacher, huh? What grade?"

I playfully kick him with my foot. "You're relentless."

He catches my foot, his grip warm and firm. A quiet sigh escapes when he presses his thumb into the pad of my foot. "More like curious."

If he continues massaging my foot like that, I'll reveal all my secrets. "First through third," I admit, unable to hide my smile. "I love kids. I love when their little faces light up when they learn new things. They're funny, and their excitement is infectious."

He chuckles, shaking his head. "And in between all that, they're little assholes."

I slap him on the arm, gasping. "They are not! You can't tell me that Presley isn't perfect."

His smile softens. "I love that little girl with every fiber in my body," he begins. "But let's be real, she can absolutely be a little shit sometimes."

Our laughter fades as we settle into the gentle ride of the boat. The salty, warm breeze brushes over us, and the rhythmic sway of the waves is almost hypnotic. I close my eyes, basking in the moment, in his touch, in his closeness.

"Too bad I didn't pack a bathing suit," I murmur, my eyes still closed.

"There's one downstairs you can use."

I jerk my head toward him, twisting my body. "I do not want to wear some left-behind swimsuit of one of your boat bunnies."

"Boat bunnies?" he repeats.

He heard me loud and clear. The wind tosses a loose strand of my hair around and he reaches out and wraps it around my ear. He did the same thing yesterday at the wedding, and the simple, sweet gesture sends a surge of chills up and down my back.

"The only used swimsuits on board won't fit you," he says, his lips curling into a slow, teasing grin. "Unless you're an adolescent, which, I assure you, is most definitely not the case."

Still not convinced that one of his groupies didn't leave the swimsuit behind—*because gross*—I ask, "So where did it come from?"

His face shifts into uncertainty. He rubs the back of his neck, a telltale sign I've already seen a few times when he's unsure how I'll react. Like when he called the doctor or grabbed my bag from my hotel. I angle my head, wondering what he did this time.

He clears his throat, looking off briefly. "I might have gotten Charli's number from your phone while you took a shower and texted her to ask your size in a bathing suit."

My brows shoot up. "You what?"

"And then," he continues, trying to get it all out before I explode. "I might have had my assistant run to the store to pick up a couple of bathing suits for you."

I blink at him, floored. "Seriously? You are the most inva-sive man I've ever met."

That's why we have passwords. Charli's voice pops in my head. She's always hounding me to set one up.

As much as I want to be annoyed by his overbearing tenden-cies, I'm not. Because as invasive as he's been, everything he's done, it's been for my benefit. I've yet to decide if I find it a flaw or one of his strengths.

Okay, I'm lying.

His attentiveness is sexy as hell, definitely a strength.

Most men I've dated only consider themselves or what they could gain from the situation. Not to say this whole swimsuit thing isn't self-serving. There's a solid chance the bathing suits are basically three strings and a prayer.

But we're not dating.

He settles back with one hand behind his head, unbothered by my reactions now. "What? You're my wife. I should know these things."

I drop my head, shaking it. "I'm starting to think you like saying that."

"It's growing on me," he says, unapologetic.

"Why did I agree to this?" I mutter, scooting to the end of the lounger. I glance behind me. "Were you even drunk that night? A mail-order bride would've been easier."

"Yep. When you stole my coffee, I knew immediately I wanted a thief for my wife. Just what a billionaire wants in his life." His tone is dripping with a mix of sarcasm and humor.

"And yet, here we are," I counter.

"Which is proof I was piss drunk that night." He lifts that perfectly groomed brow over the rim of his sunglasses. "A mail-order bride would've cost me a fortune. This one just cost me a coffee."

Did he just call me cheap?

I am not cheap.

I kick his foot with mine. "That's it. I'm taking the yacht." With a dramatic twirl, I march to the stairs, my head held high. I stop on the first stair and ask, "Where am I finding this *new* bathing suit?"

He grins. "Bottom level. Last room on the left."

FIFTEEN MINUTES LATER, I'm walking up those same stairs, trying not to burst out laughing at the ridiculousness of this swimsuit. Who bought this thing? To her credit, at least it fits. But evidently, whoever it is hates me. Wait a minute. It had to be his assistant, the one who kept telling me he was "busy."

She would do this.

As soon as Brooks sees me, he slides his sunglasses down his nose with a single finger. His smile falters for a fraction of a second before a forced, fake grin takes its place. *He thinks I might like this.*

I scrunch my nose and do a slow spin, letting him appreciate the full ensemble. "Your assistant sure knows how to pick them." I tug on the annoyingly tight mock neck. "It's a little warm." The long-sleeve swim shirt is not the worst thing in the world, it's more hilariously out of place.

"Well…" He pauses, biting his bottom lip to suppress his amusement. "I won't lose you."

"Why? Because I resemble *Where's Waldo?*" I deadpan. Who could go missing wearing a red-and-white striped top paired with black boy shorts? It's as if I popped right off a page out of the book. It's practical, I guess. "At least I won't get sunburnt."

He's biting his knuckle now. "I bet you're regretting not having one of those boat bunny suits right now."

"Nope. A Waldo suit is still better than a trip to my gyno."

"Wow," he mouths, eyes sparkling with amusement. "Just so we're clear, I'm clean."

Blood drains from my face. *Way to stick your foot in your mouth, Gray.* "I didn't mean to insinuate…"

He cuts me off with a sly grin. "Your assessment's fair. I know my reputation precedes me. But I haven't been that guy in years. Well, *until recently.*"

Like I have any room to talk about the women who throw themselves at Brooks. Considering I practically wrapped myself in a bow and said *I'm yours* after meeting him for five minutes, it doesn't say a lot about *my* character.

I sit next to him again. "Seems we bring out the worst in each other."

"The worst?" He leans in closer, kissing my shoulder. "Pretty sure I brought out the best of you. Multiple times, if I recall."

My stomach flutters. Definitely multiple times.

I turn my head, catching him staring at me. "What?" I expected to see desire, not confusion.

"Is that really the suit she bought?"

My eyes widen. "You think this is mine?"

He shakes his head in mock irritation. "I'm going to fire Hattie tomorrow."

I roll over, straddling him. "You're not firing anyone." My hands rest on his chest, and he stares up at me, heat simmering just beneath the surface. I trail a finger around the tattoo on his pec. How could I forget he had these? He has three of them. One on each shoulder and then his entire right pec.

The long sleeves of this ridiculous swim shirt are suffocating now, especially under his intense stare. His hands settle firmly on my hips, pulling me closer. We're drifting in open waters now. Nothing but endless blue surrounds us, and there aren't any boats that are close to us.

"Paul won't come up here, right?"

"If he wants to keep his job, he won't."

I wiggle my hips against his hardness and take off my sunglasses. I grab the edge of the swim shirt and pull it over my head, tossing it to the side. It's way too hot for this. The warm breeze kisses my bare skin, and his gaze drops to my breasts, darkening with desire.

"Better?" I murmur seductively.

"I'm not complaining, but you're beautiful in anything."

I lean over, placing my hands on each side of his head, hovering. "I'm going to need you to stop being so sweet," I whisper in his ear. "When I leave here, I need to hate you."

"And what exactly do I need to do for you to hate me?"

I twist my lips, coming up empty. Tossing me overboard might do it, but I'd like to leave here alive. "How about we just have sex? Raw, heart-pounding, unadulterated fucking. No more sweet nothings."

His smile grows as his fingers dig into my hips. "And here I thought *sober Gray* was going to be boring."

In one quick maneuver, he flips us, and his lips come crashing down against mine hungrily. The kiss was exactly what I asked for. Demanding. Feral. He continues kissing me along my collarbone, slow and deliberate, his breath hot against my skin. I arch into him as his mouth explores, moving down to my boobs, unraveling me more each second.

Warm wind sweeps over us, making everything seem that much more electric. It heightens every sensation, the contrast of the soft breeze against the heat radiating between us. His lips move down, and he stops for a quick kiss on my belly button before continuing down south. His teeth catch the edge of the boy shorts, tugging them down with almost agonizing patience.

He just looks up at me, his gaze dark and intense, as if he's savoring the view. I feel exposed, vulnerable, but there's a thrill in the way he's taking his time, like I'm something he wants to memorize. And then he leans down, his mouth grazing my inner thigh. His tongue flicks my swollen clit, and I mewl.

This. *This is why I married the man.*

His tongue is magical, and he knows exactly what he's doing. Every flick, every teasing stroke, drives me further to the edge. There's something about being out in the open, the rush of someone catching us, and his well-defined skills that push me over the edge. My fingers squeeze around the pillow as a wave of heat rips through my center, and my hips buck against his mouth.

Holy hell.

He must've asked me to marry him right after this. The exact moment where I'm floating in orgasmic bliss. Because, right now, I'd say yes to anything.

Movement brings me back into the present, and I watch as he shoves his board shorts down. With his gaze locked on mine, he pumps his hard cock in his hand twice. His body is the personification of a sculpted Greek god.

"It's so hard, it almost hurts," he mutters through clenched teeth.

He bends to grab a condom from his shorts, sliding it down his shaft. The wind tousles his hair, and I can't take my eyes off him, my body already aching in anticipation. Crawling forward on his knees, he reaches for me and pulls me upright.

He sits back, guiding me to straddle him, his large hands lifting me over his cock. A soft moan escapes my lips as I lower myself onto him, the intoxicating fullness sending a dizzying rush through me. The world around us fades, the open expanse of water and the possibility of being seen forgotten.

"You're so beautiful," he whispers into my ear.

His grip tightens on my ass, and I lift and grind my hips against him as I lower onto him, my body convulsing against him. He lets out a low, guttural groan, nipping my collarbone. I hold on to his neck for balance, my fingers curling into his skin. My heart pounds in my chest as his lips trail up my neck, his tongue flicking the sensitive spot behind my ear.

"Do you have any idea what you do to me?" he growls, his voice strained, raw.

I tilt my head back, giving him easier access, and my body trembles at his words. "Show me," I whisper, daring him, craving more, wanting to lose myself in him entirely.

His hands slide up my back, holding me as he lays me back, taking control, driving his thrusts upward, filling me so deeply I can't hold back the moans that slip from my lips. He falls forward, his mouth capturing mine, swallowing the sound, his kiss hungry and desperate.

His movements quicken, becoming almost primal. Each thrust sends a shockwave coursing through me, the intensity building with every stroke. My nails rake down his back, desperate to hold on as he drives me closer to the edge again.

"There is no way you could forget this." His voice is rough and commanding, as if driving the point with his dick. He pushes up again, his hands spreading me wider as he plunges even deeper, the friction between us sparking something wild and uncontrollable.

He's right. Un-freaking-forgettable.

My vision blurs as I shatter around him, screaming his name, my release barreling through me. He follows moments later, his body tensing through his own release, before collapsing against mine.

For a moment, neither of us moves. The only sounds are the soft lapping of the waves against the boat, the heavy cadence of our breathing, and the soft whistle of the wind. The breeze glides across my overheated skin as I stare up at the sky.

Brooks leans over and presses a kiss to my temple, his lips lingering there. "You're a lousy fuck," he murmurs, his voice dripping with smug satisfaction.

My jaw drops, but then my brain catches up. Liar. I bite back my laugh. "Maybe if your dick wasn't pencil-thin, you might've felt something," I shoot back.

He roars with laughter, deep and unrestrained, as he pushes up and scoots off the lounger, disposing of the condom, before crawling back. "Pencil-thin?" he repeats in mock offense. "Funny, I don't recall you complaining a few minutes ago when you were screaming my name loud enough to scare the fish."

I wasn't *that* loud. I raise a brow, my lips curving into a taunting smile. "Haven't you ever heard of a woman faking it?"

In a swift motion, he rolls on me, pinning my hands above my head. "I know damn straight you were not faking it."

I shrug, knowing it's killing him.

"Woman," he warns, the attempt of having me hate him not going his way. "Admit it."

I shake my head, and he playfully bites my chin in response. When I shake my head again, he bites somewhere else. My earlobe. My collarbone. My nipple. My stomach. Every inch of my body heats back up.

Eventually, my resistance melts into slow, teasing shakes, each one daring him to move lower. Anticipation coils inside of me, a deliciously wicked game we both know I'll lose.

So much for trying to leave hating him.

Because by the time I walk away, I'm certain his dick isn't pencil-thin, and he knows damn well my orgasms were real.

I GRIP the handle of my suitcase, my chest tightening as I wrestle with the words to say goodbye to the most infuriating, perfect man. The regret claws at me, and I haven't even left him yet.

"Thanks for…" I pause, searching for the right words. "The perfect day."

He nods, leaning against the car with a casual ease that makes my pulse race. Hands tucked in his pockets, legs crossed, that devastatingly sexy, effortless charm radiating off him. He's perfected it. "Thanks for being a degenerate."

"What? I am not!"

"You so are. You're a wedding crasher and a thief," he points out with a teasing grin.

"You drove me to a life of crime." I shrug, poking him in the chest. "Thank God we're getting that annulment. I'd hate to see what you'll have me doing next."

His smile wavers, and his sigh lingers in the air, heavy and loaded, leaving an awkward moment between us. We both feel it. But what is it exactly?

It's lust.

It's great, unforgettable sex.

It's fun.

But it's not love.

It can't be love. Spending three whirlwind days with a man should not leave me feeling regret or teetering on the edge of heartbreak. So, what is this? Why am I feeling anything other than being sexually satiated?

"Guess I'll see you next month in court." I turn to walk toward the sliding glass doors but then pause and look over my shoulder. "Well, unless you send *your* attorney."

Still rooted against the car, he winks and replies, "I'll be there."

Five more weeks. I can handle five more weeks of being married to this man.

Right?

CHAPTER 12

BROOKS

I never considered parenting to be hard. Actually, I never considered parenting at all. Being a dad wasn't in my DNA. My parents didn't want me, which is how I ended up adopted. My biological father and I have somewhat of a relationship, so I understand why he did it. It's the exact reason I didn't want kids.

Leverage.

People will use the one thing that means the most to you to take advantage of you. And women? They're as ruthless as the criminals my real father deals with. At least in my pretentious world. Before Presley, I reveled in the attention women gave me. Money, sex, and success. Just a man living his best life.

Then bam.

"Jessie had a baby. And we think it's yours."

The words that changed my life forever. Sounds dramatic, but it's the hard truth. I met Jessie at a bar one night. Slept with her a few times, and then she disappeared. I never had a second thought about her again. She was like the rest of the women I slept with, *forgettable*.

Until a stranger walked into my office with news that cracked my life wide open. First, this stranger ended up being my sister. A sister I was unaware of. And second, Jessie had a baby. A baby who was apparently mine. Turns out, Jessie was playing a game, and I was a pawn. She meant to destroy my sister's life, but in the end, it was hers that she ruined.

When the dust settled, I had a screaming seven-pound banshee, otherwise known as baby Presley. And my guilty pleasure of getting lost in womens' arms became a distant memory. But I never once regretted Presley. The unconditional love I had for her the second I laid eyes on her is the eighth wonder of the world. There are days it stops me in my tracks. It's a powerful emotion that brings out the best and worst in me.

She became my sole focus.

No more women.

Until…

"Daddy, I like Gracyn."

Sigh. *Yeah, kid. Me too.*

Dancing with her in my arms felt invigorating. Powerful. Everyone was watching and not a single person knew that she was my wife. My. Fucking. Wife. I wasn't lying when I told her about the rush I felt. In hindsight, I should've thought of a better word than owned. Little of my adult life has been my own, much to my credit. After being titled New York's Bachelor of the Year when our business took off, at the ripe age of twenty-three, I craved being in the spotlight. I ultimately paid the price by giving up my privacy.

I should've been more careful with Gracyn. Or rather, let her leave after the wedding. People will question who she is. I wonder how much damage control I need to do. The annulment can't come fast enough.

Except, I can't stop thinking about her. She possesses the qualities I'd want my future wife to have. Confidence, caring, nurturing, and someone I can be myself around. To make matters worse, she wants to be a teacher. Which means my mom would approve. But that means nothing. I've known her for less than a month and have only spent three days with her. How much do I *really* know about her? Not enough to believe our marriage was destiny calling. A drunken night with a beautiful woman didn't send my life on a different trajectory.

And Gracyn agrees.

Mistake.

End of story.

I peer down at Presley, who desperately wants a mom. "You met her once."

I want to tell her that's ridiculous. *But is it?* It only took me one night.

Presley skips around, grabbing her dance stuff as she goes, her ponytail swishing back and forth. "She was nice to me, and she's very pretty." That she is. I wonder if our shared attraction to the stranger is on a biological level. "You liked her too," Presley sings. Little girls pick up on the tiniest details. It's as if they're wired to hear or see things they shouldn't.

"Presley. She was only here for the wedding." I squat, pulling her in between my legs. "And what have I told you about talking to strangers?"

Her squeals fill the room as I tickle her. Judith, Presley's nanny, advises me to be more serious when reprimanding her, but her innocent blue eyes melt my stern facade. She knows it too, especially when she pulls out her fake crying. I swear she's going to grow up to be an actress.

Or a con artist.

Just like her mom.

I DROP my keys on the entry table and follow my nose to the kitchen. Standing at the stove with a wooden spoon in hand is Judith, with a big smile. The scent of rich, savory sauce fills the air, and it's obvious Judith's made my all-time favorite dish, her homemade lasagna.

"What's the occasion?" I ask, leaning against the doorframe as I watch her stir the sauce.

She shrugs one shoulder. "I'm just happy. The wedding was magical this weekend, and it put me in a great mood. And I haven't made it for you two in a while."

"Well, you made my day," I say, my stomach growling in agreement.

"I always love how much you enjoy my mom's recipe." She turns to check the noodles. "Oh, I meant to ask, was that woman okay?"

I try to recall if there was an incident at work today but draw a blank. "What woman?"

"The one you carried out of the wedding." Her expression shifts to something between concern and mild embarrassment. "Was she *that* drunk?"

My head tilts, confused. "How did you see that?" She left with Presley at least thirty minutes before that happened.

"Sadie saw you leave with her," she adds. "Don't worry, she won't tell anyone. She was just concerned."

I sigh, irritated that Jared's house manager is swapping stories with my nanny. They both signed NDAs, so they really shouldn't be discussing anything they see.

"The lady was okay. A little too much of the open bar," I say as I dip a spoon into the meat sauce, taking a small taste. "Hey, how's Chuck?"

She playfully scoffs, rolling her eyes. "You know he's just a friend. Nice deflection, though." She leans against the counter, watching me expectantly, not letting it go. "Who was she? I've never seen her before but Presley seemed smitten. She wouldn't stop talking about her on the way home."

"She helped find Pres's stuffy. Of course, she liked her. She's her hero. But Ms. Carmichael was only in town for the wedding. I'm positive she left on a plane with a major hangover."

A Brooks hangover.

I hide the smirk tugging at the corners of my lips as I walk out of the kitchen.

"She was strikingly beautiful. I wish I could pull off a dress like that," she muses.

I flip through the pile of mail on the counter, pretending to give it my full attention. "Let me know when dinner's done," I say, already moving toward my office. I won't eat until Presley is home from dance so we can eat together, but at least I can come out of hiding.

"Sure thing," she replies to my back, amusement lacing her voice.

CHAPTER 13

BROOKS

"Lady in red, huh?" Jared quips, slapping my shoulder as he passes by.

As if I haven't spent the better half of my day trying to shove her out of my mind, people won't stop talking about her. He drops onto the maroon leather club chair across from me, sporting a smug grin plastered on his face.

I'm surprised Anabel allowed him out of the house, considering he said *I do* only three days ago. The exclusive cigar club is our sanctuary. Our monthly meeting where we can escape the scrutinizing stares of the people who work for us, women, and drama. Just cigars, whiskey, and a few hours to shoot the shit.

"Go on your honeymoon, already," I mutter, paying more attention to the cigar between my fingers.

He laughs. "Trust me, I'd love to, but someone had to make sure that deal was finalized."

I roll my eyes, biting back a retort. He knows damn well that I was capable. But I get it, he's been working on this deal for almost eight months. It's his baby. The deal was nearly finished, but whatever helps him sleep at night.

He leans back, taking a sip of his whiskey. "Anabel and I couldn't figure out who she was. Was she someone's plus one?"

And here we go.

Our friends and other top executives around the city turn their attention to me with sparked interest. Chase flicks his cigar against the edge of the ashtray. "Wasn't that the girl from Vegas?" he asks, looking straight at me.

Shit. I was afraid of this. I hoped he was too intoxicated to remember meeting her. He's the only one who met her.

I keep my face neutral, my fingers steady as I roll the cigar between them. "Who?" I shoot for ignorance.

"The girl who showed up at the bar. The one you *left* with."

Laughing, I reply, "I barely remember anything that happened that night." I lie. "Wasn't that girl's hair dark blond?" I toss in, hoping to throw him off.

Chase shakes his head. "No, bro. It was brown." I underestimated Chase's memory. "But I guess it wasn't her."

Thank you, now let's move on. "The girl from the wedding is nobody to be concerned about," I say smoothly, pulling in a long draw of the cigar. The earthy notes coat my tongue. It gives me something to focus on rather than sit here and continue to make shit up.

"You looked pretty close on that dance floor. She's definitely a *somebody*," Jared presses.

I stare up at the ceiling, exhaling a slow breath of smoke. "She was her brother's plus one. We had a quick hookup. End of story." What I don't say, *what I won't say*, is that she crashed his wedding to serve me annulment papers, and then I begged her to stay so I could have one last taste of her.

Devon leans forward, pointing his cigar at me. "The old Brooks, *pre-Presley*, that would be a typical response. But this guy"—he points his cigar at me—"doesn't *have* hookups."

Correct. I just marry them now.

"Are you guys afraid you won't be invited to the wedding? Fuck, let it go." I bring the cigar to my mouth again. I'm done with this conversation. "She doesn't even live here."

"Where's she from?" Jared asks, pushing his luck.

"I didn't ask. I didn't care." There's a finality in my tone, and I hope it'll shut them up.

The server appears with another tray of drinks, and I'm thankful for the interruption because the guys revert their attention to her. The conversation shifts to the stock market, and their words fade away as my mind drifts back. Back to her. My hands on every part of her wicked body. Her breathy moans. The way she clawed at my back, desperate for more.

I let out a long, satisfied sigh.

Sunday was a good day.

"Handley," Jenson snaps, drawing my attention back to the present.

I blink, shaking the memory loose, only to find all of them staring at me with matching smug grins. Then the chuckles start, low and knowing.

"You guys are assholes."

"ARE we going to talk about why you disappeared early from the reception?"

I pause, biting into my tuna sandwich, glancing up at Jade. Here we go again. She pops a french fry in her amused mouth. I continue to sink my teeth into the sandwich and chew slowly. She waits, but I take another large bite.

"Oh, come on." She laughs, leaning forward. "Does it have anything to do with the stunning brunette in the red dress? I think you said her name was Gray?"

I search my memories, wondering when I let her name slip. That's right. It was right after the wedding when I caught Gracyn talking to Presley. "Someone said they saw you carrying her out the door. Apparently, she looked as if she'd passed out."

How many freaking people saw me? I swallow the bite and take a drink to wash it down. "Someone drugged her."

Her eyes widen. "What? At the wedding? Who?"

"Cooper Rossman." No reason to beat around the bush.

She slams her hand on the table with a look of disgust. "That bastard. It doesn't surprise me, though, he's a douchebag. Thank God you were there. Please tell me you got it on video to give as evidence to the cops."

I crack my neck, knowing she won't like the answer. "She didn't want to go to the cops."

Her head snaps back. "Why?"

"She isn't from here. And it's ... complicated," I add, hoping it's enough. It won't be.

She studies me for a few moments. Her mouth opens and closes, the questions piling up behind her lips. Instead, she ends with a huff, crossing her arms. "You're being super ominous with her. Is everything okay? Because honestly, this is giving me Jessie vibes."

My jaw tightens at the comparison. I glance around the packed deli, debating if I should tell her. Usually, I share everything with Jade.

Jared, Anabel, Jade, and I have been friends since freshman

year of college. Everyone assumed Jade and I would end up together after Jared and Anabel became a couple. But when Presley's mom dropped into my life like a hurricane and left me with a child to raise, Jade didn't want any part of that. And I couldn't blame her. We never clicked in that way, anyway. The occasional hookup, but that's as far as it went. She loves Presley like a niece. She just never wanted to be a mom.

Yet, I can't bring myself to admit the most reckless thing I've ever done to any of my best friends. And technically, Gracyn is my wife, and until she's not, I have to do whatever I can to protect her. Which means I have to keep our secret from everyone, including Jade.

"She's nothing like Jessie." I *might* have added a little too much protest, and Jade's brow quirks in amusement.

My phone vibrates on the table, and I glance over at the text.

Jared: My office. NOW.

Jade notices the text. "Think he heard about someone being drugged?"

"He found out *something*," I mutter, pushing my chair back and grabbing my phone. He's supposed to be working from home.

Jade stands with me, her hand gripping my arm as she levels me with a steady gaze. "What are you planning to do about Cooper?"

I lift a pointed brow. I can't say out loud what I'd like to do to him.

She leans in, her voice laced with concern. "Brooks, don't do something stupid. I know you have connections, but he's not worth jeopardizing your future."

I take her hand in mine and squeeze, leaning down so only she can hear me. "Nothing would be linked to me. Only a few people are familiar with my real father." Jade is one of them. I never asked for anything from him. But this is different. Seeing Gracyn drugged and knowing what could've happened if I hadn't been there? It's tempting.

I hold up my phone, showing her the second text I received from Jared. "I have to go." Whatever it is, it's urgent. I pause and look back at her. "By the way, take down the picture."

She snickers, shaking her head. "No. It's a great picture." I can't argue because it is. "Tell me, how many times have you stared at it?"

Countless. Too many to confess, not enough to deny. It figures she would take a picture of Gracyn in my arms on the dance floor. A moment she conspired with my daughter to make happen and then shared it to her Instagram page with all the other wedding snapshots she had taken.

I almost texted it back to Gracyn when she sent me a message about her new job, but then thought otherwise. No matter how perfect we look together, it doesn't change a damn thing. We live separate lives.

I GET a strange sense the second I step into the lobby. People are staring, and their expressions are off. Something is going on. It's the whispers that set off warning bells in my head. *For God's sake, does everyone think I drugged Gracyn?*

My phone buzzes in my pocket, but I ignore it and make a beeline for Jared's office. It goes off again as I reach for the doorknob, but I hit the side button in my pocket, ending the call, without looking at who it is. It can wait. Jared will know how to fix this. Considering it happened at his wedding.

As soon as I walk into his office and shut the door, he stands and exclaims, "You're married?"

Fuck me sideways.

Not what I was expecting.

I sigh, raking my hand through my hair. "How'd you find out?"

"Seriously? *That's* your reply?" His voice rises, and I can feel the heat behind it. "How about sorry I didn't tell you? Damn it, Handley, this could blow up in our faces. Remember, we own a business together. *A multi-million dollar business.* And you've just put it at risk. Did you even have her sign a prenup? Our attorney has already called me demanding answers. I felt like a complete fool when I told her I didn't have a clue!"

Well, that explains the whispers, the strange looks, and nonstop calls. Everyone knows. I drop into one of the two chairs across from his desk, my head falling into my hands. I don't have a good explanation. How I'm acting doesn't make sense to me either.

I lift my gaze to find his. "Don't worry, the only thing she wants from me is an annulment."

He scoffs. "The problem is, I don't think that's all you want from *her.*"

He swivels his computer screen to face me, revealing *Page Six*'s website with images of us together. One in front of the church by the road where a taxi is waiting, the reception picture from Instagram, and a picture of me helping her on my boat. In each image, I'm staring at her with a goofy grin plastered on my face. The headline reads, *"Secret Marriage: Is the Forever Bachelor of New York Finally Settling Down?"*

I groan inwardly.

"What the hell did you expect was going to happen?" The disappointment in his voice grates on my already rattled nerves. "You've been hanging out with this woman, and people are so goddamn nosy. You had to know they would figure it out."

I pinch the bridge of my nose, aware I screwed up and bracing for the storm that's coming. It had taken substantial bribes to keep Presley's name out of the headlines all these years, not to mention the considerable amount of money to bury any stories that somehow slipped through the cracks. They're there if you search hard enough, but they're not the first stories you find when searching my name.

"I haven't been under the tabloids' radar in years. How the hell was I to know they'd take an interest in me all of a sudden?"

Jared leans back, folding his arms across his chest with an almost bemused expression. "That's what happens when you show up married out of the blue. And when the hell did you get married?"

CHAPTER 14

GRACYN

Finally! Something to take my mind off him.

We'd like to welcome you to Bismarck Elementary.

I dance around the living room, rereading the last line of my official offer letter I received in my email. They contacted me this morning; however, the reality only hits me right now.

Who's an adult with a big girl job now? *Me!*

Excitement bubbles inside me as I imagine my Pinterest-perfect classroom. Bean bags in the reading corner, each wall devoted to a different subject, vibrant bursts of color everywhere. Eek! I can't wait to start!

After texting Charli, I pulled up Brooks's number. My giddiness overshadows any rational thought. Because why would I text Brooks? But I do, because he *is* my husband.

> Me: I'm officially a teacher now!

> Brooks: Congrats. Can't believe I'm married to a teacher. Never would've thought.

Me: Sorry to disappoint.

He doesn't reply, but he's not disappointed. Not after learning his mom is a teacher.

"Moooom!" I yell, walking through the front door.

"I'm in the kitchen."

I drop my purse on the entry table and grab the letter. She looks up from her puzzle and sees me waving the letter in the air.

"What's that?"

I read it out loud, and it still feels like I'm reading it for the first time.

"I'm so proud of you," she says, standing and rounding the table to pull me in for a hug. "That is so exciting! Your first real job."

I ignore her remark rather than engage in an argument about whether bartending is a legitimate job because I'm too excited. I could argue that I made more money working fewer nights a week than I will working full time as a teacher. But for her, it's all about stability and planning for the future, as she would often remind me that bartending doesn't offer either of those. Instead, I pull out my phone and open my Pinterest page.

"Look, I have an entire board dedicated to how I want to design my room. We need to go shopping."

"First, I have something for you." She walks over to her purse and pulls out an envelope. She hands it to me. "Open it. It's your graduation present." I'm confused because my graduation is Friday and the party is this weekend. "I'd prefer not to give this to you at your party with everyone watching."

I slide open the envelope and pull out a check. "Mom!" I exclaim, holding a check for twenty-five thousand dollars. "I don't—"

She shushes me. "You were always so stubborn and independent about paying your own way through college," she says, her eyes fixed on mine. "But we wanted to support you all along. Instead, we saved some money to give to you for a graduation present."

I wrap my arms around her. Tears of gratitude well up in my eyes as I hug her, with a deep sense of appreciation for everything she's done for me. "Thank you," I murmur.

She pulls back and wipes a tear off my cheek, smiling. "I couldn't have asked for a better daughter."

I wave off my emotions and point to my phone that is still in her hand. "Okay, enough mushy stuff. Look what your money is going to help me buy." As she's scrolling through my pins, a text flashes on top. When I see it's from Brooks, I snatch it back.

Brooks: I could never be disappointed in you.

How does he always find the perfect words to make my heart flutter?

It was probably better if he had ignored it.

When my mom clears her throat, my cheeks heat as I lift my gaze. Her smile reaches her eyes as she swirls her finger in a small circle in front of my face. "Well, this is new. I've never seen you smile like that before."

I turn away from her, trying to hide the giddiness by shifting my attention to a dirty spot on the counter. I scratch at it, anything to avoid her eyes.

"Is there something you forgot to tell me about your trip?"

I texted her Monday morning that I had gotten back, but between taking my last certification exam and catching up on sleep, I haven't talked with her. I shake my head, unwilling to meet her gaze. "We're still getting an annulment."

"Mm-hmm," she hums, skeptical.

"We are," I insist, looking up. "We're just ... I guess you can say friends."

She raises a brow. "I've never gotten *that* happy over one text from a friend."

"It's just a text."

"You like him." I can't hide anything from her. She can read me like an open book. "What happened on your trip?"

I sigh as I push up on a barstool. "It was amazing. *He* was amazing. Everything about him is perfect. He's attentive. *Very* attentive. Funny. And sexy as hell."

My mom nods in agreement because she's not blind or dead.

"Everything. *Except* he lives in New York and has a kid."

She doesn't miss a beat. "You want a lot of kids, so don't give me that excuse."

Four. But I guess to a woman who only had one, that's a lot. And she's right. Presley is adorable, and that's the last reason I would stay away from Brooks.

I sigh. "I'm not ready to give my life up here for a man I barely know, and he sure the hell isn't in a position to move. It is what it is. Two shooting stars crossing each other with a flash bang only to burn off into nothing. It was exciting while it lasted."

"No. No. No!" Ray screams, slamming his hand down on his desk. I flinch at the sharp, demanding tone of his voice. *No, what?* He called me to his office while I was at Mom's, and this is what I'm met with. "Gracyn Rae, you're killing me. Slowly killing me."

It must be serious. We're pulling out the middle name. "What did I do?"

"Brooks Handley?" He draws in a harsh inhale and growls through a closed mouth. My brows shoot up. I mean, I knew he wouldn't be pleased that I was irresponsible, but he's downright angry with me. "Of all the men on this earth, you had to choose that guy?"

That's a little extreme.

I chose him *that* night.

"We're getting our marriage annulled," I say, hoping it'll calm him down.

He flies out of his chair, face turning beet red as he leans his body across his desk, putting all his weight on his arms. I've heard stories about how ruthless my father can be, how a single glance can send you to hell, but I've never witnessed it first-hand. My fight-or-flight instinct tells me to get the hell out of dodge, but I'm stunned frozen in my chair.

"Married?" A string of curse words in Italian follows.

Oh. Seems his network of spies missed that *important* part of that night. I can see the flames in his eyes growing as he glares at me.

"There's no need to yell at me," I snap. If there's one thing he taught me, it's dealing with your problems head-on. "I'm a twenty-four-year-old woman, and I know I screwed up. But really? You're blowing this way out of proportion. It's not like I got knocked up and I'm stuck with the guy forever."

He stands tall, his towering six-foot figure dominating the room. The height gene clearly skipped me. His eyes darken as he places a hand over his heart, taking a few deep breaths. Despite the rage, his expression softens. "Daughter, don't say that out loud. You're going to give me a heart attack."

I blink, confused. His reaction is so off the wall that I can't process what is happening. Slowly, he transforms into the man with rock-solid control that I've always known. He adjusts his tie as he returns to his seat behind his desk.

"Do you know him?" I ask with hesitation.

"Do you?" he fires back.

"I know he's a good man. And a wonderful dad. The times we've been together, he's been nothing but a gentleman."

"Trojan horse," he mumbles under his breath as he rolls his eyes.

I throw my hands up, exasperated. "What are you talking about?"

"You're for sure getting an annulment, correct?"

Nice deflection.

"Yes. We have a court date set for next month. You still haven't answered my question."

"Next month? Couldn't good ol' Bart get you in this month? He has to be worth something." He never misses an opportunity to throw a dig in at my stepdad.

"I got myself into this mess, so I'm not asking favors from anyone," I assert, hoping he can discern my undertone because he's included in that.

A bead of sweat trails down his forehead, and he grabs a tissue to wipe it off.

"Don't you dare lay a hand on Brooks. He's all his daughter has, and I'll never forgive you if something happens to him."

Sarcastic laughter fills the rooms. "That's not an option, for reasons you'll never understand."

"Why are you being so cryptic?"

The phone rings, and my mouth gapes open when he answers.

Hello! We're in the middle of a conversation.

"Hold on," he snaps into the phone and then looks at me as if reading my mind. "Just make sure the annulment happens."

Dismissed.

Conversation over.

I stare at the backside of his chair as he continues talking on the phone. *Love you, too.* My father isn't a lovey-dovey kind of guy, but he's always been proud of me. As I walk out of his office, the weight of his disappointment settles on my shoulders. He wasn't even this mad when I forced his guy to quit.

As I exit the hotel, I regret agreeing to meet Charli to help her shop for a gala dress for her dad's charity event. I mumble a hello as I pass the bellman, who recognizes me with his overly enthusiastic greeting.

Stop being a dick, Gray. It's not that guy's fault that your dad is incredibly annoying.

I exhale deeply, trying to shake off the bad vibes. It doesn't work. I'm still annoyed he didn't tell me how he knows Brooks. He makes it sound like I'm in danger, and if that's the case, informing me would have been a wise idea. Instead, he dismissed me like I'm one of his employees.

I glance at the time on my phone. What am I going to do for an hour? I scan the familiar surroundings of the Strip. We're meeting at the mall a couple of blocks away, so there's no point in going home. The only place I'm drawn to is Starbucks.

The Starbucks.

The one that I'll always remember as the reason I'm married.

A cold chai sounds perfect right now. As I stand in line, waiting, my mind spirals in all directions. Being in here makes me think of him, and then him and Ray. I should've pushed harder for more information. Now, I'm wondering if Brooks has a gambling problem. Or worse, he'd hired my dad to do something illegal.

A woman behind me pulls me from my ridiculous thoughts.

"You're breaking up with me? I left my job, moved here, and now you're leaving me?"

I blink, caught off guard. Is this some weird glimpse into my future? Is the universe telling me what would happen if I moved to New York for Brooks?

She cries into her phone, failing to keep it quiet. *"Don't give me that bullshit line. It's not you, it's me. Just own up to being an asshole."*

Inside, I cheer her on. The last thing she needs is to think like she's drawing attention, so I keep my focus on my shoes. Her sniffles are barely audible when she hangs up. She's trying to keep it together, and it tugs at my heart.

"Ma'am, you ready?" the barista asks, snapping me out of my thoughts. My cheeks flush with embarrassment that I didn't notice the person in front of me finished as I was too busy eavesdropping. I close the gap and place my order.

The distraught lady sets her coffee down beside mine at the condiment station as I grab a straw. I hesitate for a moment but then glance over and give a small smile. "It may not seem like it right now, but everything will work out," I say, trying to offer some comfort, even if it's a bit cliché.

For a split second, her lips twitch into a halfhearted smile, but then her face twists like she ate a lemon, breaking out into an ugly cry. "I don't think it will," she bawls.

This is what you get for opening your mouth.

Misery doesn't always need company.

She shakes off the emotional outburst, takes a deep breath, and stirs her coffee, staring down at it. "Sorry. I didn't mean for that to come out," she says, lifting her head slightly. "Thank you for your kind words, though." She grabs a napkin, dabbing it under her eyes, blinking back her tears, and then takes a sip of her drink. We scoot to the side to let a guy in, who reaches for a stir stick. "Word of advice, never move for a man," she mutters, rolling her eyes. "I would've followed him anywhere. And where did it get me? Alone in a new town. Thanks, Simon." She lifts her drink in a mock toast.

Her words hit a nerve. It's frustrating. The sacrifices women often make for love, for relationships. There is no way Brooks would entertain the thought of moving here. Not that I would ever ask him because he's the one with a very successful career. And then there's me, who can work anywhere. My biggest fear is ending up like this lady. Which is why I should stop with all the what-ifs.

I glance over at her, biting my lip as I debate whether to say something, but what the hell. "Hopefully, this doesn't sound weird, but I don't have any plans for the next hour. If you want to air it all out, I'm an excellent listener."

"Oh god, I'd hate to do that to you. I'm sure you have much better things to do than listen to a stranger tell you all her problems."

I shake my head, brushing off her apology with a light laugh. "I'm Gray." I extend my hand, and she shakes it.

"Lindsey."

"See, now we're not strangers. Unless you have somewhere—"

"Nope," she snaps. "I'd love to sit and chat. Did that sound too desperate?"

I chuckle, shaking my head. "Not at all. Let's have a seat back there."

As we settle in, she dives into her story. She moved from Utah a few months ago, leaving behind a prestigious job at a large interior design firm, all for the sake of her boyfriend's promise that they'd be engaged by the end of the year if she moved here. Considering he broke up with her over the phone minutes ago, we see how that went. Throughout our conversation, I keep quiet, letting her vent. After all, it's her life and not mine.

She sighs, a mixture of sadness and frustration tangled in her words. "Know what's worse? I love living here. But now, because of that jerk, I won't be able to stay. I've yet to find a job, and there's no way I can live here without any income. He told me I needed to move my stuff out by Sunday. How embarrassing it'll be for me to move back home with my tail tucked between my legs." Her voice cracks as tears form. "Everyone warned me."

"I have an idea," I say, reaching into the side pocket of my purse. My subconscious can't help but draw comparisons, asking myself what if this was me in New York, alone? Would someone reach out and help me? I pull my phone out and hand it to her. "Give me your info. We have a family friend who owns four hotels around here with more in the works. I'm not certain if he's hiring, but I can at least get you in touch with the person who does the interior design stuff. Put a good word in for you."

She stares at my phone. "Why would you do that for me? You don't even know me."

I shrug, giving her a warm smile. "Because us women need to stick together. And I hope if I'm ever in the same spot as you, someone would be nice enough to help me."

"Wow. That's..." She pauses, her fingers hovering over the keys as she looks up at me, her face full of appreciation. "I doubt you'd ever be this stupid."

She hasn't met Brooks Handley.

I'd like to believe I wouldn't if he asked.

But he hasn't asked.

And if he did, *I might be this stupid.*

Later that night, as I'm curled up on the couch watching an episode of *Chicago PD*, my phone rings. If it wasn't Charli, I wouldn't have answered, but she is supposed to be on a date.

"Didn't I just leave you an hour ago? And is your date that bad?" A blind date set up by her mom. She's a better daughter than I am, agreeing to go on it.

She laughs into the phone. "He never showed up, so it's going great."

"Sounds like your mom picks losers, just like you."

"You are not funny. Some of us don't have the luxury of finding a gorgeous billionaire, snapping our fingers, and the next thing you know, we're married."

"You make it sound somewhat like a fairy tale. It's not. It's a pain in the ass."

"From what I heard about your weekend, the only pain in your ass would've been from him."

I gasp, my face heating. "Charli! We did not..." I stammer. "He didn't..." She cracks up. I swear I'm not telling her anything ever again. "Moving on. What are you calling for?"

"Oh, yeah. There was a reason. Has Brooks said anything about Cooper?"

I was hoping to never hear his name again. "No. Why?"

There's a brief pause. "In all my free time tonight, I figured I'd check out this Cooper asshole." Why would she waste her time on that? "You'll never believe this, someone found him in an alley, beaten to a pulp."

"What?"

"They found him this morning."

I jump up and grab my laptop. With master balancing skills, I hold the phone with my ear and type with one hand, balancing the laptop with the other as I make my way back to the couch.

"Do you think Brooks has something to do with it?"

"No!"

At least I hope not.

"Did Ray find out?"

He's alive, so no. But he has three broken ribs, a shattered arm, a busted nose, and all his front teeth are gone. He said someone with a mask cornered him in the alley and came after him with a bat.

"Wow. Can't say he didn't deserve it, though," I say, still in shock. There is zero sympathy when I think of what he's probably done to other women. The ones who weren't saved at the last minute. The ones who woke up the next morning, finding out that they had been raped. Yep, not going to lie, a part of me wants to high-five the guy who did this. "How would Ray have found out? I didn't even tell my mom."

"Well, he found out the *fuck around and find out* karma."

"That he did. So, did the loser at least call you and tell you he wasn't coming?" I click out, not wanting to focus on Cooper anymore, and go back to my news home page. A picture catches my eye at the top of the page. I pull in a sharp gasp, knowing I'll regret clicking on it, but knowing I don't have a choice. "Oh my god. Oh my god. *Oh. My. God!*"

"What? Is there an update? Did he die?"

"No. It's me. I'm on the front page of *Page Six.*"

CHAPTER 15

BROOKS

The door to my office swings open moments after my assistant gave me the heads-up about unplanned company.

"And here I thought I was the only one who could get your sister this pissed off."

I watch my brother-in-law stroll into my office, a grin on his face, loosening his tie with one hand while holding a file in the other. My pen slips from my fingers, knowing why he's here. My sister sent her husband to knock some sense into me. Just the latest in a growing list of people who've reached out to me today, including my worried mom.

Aiden unbuttons his suit jacket, takes a seat, and leans back. "Put a ring on a finger lately?"

Technically, no. But the logistics of my drunken wedding aren't the point of his question. Reading my silence, he proceeds, sliding the case file onto my desk with an FBI stamp on it. It has Gracyn's name printed on the front. I understand now. He's here to apply some pressure, making it seem official.

"Do you know anything about her?" he asks, his tone shifting to a serious note.

I hesitate. The thought of what's in that file gnaws at me, afraid they might try to tarnish my wife's reputation. I tap my finger on the file. "Is this necessary? We're getting an annulment."

He points to it. "You can thank your sister for that," he says. "The second she heard the news, there wasn't anything I could do to stop her."

I close my eyes, shaking my head.

"You can't be surprised," he says.

I open the folder, flipping through it. Pictures, random documents of Gracyn's past, a copy of our marriage license, and some pictures of her and her family when she was little. And here I was worried about paparazzi being invasive. "There's nothing in here new to me. What's this about because I have a meeting in fifteen minutes?"

He sighs and steeples his fingers in front of his mouth. "There's more."

Of course there is. He wouldn't be here if there weren't. But my patience is wearing thin, so I gesture for him to keep going.

"In the late eighties, there were two very well-known criminal organizations. One in Chicago, one in Vegas. No relation to each other." My attention sharpens at the subtle clue that he's talking about my biological dad. Aiden went undercover with the FBI to take him down eight years ago.

Since I was adopted, I wasn't aware of Travis until I was eighteen. I can't say for certain what he does, but from what I've pieced together, it's mostly illegal—guns, drug trafficking, and a few legitimate businesses thrown in to launder his gains. We have a *don't ask, don't tell* understanding. Despite our different career paths, I see a lot of myself in him. Relentless pursuit of success.

Aiden leans forward. "The cause of their conflict is still a mystery. But they started picking each other off left and right. It was a bloodbath. The police and FBI sort of stood back, letting them kill each other off. I mean, why impede bad guys from killing each other, right?"

"Law enforcement in a nutshell," I joke, and he throws his middle finger up in response.

"Then out of nowhere, it stopped. The whole thing went quiet, and they've since lived amicably."

I frown, not understanding his direction. "What does this have to do with me?"

"The bureau's afraid you're about to start that war again."

I blink. "What the hell are you talking about? I have nothing to do with Travis."

He hesitates before dropping the bombshell. "Your wife? Gracyn Rae Carmichael is Raymond Knight's daughter."

The name stirs a memory.

"He owns half of Vegas, and the man Travis was at war with."

I snap, recalling a business meeting with him a couple of years ago about doing marketing for a new hotel he was launching. After finding out that the hotel catered to some kind of seductive fantasies and had playrooms, we agreed the proposal was out of line with our brand.

"Hold on," I say as I swing back to what Aiden said. "Gracyn's dad is a judge in Vegas."

"And your dad crunches numbers for a living," he deadpans, referring to my adopted dad.

It takes a moment for my thoughts to fill in the blanks. I

raise up a hand, putting it all together. "So, your story … Travis and Raymond?" He nods in confirmation. "And now Travis's son is married to his archenemy's daughter?"

"Bingo." Anger drowns out the surprise, and I barely register Aiden's voice as he asks, "Did you—"

"Wait," I snap, needing a moment. I spin in my chair, away from his questioning eyes. His unfinished question hangs in the air. The weight of the past bears down on me, triggering a sense of déjà vu. Dulled pain from the last time a woman used me sharpens. Six years ago, I made a vow to keep women at arm's length and never be on the ass end of a conniving woman's plan again. The idea of being manipulated again infuriates me. I swear under my breath, the anger rising fast.

"Brooks, did she approach you?"

Scrubbing my beard, an icy knot in my gut tightens, and I curse under my breath again. The thunderstorm outside mirrors the chaos in my head. Slowly, I force the words out. "Yes." I whip around. "But Gracyn isn't anything like Jessie. She was the one who served me annulment papers. Why the hell would she do that if she had ulterior motives?"

He seems unconvinced, bobbing his head. "Brother, let's be honest here. When it comes to women, your judgment hasn't exactly been stellar." I raise an eyebrow, ready to remind him that Jessie was the psycho that he brought into my life. "You look pretty cozy with the woman you're supposed to be getting an annulment with," he adds, pointing to a picture of us, dancing cheek to cheek.

The photo stabs at my patience. Why does everyone keep making that assumption? Just because we had sex doesn't mean we're going to be lifelong partners. I've screwed a lot of women, and none have the last name Handley.

"Are you sure that wasn't a reason to come to New York?"

Yes.

No.

Fuck.

I throw my hands up in the air. "You seem to be the one with all the answers," I snap, a mix of irritation and confusion coloring my tone. Frustration boils over, and I grip the padding on top of the chair, needing something to help ground me.

If she's playing games, it's best she knows who she's playing with.

Leaning over my desk, I grab the office phone, pressing it to my ear as I jab my finger on my assistant's extension. "Clear my schedule for the rest of today and tomorrow. I'll be out of pocket."

"Brooks, wait," Aiden interjects, rising to his feet as soon as I hang up. "We need more information. Let's be smart about this."

Ignoring his advice, I snap open my briefcase and shove a couple of files with my current projects in it, including the FBI file. I doubt it's the original. "I'm not sure what you expected me to do, but sitting by and letting her play me isn't an option." The click of my case echoing is my resolve.

"I'd feel better if Presley stayed with us while you're away."

For once, I agree with him. "I'll arrange for Judith to bring her over tomorrow after school. I'll leave in the morning." If it weren't for Presley, I'd leave right now.

Aiden nods. "I'm also alerting the FBI in Vegas, so don't be surprised if you notice a few eyes on you."

I freeze for a moment. "That's jumping the gun. I'm sure I can handle Gracyn alone," I assert, storming out of the office.

He follows me out and puts his hand on my shoulder when

we get to the elevator. "You don't know what she's capable of. What they're planning. You'll be on their turf. I'm not doing it for you. I'm doing it for that little girl."

On the drive home, my mind won't stop spinning. She initiated the annulment. She left without wanting anything, even after our amazing weekend. If she was trying to worm her way into my life, she's going about it all wrong. But then she did text me about her job. Is she trying to keep me within arm's length?

Was that her plan all along? To make me want her so much that it's impossible to stay away? I've lost count how many times this past week I considered getting on a plane just to see her, and it's only been barely two weeks since she was underneath me.

Her plan is working.

The penthouse door slams shut with more force than intended. Judith jumps, clutching one of Presley's stuffed animals to her chest.

"Sorry. Bad day at work."

She places the stuffed animal on the shelf. "Anything I can do to help? I can take Pres to dinner if you need alone time to handle business stuff," she offers.

I let out a small growl of frustration, releasing some of the tension coiled tight in my chest. "Thanks for the offer, but I'd like to have dinner with her. I have to go out of town for a work emergency tomorrow morning. Can you take her to Addison's house after school?"

"Of course. Where are you headed?"

"Vegas."

"Oh."

I turn my head in her direction, sensing an unspoken undercurrent in her response. "Is there something wrong with that?"

She fidgets. "Sorry, no. Not at all. I just thought…" Her voice trails off, hesitating for a beat. "Last time you came back from Vegas, you told me never to let you go back."

Right. I said that, didn't I?

I sigh, leaning against the wall. "Something's come up that I have to deal with. Otherwise, it's sound advice."

Only trouble is in Vegas. And it starts with a capital G and ends in sin.

Judith finishes tidying up before heading out to pick up Presley as I pack my bag. Leaving on such short notice irks me, but I need answers. I need to find out if I'm being used as a pawn again.

I'M GREETED with the unmistakable sound of the front door slamming shut, reverberating through the penthouse. *Like father, like daughter.* Seems bad days are contagious around here. I peek around the corner from my bedroom and don't see anyone, so I walk out to the living room to find Presley by the front door. Her small fists clench by her sides, and a fiery determination blazes in her eyes. She's clearly upset.

"Hey, Snarky, what's—"

"I have a mommy and you didn't tell me!"

Fuckity, fuck, fuck, fuck.

I blink, trying to keep my composure, but my pulse is picking up speed. "Sweetheart, what are you talking about?"

She glares at me, her jaw set. "The kids at school said you got married, and now I have a mommy! Who is she?"

Those pint-sized demons.

I release a heavy sigh and crouch down to her level. She

scrunches up her little face like someone who sucked on a lemon. I've always aimed to be truthful with her, especially when she asks challenging questions. We've had conversations about her mother, discussing how she had struggled but loved her dearly. I've chosen my words carefully, not revealing that her mom is a parasite, but making sure Presley understands it was Jessie's decision not to be a part of her life.

"Presley," I start, my brain scrambling for the right words. "I fucked up."

Her eyes widen as if I told her Santa wasn't real. I never cuss around her. I'm trying to find the simplest way to explain to a six-year-old what happened. *You're doing a horrible job so far. Solid parenting move.*

"Daddy did a dumb thing. When I was in Vegas with Uncle Jared..." Words trail off as I realize there's no simple explanation for this. So, I go for plan B; lie. "It was a pretend marriage. In Vegas, you can go to this little chapel and have Elvis sing to you and have a pretend wedding. We did that, having some fun. She isn't my wife, but people are saying she is. She doesn't even live in New York."

Her gaze sharpens, and she's trying to figure out if my story makes sense. For a six-year-old who spends half her time in a world of make-believe, she's a tough crowd. "What's her name?"

It's only a matter of time until she sees the pictures, so I can't lie myself out of this one. "Gracyn."

Her entire face lights up, her lips spreading into the biggest, most delighted grin I've ever seen. *No, don't do that. Do not do that.*

"Really? Gracyn is my pretend mom?" She squeals, vibrating with excitement.

"Snarky," I say, drawing out her name. "She is not your mom. At all." If there is anything I need her to understand, it's this.

"But she wouldn't have pretended to marry you if she didn't like you," she counters, her little head weaving from side to side in that sassy way she's perfected. Under different circumstances, it'd be funny. "And I know you like her."

How? How in the hell does she know that? She saw us together for five minutes. One dance.

"It was pretend," I insist. "Just like you play pretend when you dress up like a superhero or a princess. Something silly we did."

She nods, her face calm, and for a second, it seems she gets it. But then I see those little wheels turning in her head. I brace myself as her mouth opens. "I'll take a pretend mom over no mom."

Her words slice through me, and my shoulders slump as I sigh, taking her small hands in mine. "I get it. You want a mom, and someday, I hope to give you one. One that we'll both love and live here forever with us. But that is not Gracyn. Someday, you'll understand what happened."

Her eyes fill with tears, big and round, and I can see the heartbreak as clearly as I feel it. One tear slips free, sliding down her cheek and hitting me in the heart. I gently wipe it away, and the tear of disappointment burns my skin.

"For now, I'll have to be enough for you," I whisper and scoop her into my arms and hug her tightly. "I love you, Presley."

She digs her little head into my chest, and her voice is so small when she says, "I love you too, Daddy."

CHAPTER 16

GRACYN

> Me: We need to talk about Cooper.

S taring at the unsent text, my thumb hovers over the screen. Imagining Brooks doing something reckless, something that could destroy his life just for me, is insane. What the hell am I doing? Common sense hits me smack in the head, and I erase the text before sending it. If he had anything to do with it, putting it in writing isn't smart.

My phone buzzes in my hand, startling me. It's a New York number, but I don't recognize it.

"Hello," I answer.

"Is Gracyn there?" It's a young girl's voice.

I hold my breath, hoping and praying it's not who I think it is. "This is her."

"Hi, Gracyn. This is Presley."

Shit.

Shit.

All the shit.

"Hiiii." I drag the word out, trying to sound casual while my mind races. Brooks can't be okay with this. "Is everything okay?"

"Yep," she chirps. "My daddy left for a work trip. But I found your number on his phone. I wanted to tell you how happy I am that you're my new mom."

The air vanishes from my lungs. Nooo. No. No. No. No. This isn't happening.

"My dad told me it was a mistake, but he's wrong. He really likes you. And so do I."

Her words hit me like a freight train, and I struggle to find something, *anything*, to say that won't make this situation worse.

Who am I kidding?

This can't get any worse.

"Um … hmm … well, first off, I like you too, Presley. But sometimes, adults do things that shouldn't have happened. Your dad and I made a terrible decision."

"No. Don't say that," she cries. "You two can make it work. I know you can!"

"*Presley, my mom is waiting for us,*" I overhear a woman's voice in the background say. "*Are you on the phone? Who are you on the phone with?*"

The sound of shuffling follows, and then a woman's voice. "Hello. Who is this?"

Panicking, I hang up and stare at the phone, expecting whoever it was to call back. After a few minutes of deafening silence, the weight of it all crashes down on me. I crumple, bending at the waist and leaning against the counter, tears streaming down my cheeks. Our simple mess just spiraled into a full-blown catastrophe.

Kids are resilient.

She'll forget about me by next week.

I focus on those words because I'm having a hard time believing it. Where the hell was the warning from Brooks that she found out?

I fumble for my phone, finding his number with trembling fingers. I press call, my heart racing as I try to figure out what to say. Honestly, what's there to say? Maybe that's why he didn't call. He didn't want to bother me with a situation I have no control over. The call goes straight to voicemail, and I hang up without leaving a message.

The entire afternoon slips away as I pace around, waiting for Brooks to call. He knows I called. He has to. Presley's innocent, hopeful words haunt me: *"I'm happy you're my new mom."*

In a moment of desperation, I call my mom. I wanted to keep her out of my screw-up, but she always knows what to do.

"This is horrible," I sob into the phone after telling her what happened.

"I know you're a party to the problem, but you can't fix this." I hear her words. *I've thought of them myself*, but they've yet to release this knot in my chest. "But you're right, she will move on quick. Little girls focus on what's in front of them, not what's behind them. It'll be okay, hun. You didn't ruin a child's life."

It feels like it.

A couple of sharp knocks at the door reverberate through the apartment, likely Charli, irritated that I've been ignoring her texts all day. I don't have the energy to deal with my real life.

Just the fake one.

"Mom, I'll call you later after I talk to Brooks. Charli is here. Love you," I say, making my way to the door. I swipe away the tears staining my cheeks before peering through the peephole. I do a double take. Definitely not a blond with her iconic red lips. When I open the door, Brooks is in a defensive stance, his lips pressed in a hard line and his hands shoved deep into the pockets of his jeans.

"Brooks," I stammer, confused why he's here. "I guess we need to talk."

He stares at me, and his jaw tics. I step aside and push the door open wider. Without a word, he strides past me, his anger trailing behind him like a storm cloud. The air is heavy, suffocating, as he brushes past me, his forceful presence enough to knock me off balance. He must have found out that Presley had called, but why didn't he pick up his phone?

As soon as I shut the door and turn around, he's towering over me. I take a step back until my back meets the wooden door with a thud. Brooks's thunderous expression is mere inches from my face.

"Who the hell are you?" His voice is sharp, slicing through the air like a knife.

I stare at him in disbelief. I'm caught off guard by his abrasiveness. "What are you talking about?" I manage.

"Don't play games with me, Gracyn," he growls, planting both hands on the wall, caging me in. "I won't ask again. What do you want with me?"

It takes a few beats for the cylinders in my brain to restart, but the second they do, alarm bells blare. Cooper and how he was found fill my head. My dad was right—Brooks isn't the man I thought he was.

Panic swells in my chest as I feel trapped. "Move, Brooks," I demand.

His solid, unmoving body overshadows mine in height and weight.

"No," he spits out, his voice laced with venom.

Terrified, I duck under his arm and run, grabbing the first thing within reach.

An umbrella.

I lunge for it, gripping its smooth handle as if it was going to save my life. What on earth am I going to do with an umbrella? *It'll have to do.* My hands tremble as I whip around to face him, pointing the metal tip inches from his body. His face is redder than a tomato, with a vein in his forehead about to pop.

"You should leave," I rasp, my voice shaking with adrenaline as I throw open the door. Breathless and seething with rage, he glares at me before storming out. "You want to talk to me?" I yell out after he crosses the threshold and is a safe distance away from me. "Ask me questions? Then don't come back until you've calmed down and not act like an escaped gorilla."

I slam the door and lock it, twisting the deadbolt into place. My breath comes in quick gasps as I lean my forehead against the wood, clutching the umbrella in a death grip.

Fuming, I push off the door and pace the entire length of the living room. Who does he think he is, barging into my home and demanding to know who *I am*? Who the hell does he think I am? Two weeks ago, he sure the hell didn't care who I was when I was in his bed. Well, I'm not one to let a man hurt me, that's for damn sure.

Not now. Not ever.

His daughter knows. The entire world knows. He can be mad at that. But I'll be damned if he casts me as the villain in this story. It takes two to tango.

And I don't even *remember* dancing!

Thirty minutes later, my phone buzzes. I squeeze it tight in my fist, still grappling with my emotions, when I see it's him. Nope. Not ready to talk yet. I hit ignore. It buzzes once. This time with a text.

> Brooks: I'm sorry.

A bitter laugh escapes me. Sorry? He comes in hot and heavy, boxing me in and talking crazy, and then expecting a simple sorry will magically fix everything?

The phone buzzes again.

> Brooks: Can I come up?

I scoff, typing out an immediate response.

> Me: No

I close my eyes and press the phone to my temple, knowing we can't leave it like this. But there is no way in hell I'm about to be alone with him right now. Where is somewhere close to people? Somewhere public, somewhere safe. I let him stew a bit longer before texting again.

> Me: Meet me at the community park in an hour. It's right down the street.

When I arrive at the park, I scan the area until I spot Brooks, sitting on a bench with his head in his hands, hunched over. I blow out a long-winded sigh, not sure there's been enough time for me to stop wanting to jam my thumbs into his eyeballs.

I glance around at all the kids playing at the playground not too far from the bench. Maybe this wasn't the best place to meet.

I chew on my bottom lip before forcing myself to walk toward him. One conversation. *That's all.*

I take a seat on the opposite end of the bench, leaving plenty of space between us. An invisible barrier that I hope he respects. He looks up, and our eyes meet. I shake my head at the remorse in his expression, annoyed with myself for sympathizing with him.

He wrings his hands. "I'm so sorry," he says, voice raw, thick with regret. He rubs his hands over his face, struggling to meet my eyes. He pauses, his throat bobbing as he swallows hard. "I've never talked to a woman like that before."

"And you'll never do it again," I assert, leaving no room for misinterpretation.

He closes his eyes and tilts his head upward, releasing a slow, shaky breath. "Did you … did you already know who I was in the coffee shop?" His voice cracks as he wrestles with whatever is inside his head.

What kind of question is that? "No."

He turns his intense gaze on me, like he's weighing every syllable I've spoken. "I know who your father is."

Most people who mention my father are referring to Bart Carmichael. But Brooks is not talking about Bart. He's talking about Raymond. But what does that have to do with him?

"And?" I say, throwing my hands up. "You're not the only one. It's not exactly a well-kept secret."

"Do you work for Raymond?"

For a moment, all I can do is stare at him, confused. Why does that matter? "I worked as a bartender at one of his casino's nightclubs for four years. But I quit last month." I blink, waiting for his response. His silence grates on me, so I press further. "What is it you believe I do for him, Brooks?"

"Our fathers are acquaintances," he murmurs.

My brows shoot up. Is that why Ray didn't want me with Brooks? "Wait, is your dad Ray's accountant or something?"

He twists his body toward me, draping his arm across the back of the bench, and picks at a splinter in the wood for a few moments before asking, "You really don't know?"

I squeeze the bridge of my nose, trying to quell my irritation. "This is insane. Raymond's furious at me for *choosing* you. You're furious with me for ... I've yet to find out. Why is everyone mad at me? The only thing I did was fall for a smooth talker that talked me into marrying him. For which I still can't remember." I let out a sarcastic laugh as I realize something. "It's somewhat amusing, however, that you both arrived at the same conclusion. He thought you were a plant. *A Trojan horse.* And you thought the same thing. But for the love of God, will someone please tell me why?"

His fingers mess with the splintered wood again. "I just... I've been burned before by a woman, and it turned my world upside down. I swore off women after her. And then you came into my life like a tornado, turning it upside down, again." Presley's mom. She must've done a real number on him. "And then" —his eyes find mine—"I find out that this whole thing could've been a setup. I reacted."

I shake my head. "More like overreacted. Brooks, I'm not

part of any big scheme. Why would you come to that conclusion?"

"The FBI."

Holding up a finger to take a moment to let this all sink in, the absurdity of it all catches up to me, and I can't help but laugh. "Seriously? I'm a college student turning into a teacher. I've never done anything except *maybe* steal a coffee."

His eyes narrow. "There is no *maybe* about it."

I scrunch my nose at him. He must feel I opened the door for him because he scoots over. Closer. Still holding my finger up, I shake my head. "Too soon."

He deflates and scoots to his original spot.

A chorus of "oohs" and "ouches" rises from a group of preteens hanging out on the monkey bars, staring at us, like we're the main act in their favorite drama. Great. Now we have an audience.

"C'mon, you can see he's sorry," one girl says as the rest of the group nods their little heads in agreement, as if they're a jury delivering their verdict.

I scoff silently. There's no way I'm caving to the pressure from a gaggle of prepubescent kids. Ignoring their commentary, I turn to see Brooks grinning like a fool. Of course he's eating this up, they're on his side. But if they saw him a while ago, they wouldn't be.

I refocus on Brooks. "Anyway. Why would I be on the FBI's radar?"

His grin falls, and he shifts. "My brother's FBI."

I press my lips together. That's a bit different from *the FBI*. It sounds like his brother is concerned, and he has the resources to dig into me.

But as he continues to explain what his sister found and her

FBI agent husband told him, I begin to grasp why he was skeptical of our meeting. The timing, the coincidences, the connections. Still doesn't justify him acting like a rabid animal.

Our marriage gets crazier by the day.

And we've only been married for four weeks.

"Wow." It takes a minute for me to process everything. "So, let me get this straight. Both our real fathers are criminal enemies, your sister is overprotective, and now your daughter is calling me saying she's happy I'm her mom. Did I miss anything?"

"She did what?" Brooks spits out, straightening up like a coiled spring ready to launch.

I hesitate because, let's be honest, I don't like Brooks when he's mad. And he looks mad. "She called me earlier. That's why I figured you were here. Buuutt." I wave a hand toward him, shrugging nonchalantly. "I guess not."

His jaw tightens, and he takes a moment to rein in his temper. Finally, he exhales, his shoulders sagging. "I'm sorry about the call. She must've done it after I left," he says. "And about the outburst." He glances at me, his expression softening with regret. "And for the temper."

I don't apologize for kicking him out.

That was deserved.

"It's crazy our dads know each other. *Or hate each other.* How random is that?" Ray's outburst makes sense. I think about our instant attraction. "It's like karma is tap dancing on their ruthless souls."

He chuckles. "That's one way to look at it." Pulling his phone out of his pocket, he sighs. "I need to call Pres to make sure she's okay." He gets up and strolls down the sidewalk, leaving me alone.

I turn my attention to the preteens, wondering if they've found something better to do than watch my life unravel. Nope. They're all staring, all of them smiling at me like they're in the front row at a circus. I'm act one.

Thankfully, they're far enough away to have not heard what we were saying. I stand and head toward them, squinting my eyes playfully. "Are we that interesting?"

"Ahh, yeah," the little blond with a high ponytail replies. "We've got a bet going on whether you're going to dump him. Not me, though," she clarifies, jerking her thumb toward the three boys. "It's them. I'm rooting for the guy. He was pretty messed up before you got there. Felt sorry for him." Her eyes dart between me and Brooks, who's still pacing down the sidewalk, before continuing, "When he went to slide in there, I knew I was about to win."

"But then bam! You cock-blocked him," one boy blurts out, karate-chopping the air.

My eyes widen at the inappropriate and misusage of the phrase. The other boys chuckle, giving him a high-five. Little turds. They understand it, they just misused it.

It's moments like this that have me reconsidering my career choice.

"Well, show's over, kids."

"But wait," the girl pipes up. "So, are you going to forgive him and get married and live happily ever after?"

I turn and bite back a chuckle. Wonder who would win if I told them we were already married? I spot Brooks sliding his phone into his pants pocket and walking my direction. My heart does that annoying flutter it always does when our eyes meet. Ugh. Annoyed with myself, I spin around to her and say, "Sorry, but no. He's just a friend."

Her lips fall in disappointment as the boys erupt in hoots and hollers.

I shrug. "You can't win them all."

As I walk away, I overhear her say to the boys, "She's lying. I can tell she's into him."

She's one hundred percent correct. But sometimes life isn't that simple, and all we can do to keep moving forward is tell ourselves the lies we need to believe.

"Everything good?" I ask, catching up with Brooks before he has a chance to talk to the kids.

He nods, but glances past me toward the monkey bars. "What was that about?"

I wave him off. "Nothing. Just kids being kids."

As we walk along the sidewalk toward my apartment, he fills me in. "Speaking of kids, Judith overheard the whole thing, so she took Presley to the zoo to get her mind off it. She said she was happy and tired by the time they got home."

A blush creeps up my cheeks. Judith knows it was me. And I had to freak out and hang up on her. Smooth. Real smooth. "Can you tell her I'm sorry for hanging up on her? It was a knee-jerk reaction."

He chuckles. "I'm familiar with those."

I pause at the bottom of the stairs leading up to my apartment. "Did you come here specifically to yell at me? Or are you here for business?"

"Just you," he says.

I take the first step up so we're more eye to eye. "Why?" I blurt out. "I mean, I get that you were mad. But calling would've been faster, cheaper, and easier. You're making this way more complicated than it already is. My face is already plastered all over the internet with people trying to figure out who I am. Your daughter is calling. This has gotten so out of control."

The weight of everything presses heavily on my chest, and panic creeps in. And the worst part is that even now, I still want him.

He reaches for me, but hesitation flickers across his face, and instead drops his hand to his side. "I don't know," He sighs and shakes his head at the same time. His eyes fix on mine. "I had to prove that you were nothing like Jessie."

My expression softens. Whatever we have, however tangled and messy, it isn't anywhere near what he went through with that woman. From what I heard. Curiosity sneaks in before I can stop it, and the question escapes my mouth. "Did you love her?"

His laugh is sharp, brief, and bitter. "Love her? It wasn't like that at all. We slept together a couple times, and I never saw her again. Until Presley."

I open my mouth and then shut it, realizing I'm missing a significant chunk of the story. The part I'm positive he likes to forget.

"Trust me, she's one person you don't need to worry about."

I nod, not mentioning that I already heard she's dead.

Behind Brooks, the sound of a car pulling into a parking space draws my attention. My neighbors, Lucy and her boyfriend, step out, curious about the scene they're walking up to. Considering our pictures are blasted all over the internet, I wouldn't be surprised if Lucy's seen them. As they approach, I edge to the side to let them pass. Lucy, always the nosy one, pauses in front of us, her gaze darting between Brooks and me. "Everything okay?" she asks, her tone casual, but her eyes sharp.

"I'm good," I assure her, and they disappear into their apartment. I glance up at their window, and of course, a shadow moves away. Figures, she was watching. She probably snapped a few pictures, too. We can't stay right here. "So, what now?" I ask, attempting nonchalance, though my voice comes out softer than I intended.

Despite the fact that an hour ago he practically attacked me, I'm not ready to say goodbye. I should shove him out the door and say '*see you next month at our court date*,' because that's what needs to happen. We shouldn't spend another night together. So why am I standing here, hoping his next words are going to be, '*got a place for me to crash?*'

"Yes," I blurt out.

Puzzled, a crease forms between his eyes. "Yes, what?"

Shit. I'm now saying *yes* to him before he even asks anything. I let out an awkward laugh. "Sorry. It's been a crazy day."

His eyes hold mine, searching, questioning, as he puts one leg on the stair. It brushes against my thigh, and he grabs the rail as if he's ready to pounce. "Gracyn," he rasps, undressing me by just saying my name. "What are you saying yes to?"

Goose bumps spread over my arms. I wrinkle my nose, determined not to give him the satisfaction of knowing he's got me twisted in knots. "Are you leaving tonight?"

"Do you want me to leave?"

His words hang heavy between us, their weight undeniable. It's my turn to search his eyes, trying to decide if I'm brave—*or foolish*—enough to give him the actual answer. In this instant, locked in his intense gaze, it hits me. We're the same. Irresistibly drawn to each other, and neither of us can fight it when we're near each other.

"You already know the answer to that."

He smiles and drops his hand from the rail to rest on my hip. "Go grab an overnight bag."

"And where exactly are we staying?"

"The Bellagio," he says with a hint of mischief, his fingers tightening around my waist. "I have fond memories there."

I roll my eyes. "Glad one of us does."

"We could recreate some things," he suggests, edging closer. "Try to trigger some of those hidden memories."

My heart thuds against my chest, the memories I do have vividly clear. They're impossible to forget. "You just want to bring back drunk Gray," I murmur. "Well, she's not making a comeback."

"I'd be happy with *any* Gray."

I slap his shoulder and start backing up the stairs. "Enough with the charm offensive. It's a given I'll end up in your bed tonight. So, stop with all the smooth talking."

"Charm offensive?" He chuckles, leaning against the railing, crossing his arms. "That's a new one for me."

I pause, lifting a finger. "I'm not dressing up. This Gray is going in what she's wearing." I motion to my joggers and my cropped shirt.

He gives me a once-over, and I wait for his disapproval. "You look perfect," he says.

I lift a brow, making a pointed look at his dark jeans and navy polo. Inside, I'm screaming at him to quit being so infuriatingly perfect.

"Where does this Gray want to eat?"

"The Bellagio has a great buffet," I throw out, half expecting him to make a face. I have no idea why I'm being so difficult. I hate buffets, and I'm sure he's never even stepped foot into one.

"Sounds good to me. I'm starving."

"I hate you." I laugh and spin around to go the rest of the way up. I stop and look over my shoulder and find him staring up at me.

"Your ass looks pretty fuckable right now in those joggers."

See, that's what I want.

The raw, undeniable physical craving. Make me feel like an object.

And stop making me fall in love with you.

CHAPTER 17

BROOKS

My head hurts from the relentless flip-flopping happening inside it.

I want her.

I hate her.

I need her.

What I *really* need right now is a professional to sort out the twisted mess in my brain. Perhaps it's time to use the full-time psychologist that we hired to help with employee burnout. Sure, this isn't exactly her job description, but we're paying her a small fortune to sit in an office all day.

I prop myself up against a nearby light pole and wait. A tall palm tree looms overhead, its fronds swaying in the breeze, casting flickering shadows on the ground. The complex is immaculately kept, with more greenery and plant life surrounding me than I've ever seen in the city. It's a peaceful oasis. I can see why Gracyn likes it here. Her apartment is far enough away from the Strip but right at the heart of a small, trendy downtown area.

The outdoor living area is crowded. People gather by tables, laughing and playing games, some grilling out. Does Gracyn usually join them? I've never thought about hanging out with my neighbors.

I glance up the stairs when I hear a door opening. Gray comes out, still in joggers, with a bag slung over one shoulder. Thank God she didn't change. She looks effortlessly sexy. I swallow hard, gripping the back of my neck so I don't do something stupid. Like pulling her into my arms in front of all her neighbors and showing them she's mine.

Mine.

Well … for another few weeks, at least.

She flashes a grin when she passes me, popping open the trunk of a car parked across the street. Forgetting that not everyone Ubers everywhere like I do, I push off the pole and jog over to the car.

"Yours?" I ask, eyeing the bright blue two-seater Beamer, wondering if I'll fit.

She scrunches up her freckled nose, slamming the trunk shut. "Nah. I'm stealing it."

I laugh, walking to the passenger door. "I would not be surprised. At. All."

I tuck myself into the space. And I mean tuck and roll. My knees are kissing my chest. "You could have stolen a bigger car."

Her laughter fills the car, light and easy, and it makes my tight squeeze worth it. I'm still an asshole for slamming her against the door. The memory makes my stomach churn. The way I lost control scared me more than I want to admit.

I watch her drive with ease one-handed. Her other rests on the gearshift, despite being an automatic. Her bright pink nails stand out against the black interior. She senses me watching her and glances over.

She winces when she sees my squished body. "We're almost there."

"Thank God," I mutter, shifting uncomfortably. "Because watching you drive is sexy as hell, but having a hard dick scrunched up like this is bad for my health." I tug on my jeans, trying to relieve some pressure, but it's useless. Instead, I recall the memory of walking in on my mom and dad once. I shudder at the horrible, unforgettable scene.

Yep, that did it. Softer than a pillow.

Speaking of memories. "Remember anything new from our wedding night?"

She swings into the valet and puts the car in park. "Nope."

Even though it was the most irresponsible thing I've ever done, it was one of the best nights of my life, and my ego takes a hit that she doesn't remember.

Marrying me.

As we walk through the casino, our fingers brush. I want nothing more than to lace my fingers through hers, but I can't tell if she's there yet. The attraction doesn't surprise me. Not anymore. Not with this woman.

A soft growl slips from her lips, breaking through my thoughts as she slows down. "Hey, I have to run to the bathroom. I'll be right back."

"Ooo-kay," I mutter, confused by her sudden exit. She disappears behind a row of slot machines. Glancing around the casino, the only restroom sign I notice is on the *opposite* end of the casino. What is she up to?

Walking in the direction she left, when I clear the slots, I find her talking with another man about twenty feet away. The machines jingle and clang, drowning out their conversation. The guy she's talking to looks like he came straight out of a bad mob movie. His suit's a mess. Too short at the sleeves, baggy on the bottom, and wrinkled like he pulled it out of the laundry pile this morning. A thrift store special, at best.

My jaw tightens as I take in the scene. Despite her back to me, her posture tells me everything. Arms crossed, one finger drumming against her bicep. His snide, self-satisfied smile pisses me off. I don't like this guy or the way he's looking at her. But I stand off to the side, knowing she can hold her own. This is until he grabs her waist and steps into her space.

Wrong move, asshole.

She shoves him off, and I see the sharpness in her movements. Anger, not fear. The guy jerks his head in my direction when I step behind her. She turns, shifting her attention to me, and she opens her mouth to say something, but I speak first.

"Don't fucking touch my wife again." The words spill out of my mouth. I know I said them, regretted them, but I'm too pissed to retract them. My voice is low, dangerous, and loud enough to carry over the noise of the casino.

The guy's eyes widen to saucers before flickering back to Gracyn.

"He's kidding," she sputters. Her big, beautiful green eyes plead with me, begging me to agree.

I freeze as I try to form the words, but the pause stretches too long. I shrug. *I've got nothing.*

A sneer twists across his face as he sizes me up, his lips curling like he knows something that I don't.

Come on, asshole, try something. I dare him with my glare.

"Is dear ole' daddy aware of this?"

"Justin, I was gracious once. Don't make me regret that."

Gracyn's warning snaps the guy's mouth shut. Her confidence is on par with most of the men I meet in negotiations. It's sexy as hell and reminds me of her boldness that day at the wedding. That same fire.

He glares at her for a beat, jaw tight, but it's clear who has the upper hand when he spins on his heel and stalks off. Whatever grace she gave him, I doubt he earned it.

The second he's out of sight, she whirls around, swatting me on the arm. "You are ridiculous," she scolds. "You're the most hot-and-cold guy I've ever met. There's no halfway point for you. Why would you do that?"

I thought that was obvious. "He touched you."

"Jealous much?" she asks with a wry smile.

She's boxed me in. I can't admit that, yes, seeing another man touch her makes me lose my shit because that would show she means more to me than I'm willing to confess.

"Jealousy isn't in my wheelhouse." It's not a total lie. Before her, I'd never had an itch of jealousy. Now, it seems I've got poison ivy. It fucking itches everywhere. "It seemed to me you were in trouble."

"I've proven to you I can handle myself when in trouble," she bites back, snatching her bag from my grasp.

"Gracyn, I'm sorry," I reply, catching her wrist before she can storm away. My grip is loose, but it's enough to make her pause.

She glances down at my hand for a beat, then takes a step backward, out of my reach, with a pained expression. "This was a horrible idea."

What the hell? My head reels, spinning with her sudden shift. Realization dawns on me. "Does this have to do with Raymond? I'm not afraid of him, Gracyn."

She lets out a humorless laugh. "You should be. If he learns we're together..." Her eyes scan the casino, searching. She's already gearing up for a war.

"That guy looked like he shit his pants when he left. He won't say anything."

"Maybe."

If her dad shows up, nothing will happen. He's not the only one with eyes all around.

"My stomach is about to eat itself," I say, shifting gears. "Can we please eat? And then we'll hang out in the room the rest of the night."

She exhales, her resistance faltering. She'll learn I don't give up that easily. I wouldn't be where I am today by giving in. And right now, I want Gracyn.

"Don't say I didn't warn you." She spins and heads toward the buffet.

"Good evening, Mr. Handley," the hostess greets with a smile. Gracyn lifts a brow, and I shrug. When you have money, people recognize you. But then the woman shifts her focus to Gracyn with inquisitive eyes. "To you too, Ms. Carmichael."

Gracyn's lips twitch at my confusion, and she copies my nonchalant shrug before following the hostess to our table. We settle into a booth across from each other.

"Did I marry Vegas royalty?" I joke in a quiet voice, leaning in so I don't give her a reason to be mad at me again, but I nod my head, connecting the dots. It all makes sense now. How she got into VIP, why people know her name. She wasn't kidding when she said that everyone knows who her real father is. Unlike my situation, where only a select few are aware of Travis.

She leans in too, closing the space between us until our

noses almost touch. "Are you jealous again? You can't show off?"

I laugh, my attention momentarily shifting to two men sitting at a table behind Gracyn. Their plates are stacked tall, but it's not their appetite that catches my eye. I noticed them earlier following us. One of them makes brief eye contact with me and gives the smallest nod before shoving his face with a forkful of meat.

"I'm at my best when there's competition," I say, pulling my attention back to her.

"I'm counting on it, Mr. Handley."

Without warning, she tilts closer, brushing her lips against mine in a soft, teasing kiss. It's only two seconds, but it's all I need to set my blood on fire. I try to grab her before she hops up, but she's too quick. I watch her heart-shaped ass take a plate and then peek over her shoulder at me. "I thought you were hungry?"

Hungry like a wolf.

And she's Little Red Riding Hood.

On my second plate, I lift a crab leg and snap it in half and skillfully extract the tender meat.

"Shit," Gracyn murmurs.

I lift my gaze and find her eyes fixed on something behind me. Without turning, I ask, "Raymond?"

"Yep," she snaps. She stays focused on whoever is behind me as I continue cracking legs. The last thing I want is a scene. People would whip out their phones faster than a slot machine could spin, and then I'm on the covers of all the tabloids.

Gracyn tries to shoot up out of her seat, but I grab her arm and shake my head. She lowers back down, and her gaze tracks the two guys, dressed in all black and built like linebackers, approaching our table. I don't look up. Rather, I point my crab fork over Gracyn's shoulder, gesturing to the two guys at the other table. The ones who've been shadowing us since we walked in.

"Those couple of guys right over there?" I say, cracking another crab leg. "They're FBI. So, I wouldn't try anything." Their heads both jerk in that direction, and the men at the table, their postures stiffening, both nod, watching everything ensue.

Gracyn mutters a few curse words under her breath, pulls out her phone, and holds it up to her ear. "Call your guys off," she snaps into the phone. Even from the other side of the table, I hear her dad's voice booming through the phone. I catch the word annulment and then some cursing. Her jaw tightens. "That is none of your business. I'm a grown adult. Call them off." She hangs up on him, slamming the phone down on the table. There are a few tense moments of silence before the guys get a text.

One guy gives her a chin jerk. "Gray, if you need us, you have our number."

She nods, and they disappear into the casino. And then she turns her glare at me, her eyes burning a hole through my head. "What the hell, Brooks? FBI? You said it was your brother?"

"They are one and the same," I reply, dipping a piece of meat into the butter. Her expression hardens that I'm not taking this as seriously as she thinks I should. I wipe my fingers on the napkin and meet her gaze. "I told you my brother is worried we're going to start a war. And it seems it's not a far-fetched idea considering the goons who just showed up." I stick the fork into the meat and bring the buttered piece to my mouth. "What would those guys have done, anyway?" I add, certain if her dad wants to keep in good graces with his daughter and *my dad*, he won't do anything.

"They probably would have taken you to talk to Ray. He's wondering why you're here since he knows our court date isn't for another three weeks. And now, when he finds out about them"—she jerks her thumb over her shoulder—"he's going to flip his shit."

Can't blame him. He's worried about his little girl. I don't want to imagine what I'd do if Presley married a guy that I hated.

She leans her arms on the table, her voice dropping to a hushed whisper. "Were you ever going to tell me about Cooper?"

Actually, no. I didn't want her to feel sorry for the guy. I was hoping she wouldn't find out about him. I tsk and lean forward, meeting her in the middle. "He got what he deserved."

There are zero fucks for that douchebag.

Her eyes flicker left and right before landing on mine again. "Please tell me you had nothing to do with it."

"Me? I was worried you did."

I wasn't. It might have crossed my mind how mad she was and her *supposed* connections, but it was a fleeting thought. Since finding out about her father, the last thing on my mind was Cooper, but had I known about Raymond before, I might've wondered if it was her.

Her eyes widen, and she flattens me with her stare. "I would never have someone…" She looks in all directions again before she mouths, "Almost killed."

No, she wouldn't. But her father? If he knew Cooper drugged her, he'd have dealt with him in a blink of an eye.

"I see what you're thinking. Ray didn't know about him."

He's still alive, so I believe her. Cooper pissed off a lot of people. It was only a matter of time before his bullshit caught up with him.

My phone buzzes in my pocket, and when I pull it out, I can't help but laugh out loud reading Aiden's text.

> Aiden: Kissing and holding hands? Yeah, you showed her 😒

"What's so funny?"

I shake my head and slide my phone back into my pocket. "My brother's a dick."

"'*The FBI* brother-in-law?'" She does air quotes. "I thought you were an only child. Like me."

"I am," I reply, and her brows furrow in confusion. "I grew up as an only child with my adoptive parents. When I was twenty-five, I found out that I had a half sister. That's Addison. Her husband is Aiden, *the FBI agent*."

"How weird was that, finding out you had a sister?"

"It would've gone better had I not tried flirting with her right before she told me."

She gasps, holding in her laugh with her hand. There's a lot more to the story I don't plan on sharing. It wasn't a good day, but that part, we still get a good laugh to this day.

Like every time I'm with Gracyn, our conversation flows effortlessly. She doesn't dominate with endless chatter about herself. She's just as curious about me as I am about her. Every new detail I learn makes her seem more perfect than before. I've searched for flaws, and the only one I've found so far is where she lives.

And it's a deal breaker.

After dinner, I'm too full to take her to my bed, though the idea crosses my mind. But now is a great time to test whether I can jog her memory about our wedding night.

"Feel like gambling a little?" I ask.

"Don't you know the house always wins?"

"Not always." I chuckle, remembering that night.

I lead her to a craps table and squeeze into a spot at the end. I slide five hundred dollars onto the table.

Gracyn's jaw drops as she watches the dealer exchange the cash for chips. "Do you know how much stuff I could buy with that?"

I love that my wife is frugal.

Dammit, I have to stop referring to her that way.

"What can I say? I had a good night at Chippendales."

She laughs out aloud and then covers her mouth when people glance over at us. "I forgot about that. You gave me a private show that night."

At least she remembers that. Let's see if I can coax out more of her memories.

After a few dud rolls where the people throw sevens, the stickman pushes the dice toward me. I pick up two in my hand, rolling them in between my fingers. Bringing them close to Gracyn's face, I say, "Make a wish, gorgeous."

At first she smiles, that sweet, teasing grin that always gets to me. But then, something shifts. I see it when it happens. Her brain releases a memory. Her eyes lock on my hands, her mind thrown into the past.

She gasps as she grips my arm. "Oh my god. I remember. I remember *why*."

"Make a wish, gorgeous."

She blows on my fist, closes her eyes, and murmurs, "I wish to find a good man to marry."

"I'll marry you."

She giggles and catches herself by leaning on the craps table so she doesn't tip over. I lost count of how many drinks we've had.

"How about if I roll a six, we get married?"

"That's a risky bet."

"Gray, the odds are in my favor."

Our whole marriage debacle was my fault. Well, my drunk self's fault because there's no way sober me would've done something so impulsive.

"I didn't have a job. Why the hell didn't I ask for a job?" she groans, covering her eyes with her hands.

I toss the dice, not paying attention to what rolled.

"We got married because of a bet. Nice," she says, with a heavy dose of sarcasm.

"See? The house doesn't always win."

She slaps my chest. "That's not funny."

"A little."

"No," she deadpans, narrowing her eyes at me.

I throw the dice again. Seven out. I've never been so relieved to throw a seven. I've been too busy trying to get her to remember, I forgot to place all my bets, so I'm only out fifty bucks. I trade my small chips in for large ones and take her hand, leading her to the elevators.

Her forehead wrinkles in thought as we wait for one to open. "Okay. So after we left the Aria, I'm confused. If we left to go get married, how did we end up at the Bellagio first? Is that when the taxi driver misheard us?"

I chuckle, nodding. "In my drunken state, it was a sign. I needed to get you naked before I married you."

We step into the elevator. "You're so romantic," she retorts, rolling her eyes.

"It *was* romantic. I wanted you to see that the man you were about to marry was amazing in bed. I was *totally* thinking of you. And, you know, to make sure you didn't change your mind."

The doors shut, and she steps into me, her body brushing against mine. "Here, scoot over," she says, pushing me to the side.

The elevator is empty besides us, so I raise a brow, giving her a questioning look.

"We need to make room for your confidence," she teases, her words coated with amusement.

"Am I wrong, though?" I challenge, grabbing her by the waist and drawing her against me, my thigh shifting in between her legs. "You said it yourself that my dick must've been the reason you married me."

"Not to feed the beast, but it is impressive." Her pouty red lips dust over mine, and a firecracker feels like it explodes inside me. Her fingers run down the outline of my hard cock. "We might need to revisit the night, just in case I missed some details."

I spin her around, stepping into her space until her back presses against the elevator wall. "Can't have you missing details. Like how you came three times before my dick was even inside you." Her breath hitches. "It's all in the details, babe, and I'll make sure not to miss one."

The elevator dings, and the doors slide open. The sexual tension crackles between us like a live wire, and I grin, stepping back just enough to grab her hand. "Come on." I guide her out of the elevator. "Time for a refresher course."

Chapter 18

Brooks

I pull the belt free from the hotel's plush terry-cloth robe.

"What's that for?" Gracyn asks, sprawled naked on the bed, looking like a goddess.

"You don't remember?"

She gasps. "Of course. *Drunk Gray* had you tie her up."

It's not a question. She remembers. *I never forgot.*

Climbing onto the bed, I straddle her, moving up her body until my dick rests between her glorious tits. "Hands up," I command. She raises them without hesitation, a playful grin tugging at her lips. I wrap the belt around her wrists. "Keep them above your head."

She obeys, amusement dancing in her eyes as she stretches her arms over her head. When I grab my cock and stroke it once, she licks her lips. God, she's stunning.

"You want this?" My voice is rough with desire.

Her response is in her eyes, her parted lips, her quiet surrender. I wasn't planning this so soon, but hell, I'm not about to deny her. *Or myself.* I shift forward, guiding the head of my cock to her lips. She opens, flicking her tongue out to taste me, and I growl as she takes me deep. With her hands bound, I have to take control as I rock my hips, moving in and out of her mouth.

Her tongue swirls around me, her mouth hot and eager, sending jolts of pleasure straight through me. Her eyes stay locked on mine, a mix of challenge and submission that makes my blood run hotter.

"Good girl," I murmur, and her lips curl into a faint smile around me.

I pick up the pace, thrusting deeper, testing her limits, but she never wavers. She hums around me, the vibration driving me wild.

"Gracyn," I growl.

Her eyes flash with heat, her mouth tightening around me as she sucks me in hard. I can't hold back anymore. Pulling free, my cock slips from her mouth with a wet pop, and I grip it tightly, stroking it twice before my release spills across her tits. The sight of her, her skin glistening, her lips swollen, sends a final jolt through me.

She looks up at me with a satisfied smirk.

There is no question why this woman has been in my bed three of the last five weekends. How can I resist this?

"Don't move," I say, pushing off the bed to grab a hand towel out of the bathroom. I clean her up, savoring every second of her compliance. When I reach for the ice bucket I requested be filled while we were eating, her eyes narrow with curiosity.

"Again," I say firmly, "no hands."

Her breath hitches, and she nods, her hands staying obediently above her head as I reach into the bucket, pulling out a single cube.

She shivers as I drag the ice cube up her inner thigh.

"Remember this," I murmur, circling her pussy with the cold edge before pushing it inside her. Her sharp gasp echoes in the room, her body arching off the bed. I grab another piece out of the ice bucket, this time running it over her pebbled nipple.

"You're cruel," she whispers, her voice trembling.

My tongue catches the water as it melts over her skin. I suck on her nipple, drawing out a moan from her before I move to the other one. I trail the ice cube down her stomach until it reaches her clit. She gasps again as I circle the sensitive bundle of nerves with the cold, teasing her.

I lean down to replace the ice with my tongue, and she cries out. I lap her clit until her whimpers fill the room, her thighs squeezing my head as she loses control.

That's it, babe, let go.

Her breathing becomes ragged, and I can feel her teetering on the edge. I slip a finger inside her, curling it so it hits the inner wall as I flick my tongue.

"Brooks!" she screams out, her release sudden, her entire body tensing.

She tries to pull away, but I wrap my arm around her thighs and grind my lips against her until she rides out her orgasm.

When I sit up, her face is flushed, and her lips part as she tries to catch her breath. "That was…" she murmurs. "Wow."

"There's more where that comes from," I promise, reaching for her hands. I untie the belt from her wrists, then bring them to my lips, pressing soft kisses to the insides of them. I lean against the headboard, pulling her up so she's straddling me, her body flush with mine. *Fuck. I'm in so much trouble.* I know I shouldn't do this, but the words slip out, "Are you on birth control?"

Never have I had sex bare with a woman. I wore one with Jessie, but I learned real quick that condoms aren't failproof.

She nods. "I'm on the pill," she whispers.

"Do you trust me when I tell you I'm clean?"

Another nod. Her green eyes lock with mine.

"Because I need to feel inside you. All of you. Is that okay?"

Her answer is in the way her body moves, the way her hand slips between us, guiding my dick to her entrance. And as she slides down onto me, she whispers, "Yes," against my mouth.

A guttural groan tears from my throat. Her warmth. Her tightness. The sensation of being bare is almost too much to handle. I've never felt this, and I know I won't last long. When she's fully seated, I stop her, my hands firm on her hips as I steady her. Slowly, I wrap my hand around her neck and press my forehead against hers. I close my eyes, breathing in her intoxicating scent.

"When you left a couple of weeks ago, I looked up the definition of addiction."

Her head lifts, her gaze locking with mine. I have a hard time reading her. I can't tell what she's thinking. Is this more to her, too? Or is it just sex?

"What does it mean?" she whispers as her body moves again. She pushes up, sliding back down onto me at an excruciatingly slow pace.

I can't stop the deep groan. "Compulsive engagement despite negative consequences," I rasp, my hand tightening on her hip.

She pauses for a moment, her breathing shallow. "Sounds about right," she murmurs, a sly smile tugging at the corners of her mouth. Then she moves again, this time her rhythm is quick and unrelenting, her body molding with mine as she rides me.

The room fills with a symphony of her moans blending with the sound of skin against skin. I grip her hips tighter, guiding her as she takes me deeper. I draw her in, slamming my mouth against hers, desperate and hungry. I swallow her moans as our tongues tangle in a kiss that's as wild as her movements.

When our kiss breaks, our breaths are ragged, loud, and raw. She throws her head back; her moans grow louder, her nails digging into my shoulders. We're both close.

"Come with me," I grind out.

Her body trembles, and a strangled cry escapes her lips as she comes undone in my arms, her release triggering my own. As the tremors subside, she collapses against my chest. I wrap my arms around her, holding her close, my fingers trailing up and down her back.

What the fuck am I doing?

Negative consequences for the win.

"WE MIGHT HAVE to go over all that again. You know my memory is horrible, and it's already fading."

My insatiable wife is downright gorgeous. The hotel's white robe hangs off her shoulder, barely draping across her right nipple as she stretches out on the couch. She sounds thoroughly sated despite what her mouth is saying. The sun sets behind her, past the wall of glass. It's amazing how bright the oranges and yellows are here. I thought we had decent sunsets in New York, but here, I feel I'm witnessing art unfold in real time.

I walk over and grip the tie of her robe, tugging it loose, opening it up to reveal her exquisite body that I'm addicted to. Dragging my finger across her collarbone, down over her perky breast, she lets out a moan when I pinch her nipple, enough to make her arch off the couch.

Damn, she's going to kill me. My dick is hard and raring to go again, but my head is filling with impossible things. I have to leave in the morning, and I don't want to. Whatever this is, it's on borrowed time. No matter how many times I make her yell my name—no matter how much I want to pretend otherwise—Gracyn will never be mine. And that pisses me off.

"Hey." She grabs my hand as I stand back up. "What just happened?"

I sigh, shaking off the unwelcome irritation.

She closes her robe. "Then what's wrong?"

"Truthfully?" I hesitate, meeting her gaze. She nods, but I'm not sure I can handle the truth. "Have you ever wanted to live in New York?"

I just say it.

Throw it out there.

"Hmm."

That's it? A simple hum.

"Sorry," I mutter, drawing in a harsh inhale. "I always seem to make this more complicated than it needs to be." I walk to the bedroom and slide a shirt on. Way to make things awkward.

"Brooks," she says, following me, standing in the bedroom's doorway. Her robe is loosely tied, her hair a mess, and yet she looks stunning. "You caught me off guard. For what it's worth, I have. But damn, do you know how expensive it is to live in the city? On a teacher's salary?" She strolls toward me, then wraps her arms around my waist. "I don't know if I'm ready to give up my life here for a man I barely know."

As much as I hate those words, I get it. If one of my friends packed up a woman and moved her cross-country after only meeting her a handful of times, I'd think he was crazy. Or she was after his money.

Well, call me crazy, because I would do it for her without a second thought.

"Do you want me to leave?" she whispers.

I kiss the top of her head. "No." I wish all the women from my past, the ones who accused me of being emotionally unavailable or incapable of feeling, could see me now. They'd laugh at my predicament. Because this? This sucks. "I like you. Sweet with a little dirty side." She smiles up at me. "I'll take what I can. Whatever you want to give me."

I sound desperate.

I *am* desperate.

She has my balls in a vise grip. I see it. I feel it. And yet, I can't walk away from her.

CHAPTER 19

BROOKS

My phone vibrates on the bedside table. I reach for it, and Gracyn stirs, trying to move off my chest, but I tighten my other arm around her, pinning her down. Her soft laughter vibrates against me as I stretch to grab the phone. When I see that it's Judith calling, a sense of worry slams into me. The only reason she'd be calling me past midnight is bad news. My stomach twists as I swipe to answer.

"Judith, what's wrong?" I ask, my voice sharp. Her cries fill the line, and I jerk upright. "Judith," I repeat, more forcefully this time. "What the hell is going on?"

"I'm sorry, Brooks," she sobs. "I didn't know what to do."

Her words slam into me like a freight train, and my breath catches in my throat. "What happened?"

"When …when we got back from the zoo, after we talked, Presley started feeling bad, and then she threw up her dinner. There's a stomach bug going around school. So, I called Addison and told her I'd keep her at home so she didn't spread it."

Her words tumble out in a frantic rush. But so far I haven't heard anything to explain the raw fear in her voice. My grip tightens, waiting for her to continue.

"Poor thing, wouldn't stop throwing up. I got her settled, and she seemed like she was done and fell asleep. When I checked on her a half hour later..." She breaks off, sobbing so hard that her words come out garbled, but I catch the next part clearly enough to knock the wind out of me. "Her body was limp. And she wouldn't wake up. Oh god, Brooks," she cries.

The room tilts, and I reach out, steadying myself against the wall as panic rises to a dizzying spin in my chest.

"Did you call 911?" I yell over her cries, ready to lose my mind.

"I just. This has never happened—"

"*Give me the damn phone*," Addison rumbles in the background. "She's fine, Brooks," she says matter-of-factly.

How hard was that to say? I let out a shaky exhale, relieved to hear those words, and fall back on the bed, covering my eyes with my arm. My heart tried to escape through my chest. *Breathe, Handley.*

"She's in the hospital for the night," Addison continues. "She's dehydrated. They said the stomach bug is running rampant in the schools right now."

"The hospital?" I jump up again, gathering all my stuff and shoving it in my bag. Gracyn rushes to the bathroom and comes out with my overnight bag, tossing it inside my suitcase. I mouth a quick "thank you."

"She'll be okay, Brooks. I'm not going anywhere. She'll probably be able to go home tomorrow."

"Thank you. But I'm headed home."

"How did everything go with … you know who?" She whispers the last part.

She wants to talk about this *now*?

My brain is barely functioning, and the only thing I can focus on is that my daughter is in the hospital, scared to death, and her only parent isn't there.

"Fine. Good. I'll tell you about it later," I mutter, glancing at Gracyn. "I'll call when I land. Text me the hospital and what room she's in." A text pings on my phone before I can take another breath. I glance down at it, my heart hammering.

My brain is in a scrambled state. I know who I need to call, but I can't focus long enough to make it happen. "Goddamn it!" I yell into my phone in frustration. *"Shandra Rose. Shandra Rose. Find fucking Shandra Rose,"* I murmur to myself, scrolling through my contacts like a madman. My travel agent's name pops up, and I press call.

She answers on the first ring. "I don't normally work at midnight, but then again, you've never called me at midnight." She chuckles into the phone.

"I need a flight home. Like right now," I bark.

"Is everything okay?" Concern fills her voice as the faint clatter of keys echoes through the line.

I choke up, telling her about Presley. I've failed as a father.

"Got you on a flight. It leaves in an hour and a half."

I exhale, muttering my thanks before hanging up. My mind races, spiraling through what-ifs and regrets, as I try to shove my emotions into a locked box.

Gracyn stands at the door, dressed and holding my luggage by the time I hang up. Her forehead creases with worry. "Ready?" she asks, holding her car keys up, not needing to ask a million questions, instead understanding the urgency of the situation. I like this woman more and more every time I'm with her.

The drive to the airport is a blur as my imagination runs wild, conjuring up the worst-case scenarios, each more terrifying than the last, but Gracyn lays her warm hand on my leg, grounding me in the moment, to the here and now.

I roll my head in her direction. "What if—"

Her fingers tighten. "Don't do that," she interrupts. "This will be the longest flight of your life, but try to think good thoughts. It sounds like she's in excellent hands. I have a feeling your sister will be in total control of the situation."

"I can't stop imagining my baby girl in pain."

"Keep telling yourself that she's surrounded by people that love her. She's getting what she needs in the hospital, and she'll be in your arms in a few hours."

Slumping forward in my seat, I bury my face in my hands. "I should've been there," I mutter, my voice muffled and strained. "Instead of here, blaming you for something you didn't even do. I just … I keep screwing up."

Guilt is a heavy beast.

When Gracyn pulls into the drop-off lane, I can't help but fixate on the couple in front of us. The old man dropping them off gives them tight embraces, especially the woman who I assume to be his daughter. I watch him gaze adoringly at her, waving as she walks away. I wonder if he ever experienced moments like this where guilt and fear clawed at him. Was he ever absent when his daughter needed him the most? Did he ever experience the crushing weight of wondering if he was enough?

Once he drives off, I turn to Gracyn, who's staring at me with a concerned expression, and I sigh, letting my gaze linger on her. Sexy Gray. Even when she's not trying to be. "Thank you for driving me."

"Of course."

I reach over, grabbing her hand and threading my fingers through hers. I pull her hand to my lips, kissing her knuckles. "Thank you for kicking me out. And accepting my apology. And taking me to the airport."

She smiles, then wrinkles her nose. "I don't expect you to be at the court date now. So, I guess this is goodbye."

Hello, reality.

I nod a couple of times. Since the court date is only a few weeks away, there is no way I'll be leaving Presley's side any time soon.

Silence fills the car, and not the comforting kind. The surrounding horns and bus traffic fade away. I cup her face, and with a quick tug, her lips are on mine in an instant, and that addicting taste of hers pulls out a groan from deep in my chest. I always crave more when we're together.

She jerks out of my grasp in surprise when someone knocks on her car window. A police officer's stern gaze motions for her to get moving. Her cheeks flush a deep shade of red, making me chuckle as I exit the car.

I steal one last look over my shoulder, taking her in. "Bye, beautiful thief."

She smiles, shaking her head.

"If you're ever in New York, you know my number."

As I step into the hospital room, my heart plummets into my stomach. The sight steals my breath away. My baby girl, lying perfectly still in a bed, surrounded by wires and machines, her small body barely visible in the dim light. I struggle to stay on my feet, the overwhelming fear threatening to consume me. *Pull your shit together*. I have to be strong for her, to hold her in my arms and tell her everything will be all right. Because it will. It has to.

I swallow hard, pushing down the fear clawing at my chest, and make my way to her bedside with shaky legs.

"Daddy," Presley whispers, lifting her little hand to me, and my eyes well up with tears. Judith's lying next to her on the bed. Her eyes open, and I can see the relief on her face as she slides off the bed.

I take Presley's hand, and as much as I want to crawl into the bed beside her, I fear I'm too large and don't want to pull on any of the wires, so I fall to the side of the bed, resting my head on her stomach. The last time I cried was the first time I held her, and I blink back the tears before picking my head up. "Hey, Snarky. How are you feeling?"

"Better now that my tummy isn't coming out of my mouth anymore."

"I bet." I watch her eyes flutter closed, but she fights to keep them open. "Go to sleep, baby. I'll be here when you wake up."

I wait for her breathing to slow before I stand up, but I can't stop staring at her. Judith joins me and starts tucking her blanket around her small body to keep her warm.

"Thank you. Thank you for being here for her." My voice is hoarse with emotion as I pull her into a hug. The relief that Presley's okay is overwhelming. "Are they sure it's the tummy bug?" I ask, still not ready to let her go. She's the only thing stable at the moment for me to grab onto.

Her arms tighten around my waist. "Fairly certain. They say

it might be food poisoning, but with other kids having it, they're more inclined to go with a stomach bug. But she's already so much better than when we first got here."

The hug lingers so long that it becomes awkward, so I release her and walk over to the chair, sinking into it. I slump back, exhausted. It's been a long day.

Judith grabs a blanket and hands it to me. "It reclines to a bed." She points to a lever on the side. "Addison went home about a half hour ago to grab some things, but she's coming right back. I guess I'll go home and be back in the morning. I'll bring some breakfast."

"That'd be great," I say.

She reaches for my hand and squeezes it once.

"Thank you, again. I can't even imagine what we would do without you."

CHAPTER 20

BROOKS

"Dad!" Presley bursts into our home like a tornado, flinging the front door open wide. She runs into the kitchen where Jared and I are cracking open beers.

"Hey, Pres, what are you doing here?" I glance over my shoulder, half expecting Judith to be trailing behind her, but she's nowhere in sight. The guys are coming over to watch the baseball game for the afternoon, and Presley's supposed to be hanging out with Judith. Living a couple of floors down, it's not unusual for her to go back and forth between our places, but she knows I don't like her hanging around when it's the guys. The mix of alcohol and language is not appropriate for her tiny ears, especially if our team is losing.

"She's a lot quicker than me," Judith declares, appearing around the corner, out of breath.

"We made everyone chocolate chip cookies," Presley exclaims as Judith holds up the basket.

"Snarky, you can't cook," Jared teases, giving her the side-eye.

She turns and glares at him. "Bruh. I cook better than you look."

His head falls backward with a roar of laughter, and I'm momentarily stunned and impressed by her comeback. She's honing in her skills. "When did I become a bruh?"

"Everyone is a bruh," I deadpan, hating the word, especially when she calls me that.

"Well, I see you're all better," he says, throwing a pretzel at her, and it falls to the floor. "Back to being ornery."

Without missing a beat, she picks it up, sticks her tongue out, and throws it at him. He catches it in his mouth and eats it.

"Gross! That was on the floor," she snickers.

The banter continues as Judith places the cookies with the rest of the snacks.

"Those look delicious," I comment, picking one up and taking a bite. The warm, melted chocolate hits my tongue. "Damn, those are good." The words come out muffled with a full mouth of cookie.

"I knew you would like them," she boasts, a confident grin on her face. "You've always had a weakness for anything chocolate."

"You know me too well," I reply, popping another one into my mouth.

"All right, Pres, let's get out of here so these guys can have their fun," she says, nudging her to get moving.

After the door clicks shut behind them, Jared turns to me. "Has Judith mentioned anything about Gray? About you being married?"

"Obviously, unless she's been living under a rock, she knows. But she hasn't said anything. There's no reason to act like anything has changed since it hasn't."

"So how is Gray?"

I raise a brow. He's armed with all the questions today. He pops a grape into his mouth as I collect my thoughts. That's a much harder question to answer. She's incredible. She's stubborn. She's downright hot when she's short-tempered. She doesn't hesitate to put me in my place. She's genuine.

She lives in Vegas.

Almost perfect.

I blow out a heavy breath, rubbing the back of my neck. "She's different from any woman I've ever met. I … I can't stop thinking about her."

He flashes a *told you so* smirk. "Ever think of asking her to move here?"

"She doesn't want to move here. I asked her point-blank if she ever wanted to move to New York. I got a *hmm*." It still irritates me. She flat-out denied me.

"Who the hell could be happy living in Vegas?"

"She feels the same way about New York City," I mutter, a little defensive now.

"Not every woman is perfect," he chides, popping another grape in his mouth.

"She is," I snap before I can stop myself.

His eyes widen, then his smile grows. "Wow, the last time you defended a woman … was never. She's more than a fuck to you."

His words sound archaic and grate on my nerves. I'm not a twenty-something kid anymore, even though she's ended up in my bed the three times we've been together. She's still more than that.

"Someday you'll grow up."

"What? Am I supposed to think something different? You

can't seem to stay away from a woman who lives thousands of miles away, which I *assumed* was because she was great in bed," Jared presses.

Irritated, I grab my beer and head for the living room where the game is about to start, and he's hot on my tail.

"Tell me something different, Brooks," he taunts, pushing me. "Admit that you're into this woman and do something about it. I mean, damn, she's already your wife."

I twist the cap off the bottle and take a long swig. *I want more*. That's not the problem. It's the damn distance between us that's holding me back from pursuing her.

"When do you see her next?"

"The court date is next week, I think."

I told myself I wasn't going, but with Presley fully recovered, and now that I know it was a stomach bug, I'd like to see Gracyn again. Even if it is to break the only bond between us.

Jared says nothing at first, instead watching me for a beat before saying, "You should tell her you don't want the annulment."

I laugh, not because it's funny, but because it's so absurd that laughter is my only response. We can't stay married. "I have a feeling that wouldn't go over well with her."

"Then ask for a postponement, so this gives you some time. Consider whether you genuinely want this. And pursue it."

The door swings open, and Jenson, Chase, and Devon stroll in, each carrying their drink of choice. As the night unfolds, my mind drifts elsewhere. Jared's words have lit a fire, and now I can't ignore it. He's right, I need to get off my ass and make a move, or I'll live with regrets.

I slam my empty bottle of beer down on the coffee table,

rising with a resolute air, fueled by at least six beers. All eyes turn to me.

"Decision made. I'm heading to Vegas for *my wife*."

CHAPTER 21

GRACYN

"Gray, what's it like being married to a billionaire?" Journalism has hit rock bottom. It's a constant struggle not to roll my eyes at every ridiculous question they throw at me. It's not a toss; they hurl those absurd inquiries, hitting me square in the face, every time. *A little creativity wouldn't hurt.* Charli whirls around, and I snatch her arm to stop her from doing whatever it is she's about to unleash. This is what they want. The sudden burst of a camera flash blinds both of us.

"Did that asshole take a picture of us with our mouths wide open?" she growls. "He could have at least given us a second to pose."

I don't take the time to explain they don't want a pose, they want to catch us off guard. Instead, I usher her through the front of Rarity, away from more pictures. The bouncer shakes his head at the guy, gesturing for him to step back.

It's been a little over a month since we tied the knot, but the paparazzi found out about me this week. They've become a nightmare, like relentless hound dogs, sniffing out any scoop they can get their filthy paws on, and they won't stop until they have a story locked down and tied with a big red "fuck you" bow.

Brooks, in his infinite wisdom, thought it'd be funny to send flowers for us making it over a month.

It wasn't.

Little did he know, the relentless hounds tracked me down and parked outside my apartment building. All it took was a measly twenty-dollar bribe for the delivery guy to tell them who sent the flowers. They're crafting this whimsical romance between the two of us, highlighting every time someone catches us together. Considering we live thousands of miles apart, it's been pretty frequent. Part of me wished he would've shown up at my door tonight. I almost canceled going out with Charli just in case he did.

She would've killed me. I need to get over these weekend indulgences, anyway.

"A week and a half, and you'll be a free woman again," Charli yells over the music.

"I'm a free woman *now*," I reply, and she throws me an incredulous glare. "What? I am. Look." I lift my chin toward a guy sitting at the bar. "He's cute."

"He is. Go talk to him," she dares.

As if sensing we're talking about him, he looks up and smiles.

My eyes avert past him, focusing on the bottles of liquor on the wall behind him.

"He thinks you're cute, too."

"You're an ass." I emit a resigned chuckle and pull her to the bar on the opposite end. Chelsea, the bartender, gives us high fives as a hello and takes our order. She replaced me behind the bar after I quit.

"Just admit you have a thing for Brooks."

"I do have a *thing*. A huge thing. According to Nevada law, he's my husband. And nobody will let me forget." Mom keeps asking if I've talked to him, as if we're in a relationship. Ray keeps questioning if the annulment is still going to happen because he's seen all the articles, acting as if we're really married.

I want to scream at the top of my lungs, *I'm just having fun!*

Even though it's a lie. When we finally end our marriage, the only thing left will be a broken heart. *Mine.*

When he asked me if I ever thought about living in New York, thoughts of Lindsey and her tears popped up in my head, and I freaked out inside.

"Sorry," she murmurs, sensing my irritation. She hands me my martini and picks up hers. "Cheers to annulments and great sex."

I clink my glass to hers. "*That* is something worth celebrating."

"Who asked for great sex?" Rory asks, strolling up to us. I can't help but smile at his black suit, such a contrast from the typical black torn T-shirt and jeans he's always worn behind the bar.

I straighten his tie. "I'm liking this look on you."

"Thanks to you." He leans in and gives me a side hug. "I have a table for you guys over there." He points to a two-chair high-top in the corner with a reserved sign on it. There are a couple of girls next to the table, eyeing it.

I point. "Looks like we better grab it now."

Rory bolts in that direction, making sure they don't get any ideas. We follow, but at a more leisurely pace as he secures our spot.

Charli doesn't waste time before immediately diving into our conversation. "Feels like it's been forever since we hung out."

"It has. I don't like it." We're used to seeing each other every day, but since we graduated, these moments have become rare. She's out searching for a job during the week, and I'm in bed with my husband on the weekends. Sigh. "Things will settle after the whole Brooks ordeal is over," I say.

She runs her finger over the rim of the glass. Which means she has something to say but doesn't want to say it.

"What?" I ask.

"You're not staying for me, are you?"

"What are you talking about?"

"The reason you're not taking a chance with Brooks. It's not because of me, right?"

"What? Of course not. It's because he scares me. His entire world." She waits for me to continue as I take a sip of my drink. I've thought a lot about this. How could I not? It's turned my world upside down the last month. "He has a daughter. I'd be an instant mom. That is not something I take lightly."

She nods in understanding. "Okay. I get that."

"He has freaking paparazzi all up in his business," I say, on a roll, pointing to the front door. "I'm a teacher. I am not the type to attend galas, rub shoulders with New York's elite, or set sail to St. Barts for the weekend."

"I don't know. That part sounds exciting."

"But that's what you dream of. You want the glitz and glamour of the spotlight. I don't. I want quiet moments with my husband as he whispers how much he loves me in the middle of a restaurant without the worry of someone snapping pictures of us. I've never dreamed of being the billionaire's wife and all the responsibility that comes with that."

I glance past her to the dance floor, where people move to the beat of the high energy song. My attention lingers on them as my thoughts drift to what it would be like to be with him. He said he wants an equal, and I can't shake the feeling that he might not get that from me, *a teacher*. I'd have to conform to his idea of a wife and mom, and my needs would take a back seat.

Ultimately, I fear I won't meet his expectations and end up like Lindsey.

Alone.

"Have you told him how you feel?"

"No. And I don't plan on it. I'm not going to open myself up to rejection."

She twists her lips, thinking. "If he didn't have a kid and was broke, would it be different?"

"Of course it would. That would make him normal. *Like me.*"

She finishes her drink. "Normal is boring."

I wave my hand at Chelsea as she walks by and motion for two more drinks. "Oh, look." I point to a girl sitting by herself at the bar, a surprise that I had been thinking of her, and there she is. "That's Lindsey, the girl I was telling you about, that moved here for her asshole boyfriend."

"Yeah, the one you self-projected yourself on," she says in a sarcastic voice.

I stick my tongue out at her and laugh. "C'mon, let's see if she wants to dance. I hate that she's sitting by herself."

By the time we squeeze through the crowd to where she was

sitting, the chair is empty. I do a quick scan of the bar. "Hey, Daryl, where'd the woman go that was sitting here?"

He stops wiping off the bar, looks up, and shrugs. "She paid and left." Darn it. I wish we had caught her. "You guys good?" He points at our empty hands.

"Good for now. We'll be back in a bit," I say. Because the last time I was out where I had an obnoxious amount of drinks, I ended up marrying a stranger, so I'm trying to pace myself.

"C'mon. I'm ready to sweat." I grab Charli's hand. The song's tempo is fast and pumping through the walls of the club, the vibrations tickling my insides—it's the best sweat music. We slide in with a group of girls at a bachelorette party, who all cheer us on. That's what I love about dancing; everyone is happy. We become best friends almost instantly.

A couple of guys make their way into the circle, showing off their best moves. The women inflate their ego by screaming and whistling, throwing their hands in the air. They dance with two women at first, but then slowly make their way around the circle. When one grabs me, I don't hesitate. He turns me around and dances to my back. Jokingly, I stick my ass out and shake it.

It fits the song. Everyone laughs, and then I step away, dancing by myself. He moves on to the next woman. When the song ends, I'm sweaty, breathing heavy, and thirsty.

One more drink won't hurt.

Okay, maybe two more.

As we're sitting at the table, I notice a burly guy staring at us from the bar. I angle my head, staring back. He wasn't there earlier because I would've seen him. He's hard to miss. He's sitting a few seats over from where I spotted Lindsey. Herculean strength biceps, wearing a black T-shirt, tattoos down both arms, with a scruffy black beard. It looks like he could be a bouncer or in security. A few minutes pass, and every time I glance that way, our eyes meet. *Seriously, dude, stop staring at me.*

"Who are you looking at?" Charli asks as she looks over her shoulder. She twists back in her seat. "Oh! He's like scary sexy. One you wouldn't want to meet in a dark alley, but also one that you wouldn't mind slapping your ass as he rams his enormous dick into you."

I burst out laughing, almost spewing my drink everywhere. "Oh my god, Charli!"

"What? He's dangerously hot."

He also won't stop staring at us.

"Who the hell is that guy?" Rory barks, appearing out of the blue, making us both jump. He stands between our two chairs. "His eyes haven't left you since you sat down."

"I was wondering if it was one of Ray's guys." It wouldn't surprise me.

"I know most of Ray's guys, and I've never seen him before. I'll find out his problem."

I grab Rory's arm, stopping him. "No, let me." He lifts a brow, shaking his head. "I want to know why he keeps staring at me. Or us. He's not even being discreet about it."

He growls. "Fine. But I'm staying right here and watching."

I hold my shoulders high, determined, and stride over to an empty seat, catty-corner to grumpy pants. He turns his head in my direction, eyebrows raised in a questioning expression, as if I interrupted him.

"Hi," I say.

"Hi," he replies, not moving a muscle. His fingers tent in front of him next to his drink. It looks like water. I wait for him to say more, but he doesn't. It's the most awkward stare battle ever.

Finally I blurt, "Who are you? And why are you staring at me?"

It's the first time his mouth moves from a tight-lipped expression. One side curls up for a moment. "Did Mr. Handley not tell you?"

"Brooks? Tell me what?"

"He hired me to watch over you."

Watch over me? For what?

I slide out my phone from my back pocket and text Brooks.

> Me: You could've warned me I had someone following me.

> Brooks: Sorry. Bad habit. React first, explain later.

At least he can admit his flaws.

> Me: It's later.

> Brooks: The paparazzi already posted a pic of you. I need to know you're safe. Rob will make sure no one messes with you.

How can I fault him for his flaw if he turns it into the sweetest gesture? I smile as I reread the text. Even though it's unnecessary, the thought that he cares sends a rush of warmth through me. My heart is so freaking confused.

> Me: Thank you.

Rob clears his throat, and I shake out of my dreamy bubble, dropping the giddy smile. "Did you get it all resolved?" His apathetic tone irritates me.

"I did. And that was sweet of him, but I don't need you. I have eyes on me everywhere." I point to the ceiling where there's a camera in every corner. "The owner and I are tight."

He puffs out a single chuckle. "He told me you'd try to get rid of me. But he's paying me a lot of money to sit here. And I'd be happy to call Mr. Knight and speak with him directly about making sure you are kept safe."

I narrow my eyes, hating that Ray would probably pay this guy double if he knew he was watching me. He's tried for years to hire security for me, and I don't need him getting ideas that after Brooks and I are over, I'll still need it.

> Me: You get one night of this, and that's it.

> Brooks: Maybe.

"You might want to ready yourself for the bullshit articles," Rob says, grabbing my attention again.

I tilt my head. "What articles?"

"Someone took a pic of you dancing on that guy earlier."

"I wasn't dancing on a guy," I quip defensively.

He blinks.

"It was like ten seconds." Anyone around could see that I did nothing wrong. "Everyone was dancing with those guys."

"When you're in the public eye, one fraction of a moment isn't your story, the story is the one people will make up that happened during that fraction of a moment."

This is why I can't do this. I'm not poised enough to be a public figure. It's bad enough I'll have to watch what I say and

do when I start teaching. "Shit!" I scream at no one in particular, storming back to Charli. I envision the picture and headline
and start to panic.

"What's wrong?" Rory asks, ready to go to war for me.

I wave off Rob. "He's fine. I mean, not fine, but temporary."
I blow out a grated breath and glance at Charli. "It's time to go.
Did I tell you how much I hate being in the spotlight?"

CHAPTER 22

BROOKS

"What's on the schedule for this week?" Judith asks, handing me my morning smoothie.

"I'll be working late on Wednesday, but other than that I should be home on time." I have yet to decide if I'm going to Vegas next week, but I'll need to figure my shit out soon so I can tell her. Each night is different. One moment, we're texting and flirting after I sent her flowers for our one-month anniversary, and the next, she's grinding her ass in some guy's groin, and I'm fuming, ready to put her in the past.

Jared had to remind me how news articles bend the truth for the sake of ratings and clicks. Rob confirmed it was nothing. Now I'm back to square one, unsure what to do next. I was ready to offer her my world, ready to ask her to take a chance on me, but now I have doubts.

Judith turns to clean the blender, and I return to my iPad, catching up on the morning news. Presley dances her way into the room, pausing at the table to grab a quick bite of eggs before continuing her twirling. I can't help but laugh when she suddenly strikes a Michael Jackson pose and sings, "She's bad."

"You're about to be *badly* late if we don't get moving," I say.

Judith looks at me with a quizzical expression, and her head tilts in surprise because I rarely take Presley during the week.

I swallow the last of my drink, reach over the bar, and drop my cup into the sink. "My meeting isn't until later, so I'll walk her to dance camp."

"That'd be awesome. I can attend the earlier yoga class."

Presley and I stroll hand in hand down the sidewalk. It seems hotter out here than they forecasted. A bead of sweat trickles down my temple, prompting me to loosen my tie and undo the top buttons of my shirt.

"Daddy, what's wrong? You have a weird look on your face?"

"It's just really hot. Are you hot?"

"No." She stares at me. "You look red."

Wiping the sweat from my brow, I motion for us to continue walking. The quicker I drop her off, the faster I can escape the scorching heat.

"Mr. Handley," Ms. Ramstead says, greeting me at the door of the dance facility. Concern fills her face as she holds the door for Presley. "Presley, why don't you go stretch?"

With a quick "I love you," she scurries under Ms. Ramstead's arm, but the teacher's gaze remains fixed on me. "Are you feeling all right?"

My stomach pinches. "Actually, I don't think so."

She holds the back of her hand to my forehead. "You're not hot." She takes a step backward. "Something's going around. Didn't Presley have it a week ago?"

Shit! I'm too busy to be sick.

"I think it's the weather. It's pretty hot out here," I say, clutching at any excuse, hoping she's wrong. She chuckles and shakes her head before heading inside, muttering something about NyQuil. I barely reach home, rushing to the first trash can I find.

That's how it starts.

That was the beginning of my death sentence.

I can't recall the last time I was sick with a stomach bug, but it seems to make up for lost time. It's hitting hard and fast, and I feel like I'm being run over by a train at both ends. I'm completely drained, with nothing left to offer the toilet gods.

"C'mon, make sure you're taking sips now and then." Judith came over to save me. Literally. She holds out my drink, tilting the straw to my chapped lips. It's the last thing I want to do. Drinking requires energy. I don't have any. I shake my head. "Brooks, stop being a baby and open your mouth."

I'd flip her off if I could lift my hand.

Instead, I stubbornly follow her advice and take a tiny sip of the blue liquid. The fear that it's going to come back up is instant. My stomach tightens, and I blow out heavy, quick breaths through my nose. As Judith places a cold rag on my forehead, a wave of relief washes over me. My stomach settles, and my breathing becomes more regular.

"I hate you caught whatever Presley had," she says sympathetically.

I nod weakly in response, grateful for her care and attention. I hold my hand over hers. "Thanks for staying with me."

"Of course. I'm always here for you."

My eyelids grow heavy, and I welcome the embrace of sleep. I drift in and out of consciousness, tossing and turning throughout the night. When I wake, I feel better. I'm thinking it's over. Then my insides twist. My esophagus is on fire. When is this going to end? My groan causes Judith to come running. She does all the things. Gives me meds, wraps me in blankets, and makes sure to force down more liquid.

"You're the perfect mom," I say, my body trembling. "I'm so glad me and Presley have you."

She smiles as she gives me some more meds. "You know I love both of you."

"And I love you, Gracyn," I mumble, closing my eyes again, drifting to sleep.

I RUB MY BEARD, stretching as I wake up the next morning. Rolling my head to the side, I notice it's ten o'clock already. It's not until then that I realize I'm not on death's bed anymore. My stomach grumbles, as if telling me it's better and wants something to eat.

I grab my phone to text Jared that I survived. There are a million texts, but it's the top one that grabs my attention. When I open it, I stare at the conversation between me and Gracyn. One, I have zero memory of having.

> Me: I need you. I wish you were here to take care of me.

> Coffee Thief: What? Why?

> Me: I'm dying.

> Coffee Thief: WHAT!?!?!

Me: Of the stomach bug.

Coffee Thief: You're dramatic.

Me: No, I'm lonely.

Me: And sick.

Wifey: Are you really okay?

Jesus Christ. Apparently, the stomach bug took on a mind of its own, changed her name twice, and slipped into her messages, looking for pity. I must've fallen asleep because I left her on unread. Shit. What do I do now? I tap my thumb against the edge of the phone.

Banging sounds coming from the kitchen pull my attention away from the phone. Who is being so noisy? And why?

Dragging my socks across the hardwood, I make my way out of the bedroom, tightening my robe around my waist. Judith slams a couple more cabinets and mutters under her breath to herself. When I clear my throat, she shoots me a piercing, icy glare. I may not be the most perceptive guy, but it's clear she's angry, and I suspect I'm the reason.

I regretfully ask, "Everything okay?"

"It's fine."

The universal code for *it's not.*

"I made you some oatmeal," she sneers, placing a bowl on the kitchen bar and then rolling her eyes, mumbling something again while she turns away.

"Did I do something wrong?" I wonder aloud, my mind muddled from the texts and hazy recollection of my actions over the past forty-eight hours. I raise my hands in a defensive gesture. "You can't hold me accountable for anything during the last couple of days. I was on the verge of death and barely coherent." I manage a strained chuckle as I sink onto a barstool. I lean against the bar on my elbows. "Thanks for sticking around. It means the world to me."

"You already told me that." Nothing like throwing appreciation right back in your face. "Right before you called me *Gracyn*."

Shit.

I place the spoon down, taking a moment to gather my thoughts on how to explain the unexplainable. How the demon bug went rogue, and how I lost control of my actions and words.

She clutches the countertop, takes a deep breath, and shakes off her frustration. "Brooks, were you ever going to tell me that you were married?"

I sigh, rubbing a hand over my face. "It was a mistake. There was nothing to discuss."

She levels me with her stare, obviously not believing the lie. "You're married to the woman. Don't you think that's something you should have discussed with me, considering I'm the one having to field questions from your child?"

"If she has questions, she can come to me."

"You weren't here," she snaps.

It's a good thing I'm lacking energy at the moment because if I were running on all cylinders, those would be fighting words.

But clearly I'm fucking everything up. Time I fix it.

CHAPTER 23

GRACYN

I fidget in my seat and wait.

Today is the day I put Brooks behind me.

The day I regain my single status.

The day I get my life back. I'll no longer be married to the *billionaire*. The paparazzi can finally leave me alone. They're straight-up horrible human beings. They've relentlessly harassed me ever since that photo of me dancing with that guy spread across the internet.

Charli puts her hand on my shoulder and whispers from behind, "It'll be over soon. Hang in there."

I nod without looking back. I don't know why I'm so nervous. Maybe embarrassed is a better word. I've known the judge since I could walk. My attorney, or rather *my mom*, felt I could handle this on my own. It's not like Brooks's attorney will contest anything. In other words, she wants me to experience all the humiliation that comes with making irresponsible choices.

Even though I can't remember making that choice.

The heavy wooden courtroom door opens, and I twist in my

seat, expecting to see Brooks's attorney enter. However, to my surprise, it's familiar hazel eyes that meet mine. He smiles, and that damn smile of his sends a flurry of emotions through me. He wasn't supposed to be here. I watch as he strides down the center aisle, showing no signs of nervousness.

I rise to my feet as he approaches. Awkwardly, my arms dangle to my sides, and then I cross them, unable to decide what to do with them. A snicker comes from Charli, and I shoot her a glare to stop making fun of me.

"Gracyn," Brooks's deep voice murmurs.

I rub my glossed lips together. "He lives." We both chuckle at the same time. "You said you weren't coming."

He lifts his fingers, and they tug on my side braid. "You look gorgeous," he replies, ignoring my question. "I was hoping you would've looked like you were mourning a loss."

"What? You thought I'd be in sweats and an oversized shirt with a pint of ice cream?" After the week I had, this day couldn't come faster. "You think highly of yourself," I tease.

"Someone has to," he says, and his playful demeanor shifts to something more reluctant. "There's a reason I came. I wanted to talk to you before this, but my plane was late this morning."

"About what?"

He draws in a deep breath and exhales sharply. "I'd like us to give this a real chance."

What? My mind races, struggling to find words because at this moment, there are none.

"Now?" My eyes dart around the room in panic, and I shake my head. "You're telling me this at the eleventh hour and expect me to give you an answer right now?" I question with disbelief in my voice.

The past week has been a nightmare. Countless articles

labeled me a cheater and a gold digger. I've had to hide out at my mom's house until this all dies down.

"I can't. I can't do this." I storm past him, pushing the wooden door open and step into the hallway to catch my breath. Why did he do this right now?

I quickly whip my head around when the door opens behind me, and I shoot daggers at the doorway. He could at least give me a minute.

Instead, Charli walks out with a concerned expression. "You okay? I overheard."

"No," I say, honestly. "My mind is so scattered, there's no way I can answer him in five seconds. My brain keeps telling me that there is a zero chance this could work. You read the horrible things people were saying about me, and that was from *one* photo." My voice rises an octave higher with each word until people stare. I force myself to whisper. "But every time he's standing in front of me, my heart beats faster. Things get all tingly, and I can't stop smiling." I take a few steps, shaking out my hands, and then turn back. "Okay. I need to get this over with. I can't have another week like I did last week."

We return to the courtroom just as the judge is entering. He gives me an irritated scowl as I rush down the aisle to get to my table. He sits and wrestles with some papers before raising his eyes.

"Court is now in session."

I've heard those words a million times. Growing up, I sat on the back bench, listening to my dad during his cases, yet hearing them today burdens my chest with a crushing two-ton weight. My mom knew what she was doing by making me come.

Add to that the enormous elephant in the room, towering five feet from me, wanting more, I'm teetering on the edge of a mental breakdown. My fingers tremble as I clench them into a fist under the table. I need to calm down.

The judge asks us a couple of formal questions. We answer with an easy "yes" or "no." This will be his easiest case of the day. Neither of us are contesting it. The judge sighs, bows his head to read something and then glances back up, his eyes looking over the rim of his readers, bouncing between me and Brooks. I fixate straight ahead, afraid if I look over at Brooks, I'll lose it.

The judge looks to Brooks. "Mr. Handley, you live in New York, correct?"

"Yes, your Honor."

"Why didn't you send your attorney in your place?"

My head snaps at him. Don't tell him, I plead with my eyes. Don't tell him it's because you want to try.

"I … um." Brooks stares at me for a moment before turning to the judge.

"I imagine you're a busy man, being CEO of a large company. And as you've mentioned in the complaint, you didn't know Gracyn Carmichael until just over a month and a half ago. Most men in your position wouldn't bother showing up at a court date to admit they made such an enormous mistake. Especially when they can afford an attorney."

Brooks lets out an awkward laugh and then clears his throat. "You are absolutely right, Your Honor. I am a busy man, but this mistake is ours, and I owed it to Gracyn to be here. I didn't intend for her to shoulder the responsibility alone of correcting this wrong."

Of course, his answer is perfect. The judge's lips quirk up as he gazes down, reading whatever is in front of him again. I exhale with relief, realizing I'm moments away from no longer being married. My eyes remain locked on the judge's hand, anticipating the sound of the gavel.

But then he looks up, takes off his readers, and folds his hands before him.

"Standing before me, claiming this was a mistake, is a mockery of the institution of marriage. Both of you made a choice and a commitment, and I don't believe that it was made under duress or manipulation."

It could have! I just don't remember!

"Your Honor, we were both—"

The judge raises his hand with a stern expression, halting my objection.

"Ms. Carmichael, I'm aware. But truthfully, I'm growing weary of individuals assuming they can dissolve a marriage they entered on a whim because they imagined it would be fun, only to awaken with regrets."

I turn my head and over my shoulder mouth, *"What's happening?"* to Charli. Her wide-eyed expression is as confused as I am. My mom told me I had nothing to worry about.

Well, I'm worried.

I fly out of my seat, pounding my palms on the table. "You can't force us to stay married. This is absurd."

"What's absurd is that two grown adults ended up in a situation like this," he retorts, his glare fierce. I want to cry, but I blink back my tears. "And you're right, I can't. But I can prolong the dissolution to make sure this is what everyone wants. In three months, we'll reconvene."

No!

Don't hit the gavel.

Not now.

The echo of the hit vibrates in my chest.

It's over.

And I'm still married.

What. The. Actual. Hell?

Once the judge exits the courtroom, I bolt toward the door that leads to his office without a glance toward Brooks. The officer waves me through, his eyes softening as his lips press into a faint, almost apologetic line.

"George, why are you doing this?" I say, barging into his office. The man I've known since I was five gestures for me to sit, as if expecting me. Though I'd rather keep standing, I reluctantly sit on the uncomfortable navy blue chair opposite his desk and cross my legs. "Have you seen the tabloids? They've made my life a living hell. This needs to end."

"I deal with these cases daily," he says, hanging up his robe and then taking a seat. "Never have I received, not one, but two letters asking me to not grant the annulment."

He holds up a plain white manila folder. My eyes widen as I sit up taller. Who would request something like this, and why would the judge even entertain their plea? This is unfounded, and when my dad hears what he's done, he'll be livid.

"There's usually a grain of truth in the tabloids. And I did see them. I saw the way you guys look at each other. No matter how you fight it, it's genuine. I believe it deserves a bit more time for you two to explore before reaching a final decision."

"With all due respect, that's not for you to decide," I protest.

He responds with a nonchalant shrug that irritates me even more. "In my courtroom, it is."

I groan, standing up. It's clear he won't change his mind. "Who are the letters from?"

"I'll read them to you at your next court date."

"This is ridiculous. I don't even remember getting married,"

I whine like a five-year-old, dropping my arms by my side. "You know you're going to hear from my mom."

He laughs, his head bobbing in agreement. "I have no doubt. But I think she's going to agree with me on this one."

I hate that he's right. She'll get a kick out of this. But this decision isn't theirs to make. It's mine and Brooks's.

As soon as I step off the elevator, I spot Brooks sitting alone on a wooden bench in the narrow hallway on the first floor. The letters come to mind, and I storm over to him. "Did you have something to do with this?" I blurt out, narrowing my eyes at him.

He looks up from his phone, confused. "With what?"

"Did you write a letter? I mean, Brooks, no matter how bad you want this to work, it's not going to." I pace in front of him, my frustration bubbling over. He's proven he can't stay away from me, and now he's going to force me to stay married to him. It suddenly clicks. "Did you pay him off?" I stop and stare at him. "That's the only reason he'd take your side over mine."

"You're accusing me of paying off a judge?" he responds, his eyes wide in disbelief. "I think this is asinine. I sure in the hell don't want to stay married to a woman who doesn't want to. My attorney is already drafting a response to the unprofessionalism of that judge. And what letter?"

This is pointless. I turn around to leave, but his words stop me in my tracks.

"And you think I'm full of myself? You think I'd manipulate a woman to stay married to me? Fucking, please. I'm not that hard up. I like you, Gracyn, but not that damn much. Fuck! I can't keep you, but now I can't get rid of you. Worst case of purgatory ever," he says, storming off down the hallway.

Good job, Gray. Way to make a bad situation worse.

I sink onto the bench, the wooden seat groaning under my weight. Why did Brooks even bother showing up? If his attorney had come, we would be single again.

My phone buzzes in my purse, and I grab it to find a message from my mom asking how it went. I type a response through tear-blurred vision.

Me: Still married.

CHAPTER 24

BROOKS

I'm a fucking liar.

Desperate, weak, and utterly at her mercy. We've established this. And I despise it. As I sit on the bottom step of the courthouse, I can't escape her words. The truth in them. She's right, I don't want to let her go. Not now. Not ever. To my surprise, the judge's ruling might have been a fortunate turn of events.

She's still mine.

At least for three more months.

I notice one guy hanging around with a camera, leaning against a tree, staring at me. A muscle in my jaw twitches. Asshole better keep his distance.

As soon as I watch Gracyn emerge from the courthouse doors, my mind races. A plan forms. It's half-baked, impulsive, and probably the worst plan I've ever had. Then again, getting married while being drunk wasn't exactly my crowning moment of brilliance. But this? This is a now-or-never situation. No time to think. Just act.

"Gracyn," I call, quickly crossing to the other side of the stairway entrance.

She arches an eyebrow and glares at me like she could freeze hell. She's been crying, and I resist the urge to pull her into my arms and offer comfort.

"I'm sorry for being an ass. This entire thing blindsided me. I didn't handle it right."

"It's fine. I'm used to your hot-and-cold," she retorts.

Her words leave a bitter taste in my mouth. Not an attribute that I'd like her to be used to.

She dismisses me with a casual wave. "I'll see you in three months." With that, she turns on her heels and starts down the stairs.

"Wait," I call out.

She pauses, and while I can't see her eyes, I can feel her rolling them.

"Can I hitch a ride to the airport?"

To my surprise, she pivots and says, "Whatever." There must be something seriously wrong with me clinging to the idea that we could work, like a soldier desperately holding the line when the war's been lost. She takes a few steps, then looks over her shoulder, impatience flickering in her eyes. "You coming?"

I hesitate, knowing there's no logic in chasing her. Internally I scoff, has there ever been logic used with Gracyn? The camera guy clicks away like he's trying to capture every moment of this.

"Do you want a ride or not?" she asks, sounding slightly annoyed.

Am I willing to lose?

The question hangs in the air for a second longer than it should, then I throw caution to the wind because, honestly?

Fuck it. It's clear she has feelings for me. She can try to mask it, try to push me away, but I saw it in her eyes the second I walked into the courtroom. No matter how hard she tries to pretend she hates me now, there's something here. Something real.

I catch up with her, and we fall into step together, the silence thick and heavy. I blow out a breath, needing to move past this awkwardness. When we reach the parking lot, she pulls a remote out of her purse, pressing the unlock button. To my surprise, a red Jeep's lights flash. I shoot her a curious glance and raise a questioning brow.

"The Beamer was my mom's. I had a job interview and figured it would make me seem more professional," she explains.

I can picture her in both. One, the sleek, sexy, polished side of Gracyn and the other wild, sporty, and free. They're equally my favorite.

"Mind if I drive?"

She lets out a small gasp, holding the keys to her chest. "Lucy is my baby. I'm not sure I trust you." Her lips twitch. "Do you actually know *how* to drive, Mr. New York?"

There she is, the bold and beautiful Gracyn. Her teasing tone and playful smirk. The woman who knows how to keep me on my toes.

My laughter echoes through the packed parking garage. "I started driving when I was thirteen."

She narrows her eyes as if she doesn't believe me, and I realize how little she knows about me.

"I didn't grow up in New York," I explain. "I grew up in Georgia."

"Really?"

"Why is that so shocking?"

She bites her bottom lip and shrugs. "You scream big city. Like you were born in a suit with a cell phone in one hand and a briefcase in another."

I chuckle, shaking my head. "That's funny, 'cause you haven't even seen me in a suit."

"Are you telling me you don't wear a tailored suit every day? With a matching belt and shoes? And a fancy tie to pull it all together?"

I lick my lips, owning her spot-on observation. I can't help but nod as I murmur, "Most days."

Her laughter rings out, and for a moment, the tension we've been holding onto dissipates. It's just us—teasing, flirting, and forgetting the chaos we've created. And damn, it feels good. Which makes it more important that my plan works.

"Here," she says, right before tossing me the keys.

Perfect. Nothing like the present to learn a little more about your *husband*.

I'm not on the freeway, but a few minutes before, she stares at the exit we should be taking and stiffens as she points. "Brooks, you missed the exit."

I smirk, not even trying to hide it. "Hmm. I did?"

She twists in her seat. "Where are you going?"

I shrug, staring ahead. "Grand Canyon."

"Brooks! That's like almost four hours away," she exclaims.

"I know."

Her mouth falls open, but nothing comes out. After a moment of thinking, she levels me with a raised brow. "I thought you didn't *need* to manipulate a woman to have her be with you?"

"What are you talking about? This is a court-ordered mandate." I love when she wrinkles her nose. It's cute, stubborn, and sexy all at the same time. "I understood the assignment."

She lets out a soft, frustrated hum, her gaze fixed firmly out the passenger side window. "You're prolonging the inevitable."

Maybe I am. But *maybe* the judge was on to something. Maybe he witnessed our chemistry. Perhaps he sensed the static heat between us. We just needed a little push to explore our feelings. I'm helping steer us in that direction.

The further we get from the flashing lights and clamor of the casinos, the more my shoulders loosen, releasing the tension from this morning's activities. The desert landscape passes us by in a blur of oranges and yellows as I focus on the road ahead. And her.

"Have you ever been to the Grand Canyon?" she asks, breaking the silence.

"I've seen pictures of me and my folks there when I was four, but I don't remember it," I reply. "I'm sure you've been a million times."

She tilts her head from side to side. "Not a million. But I definitely remember going."

"That's surprising. You seem to *forget* a lot of things."

She puffs out air and playfully slaps me on the arm. "That was a low blow."

I watch as the apprehension melts from her body and words. *I'm trying not to get ahead of myself, but she wants this, too.*

With her bare feet propped up on the dashboard and eyes closed, she basks in the warmth from the sun. Her dress rides up high on her thighs, revealing her tanned and toned legs, and for a split second, I forget how to breathe. When she smiled at me in the courtroom, I knew I made the right decision to come.

My phone rings. I glance down at the console, and Judith's name flashes on the screen. *Talk about ruining the moment.*

Gracyn glances at me, concerned. "What if it's about Presley?"

I shake my head, frustration building. "Presley's at Addison's house." There is no reason for her to be calling me right now. Things have been tense between us since she called me out last Friday. Maybe because she was right. Maybe because I felt ambushed, by my own nanny, of all people. But just in case there's a problem at the penthouse, I play the voicemail on speaker.

"Hey, Brooks,. I just wanted to let you know that Addison had to work late tonight so she's picking Presley up in the morning. Hope everything is going all right. I know Vegas is the last place you wanted to go so I'm here if you need anything. Okay, bye."

"Last place you wanted to go, huh?" Gracyn softly asks, adjusting in her seat so her body is facing me.

I roll my head in her direction. "She has no idea how wrong she is. I'm exactly where I want to be."

She clears her throat, a blush creeping up her neck. "Look, there's a Target. Pull in so I can get a change of clothes."

"I like where your head's at. I like to pull in … and out. Fast and hard. With you screaming my name."

"Brooks!"

"Yep. Just like that."

"Oh my god," she says, turning red as I steer the car into the parking lot. "Just park."

"Yes, ma'am."

An hour later, we're back on the road with snacks, water, and dressed more casually. As the miles roll by, memories of our childhoods, parents, and life in general flows freely. It's a change for me, as I've always guarded my personal life to prevent it from being used against me in some way. Past experiences with women have shown that they are typically uninterested in anything beyond what I can give them financially. But Gracyn's different. She listens, truly listens, her gaze unwavering. Unlike the others, she's not nodding along absentmindedly, waiting for her turn to speak. She hangs on to every word. It's unusual to have someone care about my life beyond my wallet.

Once we see signs for the Grand Canyon, Gracyn directs me to a park with a lesser-known trail. The canyon stretches out before us as we walk toward the edge. The sight that greets us is nothing short of breathtaking.

"Isn't it amazing?" she murmurs.

I nod, staring at the vast expanse of oranges and reds, following it as far as my eyes can reach. The air is different here. Thin and crisp with the altitude weighing on my chest. We casually walk along the rim of the canyon, stopping occasionally to take in the different viewpoints. Originally, we planned to walk a mile, but the more we're here, the more invested we are in continuing further. It's how I imagine our relationship. I'm not here for the short version. I'm here for the long haul.

At one point, we stop and sit down on a rocky outcropping, dangling our legs over the edge. She pulls out her phone and scoots over, resting her legs on top of mine, and takes a picture of us.

"The day we'll remember our annulment being denied," she jokes, sliding her phone back in her hidden pocket underneath her skirt.

She turns to look at me when I let out a heavy exhale. The

breeze blows her loose tendrils of hair into her face, so I run my fingers down the side of her cheek, tucking them behind her ear.

"I'm going to kiss you," I say, my voice barely above a whisper as I cradle her face.

She nods as I lean in, stopping a breath away from her lips.

"Tell me you want me," I murmur against her lips, my heart pounding in my chest.

The moment she tries to pull back and question me, I grab her and bring her close and press my lips against hers. The kiss is fierce, filled with urgency and hunger, silencing her unspoken question. Through the desperate kiss, I convey everything that I'm feeling, asking for her surrender without words. The taste of her lips and the heat of her body fill my senses, and I lose myself in the moment, driven by the intensity of our connection.

She breaks the kiss and presses her forehead gently against mine, shaking her head with a quiet sigh. "I'm afraid."

"Of what?"

"Breaking *three* hearts," she murmurs, dropping her gaze.

Therein lies the root of my obsession with her. She's putting Presley first. She truly cares about how she fits into this equation. How her choices affect the little girl who sees her as everything. Who means everything to me.

"There are thousands of miles between us." She sighs, looking away. She stares out across the canyon. "I can't give her false hope when I'm not even sure how this will work. I'll be on a teacher's budget. I can't fly out there whenever I want. When would we see each other? This sounds like a disaster from the beginning. We're trying to shove a square into a circle."

Make no mistake, we've been a disaster from the beginning. But in the wake of chaos, sometimes the most beautiful things can emerge. I stare at her profile for several moments, fixated by her, but then reach out and grab her chin, angling her face until her eyes meet mine again.

"First," I start, my voice low and deliberate, "I have plenty of money. You can come and see me anytime you want. We just need to file the edges of the square down, but I promise you, it'll fit. You fit into my life."

Her breath catches as she rests her head in my hand. "You better stop," she warns, a playful edge to her tone. "Or you're about to have me falling at your feet."

"It's about *damn* time," I say, pulling her in again, needing to taste her. She should know I built my empire on seeing the potential in things. And I'm certain about this. We're a campaign waiting to explode. And our campaign will be the most successful yet. "Trust me."

CHAPTER 25

BROOKS

Two thoughts when Gracyn walks out of the bedroom.

First, she should stop stealing stuff and become a bathing suit model.

And second, *I've reconsidered.*

"Maybe we should skip the pool."

We got back to her apartment about thirty minutes ago, and after eight hours in the car and a hike, a swim sounded like the perfect way to unwind. But I've since changed my mind.

She glances up as she finishes tying a knot in the flimsy skirt wrapped around her waist. Calling it that is generous. It's a sheer black piece of material that hides nothing.

I stride over to her, standing so close I'm able to smell the mint from her toothpaste. Reaching out, I give the knot a quick tug, releasing it, and it flutters to the floor in a soft pile.

"Really? This was your idea."

I glance down at the curve of her delicious body and smirk. "That's before you came out in that."

She stares at me. "It's a swimsuit, Brooks."

"I see that. A tiny one that makes my dick hard. I can't walk around with a perpetual hard-on."

She wrinkles her freckled nose, and her smile grows, stepping backward. "I have something that will help with that problem. There's always the swimsuit *you* bought for me."

I can't grab her hand fast enough. Why didn't she throw that thing away? "No. That's unnecessary. The one time you wore it was enough to leave a lasting impression."

She bends over and grabs her wrap, then says, "Just think about how your mom is going to love me. I can't wait to talk to her about teaching." She flashes a sweet, innocent smile.

She's evil. Nothing like the thought of my mom to ruin the moment, but I'll be the first to admit that the thought makes me happy. *Gracyn meeting my mom.*

"C'mon." She grabs my hand and pulls me outside. "I'm all sweaty and sticky from our hike. The pool sounds so good right now."

"As long as you'll let me make you sweaty and sticky later," I murmur.

She bites her lip, giving me a teasing glance over her shoulder.

You did it, Handley. Best plan ever.

As we lie on the couch, sated, relaxed, and wrapped in the long day's aftermath, I close my eyes and trace my finger down Gracyn's leg. If it were up to me, I'd be moving her to the city tomorrow, but that'll only scare her away. Despite my need to have her close to me, I need to take this slowly.

She's the one making a bigger sacrifice. Putting all her trust in me. In us. For that, I'm willing to be patient. As long as she needs me to be.

The movie *Twisters* is on in the background, but it's merely noise to me as my mind plays out our future. Vacations, kids, everyday life with her in my bed. I open my eyes and find her passed out, her chest rising and falling with each breath. *I promise, I will make this work.*

Gracyn Carmichael is mine.

Three sharp knocks echo through the room, jolting her awake. Our eyes dart to the front door. Who the hell shows up at eleven at night? Jealousy flares in my chest, tight and unwelcome. That's a move straight out of a guy's playbook.

"Expecting someone?" I ask, biting back my irritation, as she groans and shifts her legs off me.

She slides her hand through her messy hair and shakes her head. When she looks through the peephole, her body goes still, her gaze snaps back at me with confusion all over her face.

"Who is it?" I push off the couch, moving toward her.

She points to the door. "I think this is for you."

If it's paparazzi, I'm going to lose my shit. I swing the door open, ready for a fight, but freeze when I come face-to-face with two familiar figures.

"Mr. Handley," one of them says, all business. "You're needed back in New York ASAP."

I blink, attempting to make sense of the situation. "Come again?" I stare at the FBI agents that followed me last time I was here.

"Can you come outside?" one asks, glancing at Gracyn, who's standing behind me. "This is a matter best between us."

I'm sure this is under Aiden's orders, but this is ridiculous. "She's fine. Tell me what's wrong."

The agent's hesitation unnerves me. He doesn't look pleased, but he gives a small nod. "It's your daughter."

How on fucking earth does something keep happening to Presley when I'm out of town?

"She's missing."

Gracyn gasps beside me.

My mind blanks as I shake my head furiously. "No. There must be a mistake. She's probably hiding somewhere in the house. She's a pro at hide-and-seek. That's all. She's fine."

Even as the words leave my mouth, I know how ridiculous they sound. It's two in the morning over there. I grab my phone off the coffee table and press Addison's number.

"Brooks." The second I hear Aiden's voice on the line, shock slams into me, stealing all my air. "We'll find her," he snaps.

"How? And why the hell did you fucking send these guys and not call me yourself? Or Judith? Why didn't she call me right away?" I shout into the phone. Out of the corner of my eyes, I catch Gracyn shoving my stuff into the bag. I'm having a déjà vu moment. Except this time, Presley isn't okay.

My world spins under my feet.

"She called us first so we could come over right away. I told her I'd call you. But I knew it'd be faster to have them there to escort you to the plane. It's ready to take off the second you get there."

A sick feeling curls in my gut as reality hits me. "I don't understand. How can she be missing?"

"The agents will tell you everything on the plane," he says. His voice is tight, and I can hear the strain he's trying to hide. "Brooks, we have the entire state searching for her. Max and his team are headed here, too."

Gracyn hands me my bag, tears running down her face. "Go find her," she says,

I nod, still in shock.

"Are you ready, Mr. Handley?" an agent says, yanking me out of my frozen state of shock.

"Yes."

Gracyn rushes into my arms for a quick second and then pushes me toward the door. The next few hours are a blur. The agents usher me to the private airport, telling me bits and pieces, but it all feels detached, like I'm watching it happen to someone else.

Reality crashes down on me the moment the wheels hit the ground in LaGuardia. The jarring impact snaps me out of my daze. So far, they haven't told me much. She was with Judith at my place. Judith put her to bed, then took a bath. While cleaning up after, Judith opened Presley's door to slip in a toy, only to discover an empty bed.

Poof. She was gone.

I have a million questions pounding into my head. We live in a secure building. Cameras. Doorman. Locked doors. How did no one see her leave?

Unless she's in the building.

As soon as the doors open, I'm taking two steps at a time down the ramp, my heart pounding so hard it echoes in my ears. I sprint toward the waiting black SUV, spotting Max leaning against the hood. Relief washes over me at the sight of him. My brother-in-law's best friend, who runs one of the most successful security firms in the country, gives me a nod as I slide in the front seat. He reaches over to squeeze my arm, a silent reassurance that I desperately cling to.

If anyone can find Presley, it's Max.

"Are we tearing up the building looking for her?" I fire off, clicking my seat belt. "If no one saw her leave, she has to be there somewhere."

Max doesn't waste time. He throws the car in drive, the tires screeching as he hauls ass out of the airport. "We got the security tape," he says, cutting straight to the point. "She's seen walking out on her own through the building and exiting the side entrance of the building at ten o'clock and getting into a white car."

All the air leaves my lungs in one sharp exhale. "What white car?" I yell.

Max doesn't flinch. Despite my panic, Max's voice stays informative and calm. "The license plates were fake," he says, taking a hard turn. "But I have Stone reviewing more security cameras. We know she left willingly. Like she knew her."

Murdering rage fills my veins. "Her?"

"It's not *her*," he assures me, reading my thoughts. "At least the woman driving the car wasn't her."

CHAPTER 26

GRACYN

"I need your help," I plead, my voice edged with desperation as I burst into Ray's office. I figured I'd find him here, considering his business hours cater to the night.

The entire drive over, I found myself caught in a whirlwind of thoughts, wrestling with the decision to involve him. Ray has contacts all over the world, but a nagging doubt takes hold because Brooks is well aware that his connections don't walk the straight and narrow.

Did Brooks tell his real dad?

But then, the thought of Presley out there, scared and alone, pushes all the hesitation aside. If it was my child missing? I'd sell my soul to the devil to find her.

He releases a deep sigh, taking a slow sip from the coffee in his hand. His face is unreadable, but there's a flicker of concern in his eyes. He sets the mug down and walks toward me. "I already heard, and I've already contacted everyone in New York to keep their eyes and ears open."

"How…" I pause with a tilt of my head. "How did you find out? We just found out an hour ago that she was missing."

Ray leans against the edge of his desk, crossing his arms. "Travis called me."

My mind scrambles to make sense of this revelation. Aren't they enemies? But the tone in his voice tells a different story. It's not hatred, it's sorrow.

"Who is Travis to you?" I ask, narrowing my eyes.

"Aye Aye … um…" He stalls, dropping his gaze to the floor for a beat. "Travis and I grew up together."

My eyes widen to saucers behind a look of disbelief. I thought the story was crazy before.

"We were best friends once upon a time. Our dads, yours and Brooks's grandfathers, were business partners." *No shit?* He pauses for a second, watching shock play across my face as my mouth gapes open. "Travis and I went our own separate ways in the business after college." His jaw tightens. "It was all my fault. Our feud. I let greed impede our friendship. I wanted more."

I'm still stuck on *"our grandfathers were business partners."*

"When I heard about Brooks…" He shrugs. "Now you understand my reaction. I don't believe in coincidences."

"You weren't the only one," I murmur. "That's why Brooks was here a couple of weeks ago. That's why the FBI was here. But it was just that. A coincidence. He was a stranger in a coffee shop who caught my eye."

He lets out a single chuckle, humorless and bitter. "I think your grandfathers were whispering in your ears that day. They are probably celebrating in hell together."

My phone buzzes in my pocket. It's the Google email alert I

set up to notify me whenever Brooks's name hits the news. Dread fills my heart as I open the email, my hands trembling. My emotions well up in my throat as I read the headline. It's about Presley. Her name. Her description. Her picture.

Confirmation of the nightmare.

This can't be happening.

My knees buckle, but my dad steadies me, wrapping his arms around me, an uncharacteristic show of comfort. "I don't know what to do," I cry into his chest. "I want to be there for Brooks. But what if he doesn't want me there?"

He pulls back enough to look me in the eye. "Gracyn, you are a Knight. We don't sit on the sideline. We fight for what we want. If you want to be by his side through this, let's get on a plane."

"Let's?" I ask slowly, looking up at him, regaining my control.

He nods, his jaw set tight. "I need to make sure Travis knows he has my full support. I'm sure he'll be there."

I lift a brow. After Brooks told me that their relationship is volatile, to say the least, I'm not sure if this will make things worse.

Sensing my concern, he adds, "I'll stay out of sight. If you need me, I'll be close."

I swallow hard and nod, still uncertain this is a good idea, but it's the only idea that I have. "I'll meet you at the plane," I say, heading for the door.

My dad has owned his own plane for as long as I can remember, but this will be the first time I'll step foot on it. Growing up, my mom made it her life's mission to keep me as far away from his world as possible. She didn't want me anywhere near the shadows that seemed to follow him, or the deals whispered behind closed doors, or the loyalty and power plays that seem more like war strategies than business.

It's why she hated that I worked at one of his hotels. She feared I was trying to edge my way into the family business. But I was a bartender, not a soldier. I rarely even saw him.

THE PLANE DARTS through the inky darkness, carrying us toward uncertainty. Will Brooks ask me to leave? He wants me to trust him and to give us a chance, but is it only in my world? Will I be an intruder at a time he needs control and clarity, not chaos? The thoughts of doubt sink heavy in my belly. The knot twists, making me nauseous. It's a good thing I'm not in a car or I'd turn around.

A chessboard is placed on the table between us. I stare at the black and white squares.

"Do you remember how to play?" Ray asks.

I raise one shoulder in a casual shrug. "I might remember a few things."

He taught me to play when I was five, and what he doesn't know is that I continued playing well into college. Secretly, it was the one thing that kept us connected, even though we never played again. I can't recall the last time we were together longer than a few minutes. Our conversations are kept to phone calls or quick meet-ups in his office.

As he places the last pieces on the board, I say, "Did I tell you I got offered a job?"

Without looking up, he continues to set the board up, he replies, "You didn't. I hope it's not another bartender job."

I playfully scowl at him when he glances up. "No. It's a grown-up job. Teaching first graders."

He hesitates for a moment. His eyes meet mine before nodding in approval. There's a sense of pride in his expression. "Congratulations. I hope they aren't as wild as you were when you were six." As if he would know. He reads my silence, sitting back, and his expression softens. "Don't assume my absence meant I wasn't keeping tabs on you."

"Why is that? Why did you keep your distance?"

He angles his head. "You know why. For your safety, of course. Your mom and I both agreed it was for the best. It's about the only thing we agreed on. That woman is strung tighter than a tightly wound coil."

I chuckle in agreement. She is a worrywart. *About everything.* But I don't blame her. Even though she's been married to two polar opposite men, both gave her a glimpse of the worst the world has to offer. That tends to harden your shell. And constantly worrying about your only child.

After a couple of hours, I try to sleep, but it's useless. The knots in my stomach keep me up.

By the time the plane touches down, it's seven in the morning local time. "Do you want a room at the hotel? To freshen up, or take a quick nap?" Ray asks.

I scrub my exhausted face and nod. "There's no way I can sleep, but I can at least shower and change clothes." Also, having a place to retreat if things don't go well might be a good idea.

CHAPTER 27

GRACYN

By nine, Ray arranged a car to take me to Brooks. I nibbled on the breakfast he sent over, but my nerves were still shot. I couldn't eat much. As the car stops in front of Brooks's building, I swallow hard. *You're here for him. That's all that matters.*

The bellman opens the door for me, a questioning expression on his face, and I wonder if he recognizes me. The entire building, both inside and out, is swarming with uniformed police officers. The weight of their presence bears down on me, amplifying the panic. My heart races as I approach the security guard's desk. He looks disheveled and tired when he glances up at me.

"I'm sorry, ma'am. We're not allowing visitors into the building at the moment."

I glance around nervously, my mouth parched. How do I introduce myself? Well, the headlines have already spilled our secret, so I may as well use it to my advantage. "I'm Gracyn Carmichael, Brooks Handley's wife," I say, watching the security guard's eyes widen as he looks around, unsure of what to do.

You and me both, buddy.

"One moment," he mutters before darting to a police officer. Their conversation is too low for me to catch, but the officer gives me a measured glance, sending a ripple of unease through me, before he angles his head and speaks into his radio. The security guard returns and gestures to the chairs in the lobby. "Have a seat. Someone will be down shortly to assist you."

I walk over and force myself into a chair. Minutes crawl by, my nerves twisting tighter with each passing second. I can't stop fidgeting, wondering if Brooks decided to not let me up.

The elevator dings, and my eyes snap up, but a woman steps off. A sigh of disappointment escapes my lips, and I return my gaze to my phone. Charli texted me she saw the same Google Alert and wants to know what's happening. In all the chaos, I forgot to let her know.

"Gracyn Carmichael?"

I pause writing Charli back, and lift my head to find the woman who just got off the elevator staring down at me. With a quick nod, I tuck my phone into my purse and rise to my feet. "Yes, that's me," I reply. She's dressed in plain clothes, but now I notice the NYPD badge clipped to her hip.

She extends her hand with a warm smile. "I'm Addison Roberts," she introduces herself. I grasp her hand, wondering why her name seems familiar. "I'm Brooks's sister."

The hint of judgment in her eyes, mixed with a touch of curiosity, makes sense now. Who could blame her?

"Oh. Hi. Call me Gray," I say, hoping to avoid a lecture about our irresponsible choices. I'm not in the mood. "How's Brooks?"

Her shoulders rise and fall with a heavy sigh. "A mess. So, tread lightly when you see him."

Her words catch me off guard. I was ready to be sent away. "You're taking me up?"

"Isn't that why you came?"

"Yes," I reply, bending to grab my bag. We step into the elevator. "I thought maybe he wouldn't wa—"

"He doesn't know you're here yet," she cuts in, her tone matter-of-fact.

Her words resonate in the elevator's confined space. Why wouldn't they tell him I'm here first?

I shift uncomfortably, leaning against the cool metal wall. "What if he doesn't want me here?" I whisper.

Addison doesn't sugarcoat it. "He might not," she says bluntly. I like no bullshit answers, but ouch. "But that's okay. You're not here for what he wants right now. You're here for when he needs you. And I promise he's going to need you."

Her words hit something deep inside me, reassuring and grounding. I take a steady breath and nod. *I hope she's right.* I clutch the strap of my bag as the elevator door opens.

Stepping into Brooks's place is like crossing the threshold into the calm center of a raging storm. The air hums with a heavy, foreboding atmosphere, sending a chill down my spine. The room falls silent as soon as we close the door, and all eyes turn on me. I search for the only face that means everything to me in a sea of strangers.

As Brooks emerges from the kitchen, his gaze locks with mine, and my worries and doubts melt away in the intensity of that moment. Without uttering a single word, he rushes toward me and pulls me in a tight, wordless hug. It's brief, but in those fleeting moments, I sense the depth of his pain etched in my own heart. He turns and returns to the kitchen table, leaning over the shoulder of a man working on a computer.

It's not a rejection. I exhale, making myself breathe.

"Okay. What can I do to help?" I ask Addison, my confidence returning.

"Let's introduce you to everyone first."

The names flow in one ear and out the other while we navigate the room. My focus is on Brooks and trying to listen to the updates. There's a mix of local police, FBI, and a security team. The security team they hired is slightly intimidating, their assessing stares lingering on me as I move around. They make Ray's security guards seem unimposing. These men are built like tanks with tats up and down their arms, taking up a lot of room at the kitchen table, except the computer guy. He's muscular, but tall and thin. The last person I meet is Aiden, Addison's husband—the *FBI*.

"I apologize for jumping to conclusions," he says, shaking my hand. "I've learned that coincidences sometimes happen." He shoots a meaningful glance at Addison, and she nods.

"It's okay. It's still hard for *me* to believe."

"Since you're here, do you mind if I ask you some questions?"

"What the fuck!" Brooks roars, startling me. "She has nothing to do with this." Aiden maintains his gaze with him as he storms over. "She was with me when it happened, in a different state." He goes toe-to-toe with Aiden.

"Hey," I whisper, placing my hand on Brooks's tense bicep. "It's okay. I don't mind."

He jerks his head toward me. "I do."

I lift my hand, touching his beard, tears welling up from the sight of his brokenness. "If they have questions, I want to help. I'll do whatever I can to find Presley."

He closes his eyes for a moment, pulling in a sharp inhale and blowing it out slowly. He gives Aiden a hard nod, leaving as fast as he got there.

Aiden gestures for me to sit on the couch in the living room. The whirlwind of events since the last time I sat on this couch feels like an eternity has passed, yet it was only weeks ago.

Nothing I have to say is anything of importance. But as he's finishing up asking me questions, an attractive woman enters through the front door, carrying a stack of papers. Her dark blond hair is up in a messy bun, but not messy enough that it was done haphazardly. She knows who I am because the moment her eyes lock with mine, I can see her hackles raise. She proceeds to the kitchen, and as she disappears out of view, Aiden and I exchange a look.

"Please tell me that's not an ex or something."

He rolls his eyes, shaking his head. "That's Judith."

The nanny. I nod in understanding, her reaction making more sense. But I don't know why I'm surprised that she's so pretty. Of course, Brooks would hire an attractive nanny. I guess when I heard her name was Judith, my mind imagined a cute older lady.

"She's probably surprised you're here. But don't pay any attention to her." He leans closer and whispers, "He's glad you're here, and so are we."

I wouldn't go that far to say he's glad, but I appreciate the words.

He stands up and motions for us to join the others. "Let's tell Brooks we're done, so he's not in there fuming the entire time."

As we enter the kitchen, Judith stands right next to Brooks, her head leaning against his arm as they stare out the window. Their backs are to us.

"We're done," Aiden states, causing Brooks to spin around.

He heads in our direction. Judith's sneer is quick, but I caught it. I stare at her a moment, lifting a brow, as if asking her what her freaking problem is. Her gaze falls to the papers in her hand, and she acts like she's searching for something in the pile, knowing she was caught.

Brooks's large frame stands close, and he leans down, whispering, "Sorry I didn't say it earlier, but thanks for coming." Our fingers brush against each other, so I grab his hand and squeeze.

"Hi, I'm Judith. You must be Gracyn," Judith says, walking up to us. Brooks tightens his grip as we turn toward her. I can't tell if it's intentional or he just doesn't want to let go.

I see the worry in her reddened eyes. Despite her clear displeasure with me being here, I swallow any irritation and offer a warm smile. I'm sure she's in hell, too. "Please, call me Gray," I reply. "It's nice to meet you. Do you need any help with those?" I glance between the two of them.

She lifts the stack of papers, and her body language remains frosty as she attempts to be friendly. "I printed off flyers to pass around. Would you mind passing them out throughout the neighborhood?"

I don't care if she's trying to test my intentions or get rid of me. I'm not here to play tug-of-war with Brooks. I'm here to help. "Not at all," I reply, taking the flyers from her.

She looks at me with a hint of surprise, as if she was expecting me to fight to stay near Brooks.

I turn to Addison, who has joined us. "Should I start by going door-to-door in the building?"

"No, the police have already done that," she says. "Since you're not familiar with the area, I'll go with you." She places her hand on Brooks's shoulder. "You need anything?"

He shakes his head, the corners of his mouth turned down, not able to hide the worry etched across his features. I have the urge to reach out to him as he walks past us and give him a reassuring hug. But I can't. Not when I have no idea how much danger Presley might be in.

He paces restlessly behind the others, and I glance at Addison, whispering, "How could she have just vanished?" With all the technology and cameras around, I'm having a hard time understanding how someone got away with the perfect crime.

Her jaw tightens, and she exhales. "There are no perfect crimes. We'll find her," she states, her voice heavy with frustration and determination.

Once we hand out the last of the flyers, a cloud of failure settles over me. I'd been clinging to the hope of finding a lead. Hoping someone might glance at the flyer and it would jog a memory, bringing us closer to Presley. But nothing. I *probably* toed the line of harassment, demanding people look at the picture, but damn them for not caring enough to give me five seconds of their busy life. A certain lady, in particular, didn't like when I stuffed the flyer into her Gucci bag. But again, screw her and her self-absorbed attitude.

We return to the penthouse a little before lunchtime. There's no new information, and I feel in the way, so I stand to the side, studying the whiteboard, separating the dining area and the living room.

My eyes scan over the names, timelines, and connections.

There's a picture that catches my attention. Brows furrow as I step closer. It's a mugshot of a blonde woman with hollow, dark bags under her eyes and an expression that could rival stone.

"Who's that?" I ask, breaking the room's silence. There's a line pointing to her with question marks. Something about her feels *familiar*.

Addison steps up beside me. "That's Jessie. Presley's mom."

My brows knit together in surprise, looking at the worn, tired face on the board. "I thought she was dead."

"If only," Brooks mutters under his breath, joining us.

Addison points her glare at him, and he throws his hands in the air.

"It'd make my life easier," he says, unapologetic.

I stare at the picture, recalling the conversation at the wedding with my chatty neighbor.

"Why did you think she was dead?" Aiden asks, startling me as he stands on my other side.

"I guess it was just gossip. I was told at Jared's wedding that she tried to kill Addison and then killed herself."

Addison lets out a sound somewhere between a grunt and a scoff as she walks away. "It's half right," she calls over her shoulder.

My eyes widen, and my gaze jumps from her to Aiden and back to her. Jessie's alive, so I can assume which half is right.

"Yeah, that wasn't one of my best days," Aiden adds, irritated.

You don't say.

"So, do y'all think she has Presley?"

Aiden hums. "She's our top suspect. No one has seen her for two months."

"I don't understand why Presley would go to the vehicle like she knew her," Judith chokes out, her voice trembling. She turns to Brooks, her tear-filled eyes pleading with him. "I just want our girl back."

Our? I don't like that woman. She's trying hard to remind me of her place here. But the pointless emphasis isn't necessary. I get it. She's been in Presley's life since she was one. She's practically her mom. *I'm the outsider.*

Brooks's shoulders droop, and he nods. He's exhausted. He hasn't said much since this morning. Just pacing nonstop, gripping onto his phone like it's his lifeline. When the door opens, every head whips in that direction.

"I got food," a woman says, in a sad singsong voice, hidden behind a tall stack of pizza boxes.

My jaw drops open when she drops the boxes on the table. "Is that…" I whisper to Addison.

She nods, grabbing my hand. I've never experienced a confusing swirl of worry and excitement at the same time. The emotions are confusing. Thank God my brain has enough sense to keep from fangirling right now.

"Sydney, this is Gray. Brooks's, *you know…*" She mutters the last part as if I'm the surprise here.

I blink, trying to process the fact that I'm standing right next to Sky Owen—*the famous country star*—who I paid an exorbitant amount last year to see in concert.

"Ohhh," she replies, giving me a once-over. "It's nice to finally meet you, Gray." She sticks out her hand, and I shake it. "You've met Max, right? He belongs to me."

This is surreal. Sky knew about me? I'm stunned stupid and nod. I force myself to focus, snapping out of my daze. *Not the time nor the place, Gray.* Relief washes over me when she turns away, giving me a moment to collect myself.

"All right, everyone, eat," she announces to the room in a sweet Southern accent. "Brooks, you too."

He mumbles a string of curse words under his breath and storms into the hallway, disappearing into his room, slamming the door behind him. Judith stands and stares in that direction. As she takes a step toward it, Addison stops her.

"Judith, can you help me get plates and drinks out?"

She turns and looks at her. Not a blank stare, but an annoyed one.

"You know where everything is," Addison reminds her, pretending she doesn't see her irritation. I've learned that Addison sees everything.

Judith scans the group of people in the room as if to see who's watching. When she sees it's more than just Addison and me, she walks to the kitchen. When I peek over at Addison, she jerks her head toward the bedroom. "Go," she mouths.

I take slow, calculated steps to his door and knock twice. "I'm coming in," I warn.

Whether or not you like it. His back is to me as he sits on the edge of his king-size bed, his head hung between his shoulders. He doesn't move, so I step inside and ease the door closed. My footsteps brush against the wooden floor. Chewing on my inner cheek, I stand in front of him and wait.

He lifts his head, and angry tears fall. His strength hangs from a thin string, fraying in the middle. I take a step forward and raise my hand. His beard is rough against my palm, and I wait for him to pull back.

He doesn't. His exhale is rough as he falls forward, digging his face into my stomach, and I let out the breath I'd been holding. His arms wrap around my waist, and my fingers dig through his hair.

"They'll find her. They have to."

"She can't have her," he says, choking up. "She's mine."

The string breaks, and he's ripped in two. His raw emotions blanket me as he cries without a sound. In this fractured moment, our hearts bleed a river, and we're both drowning.

"I'm so sorry," I whisper.

After a couple of beats of silence, the weight of his body heavies. He's exhausted from being up all night. "Brooks, lie down."

He refuses with a stubborn tilt of his head, clinging to me like a child holding onto his mom. "I'm comfortable right here."

"I'll lie down with you."

He releases me, but only long enough to pull me onto the bed with him. He draws me into him, my back to his chest, with a tight grip around my waist. Within a few deep breaths, his grip loosens, and we both fall asleep.

CHAPTER 28

GRACYN

B rooks is still asleep when I stir awake, so I roll over and watch him, syncing my breathing with his. The disarray of his thick hair is a wild mess. His eyelids flutter, and I can only imagine the terror behind them. He's living his nightmare. It's only been a couple of hours, but he needed this time to recoup. He's going to need his energy.

"Thank you," he whispers, eyes still closed.

"For what?"

Dull hazel eyes peek out under heavy, sleepy lids. It's hard to watch a strong man crumble. "Coming," he replies.

As if I had a choice. "I needed to know you *both* are okay. And as you're already aware, patience has never been my strong suit." My hand rests on his cheek as he gives me a subtle nod. Glancing past him at the closed door, I ask, "Ready to go back out?"

He presses his lips in a tight line, inhales deeply, and nods. As we step into the living room, the hushed chatter among the guys dwindles into silence. Not that I'm worried about how I look, but when everyone stares at you, it sparks a twinge of self-consciousness. I run my fingers through my hair and pull it into a ponytail.

"Anything?" Brooks inquires, joining the guys at the kitchen table. I spot Addison, sitting on top of the kitchen island, and she shakes her head, her lips pressed into a thin line. Isn't there supposed to be a phone call by now asking for a ransom? *Something?*

My stomach grumbles, a reminder that the few nibbles from breakfast aren't cutting it. I make my way into the kitchen, snag a piece of cold cheese pizza, and sink my teeth down into it. As I chew, I study the room. There are fewer officers than before. Four large men sit at the table, straining the legs of the chairs. I'm especially afraid for Max's chair. Addison moved, now hovering over Aiden's shoulder as they survey a map of the city. Her finger follows a trail. Stone marked the path the kidnapper took, ending with an abrupt stop. Everyone is hoping she's somewhere in that area, but so far, nothing. Sydney, *or Sky,* I'm not even sure what to call her, left, and Judith sits on the couch blankly staring out the window.

Doing my best to stay out of the way, I walk over and sit beside Judith. "Anything else I can do?"

She turns to me and pointedly murmurs, "Leave."

I jerk in surprise. "Excuse me?"

She shakes the venom from her expression. "Sorry, that was uncalled for." *You think?* "I meant you don't have to attend to me. You're here for Brooks."

That is not what she meant. But whatever.

I don't want to make this awkward, so I let it slide. Everyone deals with stress differently, and clearly, Judith's way involves passive-aggressive jabs. "I'm here to help however I can. So, if you need anything, please ask. I'm great at getting coffee."

She nods and turns away from me, returning her gaze outside as if I'm already forgotten. *Fine by me.* When I push off the couch, her hand stops me. I look back at her, and she murmurs, "Coffee sounds great."

"You got it," I say, relieved I have something to do. "I'm making a coffee run. Would anyone else like something?"

The guys rattle off their orders, and I can't help the small smile when Brooks gives me his. His lips quirk up on one side with a knowing expression, but it's replaced with the heavy shadow of worry hanging over him.

"I'll go with you," Addison says, grabbing her bag. "I could use some air."

We exit out the rear of the building to avoid the media frenzy out front. I glance over at Addison as we walk. She's been quiet since we left. "How are you doing?" It has to be hard on her, too. Presley is her niece. She's handling it a lot better than I would be.

She exhales, her cheeks puffing out. "I'm trying to stay strong for Brooks. But inside, I'm fighting some demons." She wipes away a fallen tear, and my heart aches for her. She stops on the sidewalk and turns to me, biting her lip, struggling to keep her emotions in. "All those horrible scenarios Brooks is imagining? I've lived that nightmare. I know what could happen to someone who's been taken."

My chest tightens. I hold my breath, afraid whatever I say won't be right.

"And when Brooks looks at me," she continues, her voice breaking, "searching for confirmation that his worst fears might be true, I can't..." She pauses, fisting her hands. "*I won't* give it to him. I have to be strong. For him. And Presley."

I throw my arms around her in a tight hug. "You're the strongest woman I've ever met," I whisper, not caring if she's a hugger or not, or that we're practically strangers. Right now, she needs someone to hold her up, even if for a second.

"Thank you," she murmurs, pulling away with a shaky sigh. A bitter laugh slips from her lips. "I didn't know letting that out would help." She turns to walk down the sidewalk, and I fall in step beside her.

"I know we just met, but if you ever need a second to let things out, I'm here."

Her lips curve into an appreciative closed smile, her wall of steel already sliding into place. "When I heard you crashed a wedding to serve my brother annulment papers, I had a feeling I'd like you."

I let out a short laugh, surprised by her bluntness. "That's definitely one way to make an impression," I say as we push through the door of the coffee shop. The crisp chill of the AC hits my face, and I sigh in relief. *How am I sweating? I never sweat?* I grab a napkin and dab my forehead. This humid heat will be the death of me.

Addison smiles. "You'll get used to it."

Standing in line, I bite my inner cheek, wondering if now would be a good time to ask the question gnawing at me since this morning. "Shouldn't there be a ransom already? It's been almost twenty-four hours," I ask, keeping my voice low.

She stares at the menu board. "This is personal. Presley was familiar with the person in that car. Which points to a family member. But we're all here." She finally turns toward me.

"*Except Jessie*. But Presley's never met her. I still think she's involved, somehow."

I want to ask more about Jessie. Why isn't she involved with Presley? Where does she live? I have so many questions after learning that she's still alive, but she has to be a hot button for Addison. I'd hate the woman who once tried to kill me.

"Does Jessie live around here?" I ask with a slight hesitation, trying not to push too hard.

She shakes her head again. "Not that we're aware of. Last we heard, she was working for an interior design firm on the West Coast."

Her voice falters at the end as her eyes fixate past me with a questioning expression. I glance over my shoulder to see what she's looking at. Two police officers stand in the doorway, staring at us.

A fragment of memory tugs at the edges of my mind, refusing to take shape.

"C'mon, let's go find out what's up," she says, already striding toward the officers.

I love her take-charge attitude. She's my kind of person.

"Hey, Evans. Did you guys find her?"

The dark-haired guy with the bushy mustache shakes his head.

"So, what's going on?" she asks.

Meanwhile, my mind is still trying to piece together the memory. It's important, I feel it. It's right there, so I ignore the cops and grab Addison's arm. "What did you just say earlier? Something about it sparked a memory, and I can't for the life of me figure out why."

She stares at me, confused.

"When you said something about Jessie?"

"She's on the West Coast?"

I shake my head. That's not it.

"She's an interior designer."

"That's it!" The memory snaps in place, and my heart skips a beat. That's why that picture of Jessie looked familiar. She's Lindsey. Just with a different hair color. "We have to go. I know where Jessie is."

Addison's eyes widen. "Where?"

"I think I got her a job at the new hotel going up in Vegas," I say, the words tumbling out.

"You know her?"

I nod. "When I saw Jessie's picture, she seemed familiar. But she looks different. I'm almost certain it's her."

Addison's expression hardens. She grabs my arm and drags me out of the coffee shop, leaving the drinks behind.

"Wait, we have some questions for Gracyn Carmichael," an officer shouts from behind us, his voice growing louder as he rushes after us.

Wait. *That's me.*

I stop and spin around. "For me? Why?"

"We need to talk to you about Cooper Rossman."

Addison lets out a frustrated sigh at the interruption. "Why in the hell are you questioning her about Cooper Rossman? She's never even met the guy."

But I have.

"We're following up on a tip."

Addison sends me a confused glance. She catches my panic and takes a slow, calculated breath, standing taller. "Are you arresting her?"

I gasp, whipping my face toward her. *Why would they arrest me?*

"No. We just need to talk," the officer with the bushy mustache replies, turning his attention to me.

Addison scoffs. "Then follow us. We just had a huge development in the kidnapping case of Presley Handley." She doesn't give them any other option as she spins on her toes and calls over her shoulder, "Let's go!"

On the way, I tell Addison everything about running into Lindsey, who I think is Jessie. But after, my thoughts jumble together. *Did Jessie search me out? How do the cops know about me and Cooper? Was her boyfriend all a lie? Do they think I beat him up?*

The elevator ride up is uncomfortably silent. I clutch my bag close to my hip as I sense the officer's eyes on me.

As soon as the elevator doors slide open, Addison storms through the hallway and throws open the front door with so much force it bangs against the wall. "She friended Gray!" she barks.

Everyone stops what they're doing. The guys at the table stand, their expressions a mix of confusion and alarm as they look between Addison, me, and the police officers.

"FBI Agent Roberts," Aiden says, stepping forward and introducing himself to the officers. "Can I help you?"

Addison doesn't even pay attention to them. "Don't worry about them right now. Gray, tell them what you told me."

Still stunned that I'm being questioned about Cooper, I take a second to catch up. "Right," I manage, fumbling with my phone, almost dropping it. I had sent Ray a text on the way here to see if he could get me the picture of Lindsey that they used for her badge.

I stare at the image he sent, my stomach flipping. It's her.

I hold my phone up, showing it to Aiden.

"Fuck," he snaps.

A bomb of commotion blows up. The guys talk all at once. Orders are barked out while others make phone calls.

Brooks throws out a slew of curse words, pacing again. "Why is she doing this to me? She's the one who wanted nothing to do with her own child."

"Gray, tell me about her," Max asks, walking up to me, his enormous frame towering over me.

I recap our brief encounters at the coffee shop and spotting her at the bar, but how she left before I could talk to her. Aside from that, we'd only talked on the phone once about the job. We hadn't had a chance to meet up for dinner like we talked about.

"She was in Vegas for a reason. Which was you," Max states. His piercing gaze locks onto mine, and I feel small.

Like a mouse to an elephant. For my safety, I take a step backward.

"But why? Why come after you?"

Good question. Why me? Did she find out Brooks and I were married?

"Why are they here?" he asks, jerking his chin toward the two officers standing at the door, waiting patiently.

"I'm not sure of that either," I admit with a wince, afraid I'm derailing the focus on Presley. "They want to talk to me."

"Aiden," Max barks, startling me.

Aiden walks over.

"Stay with her while the cops talk to her."

He looks down at me, confused. "They're here for you?"

I nod. *That's what I hear.*

"Outside, now," he demands.

I follow him, and he gestures for the officers to follow as we pass them. The hallway outside the door is quiet, and I shrink back when the officers both look at me. Even though I had nothing to do with Cooper getting the shit beat out of him, chills run along my spine, afraid of what they're going to ask.

"Ms. Carmichael, as we stated earlier, we're following up on a tip," the officer states, pulling out a little notebook. "Were you in New York City on May 17 attending a wedding for a Jared Rice?"

I swallow hard. "I was."

"Did you have an altercation with Mr. Rossman that night?"

Altercation?

"What the hell, Officer Evans?" Aiden jumps in, his tone crackling with irritation as he stands in front of me, shielding me. "Does Gray need an attorney?"

The young cop looks like he's about to say something, but Evans lifts his hand to silence him. "It's procedure. Ms. Carmichael is not under arrest."

"It's all right," I say, stepping out from behind him. If he wasn't here, I'm not sure I could be so confident. "I wouldn't say it was an altercation. He roofied my drink. Before I could pass out, Brooks was there to save me."

"And you're certain it was Mr. Rossman who put a drug in your drink?"

Yes. I open my mouth to say Brooks has it on tape but then snap it shut. I have an alibi the night of his beating *in a different state*, but I'm not sure Brooks does. And if I admit we have proof, they'll wonder why I didn't go to the cops. "Not a hundred percent. He was aggressively trying to get me to leave the party and got mad when I didn't. That's when Brooks stepped in. We both assumed it was him."

Officer Evans's brow furrows, his pen hovering over the small notepad in his hand. "Why didn't you go to the police?"

"Because I wasn't sure. There wasn't any proof."

He jots down a couple of notes. I steal a glance at Aiden, who's watching them both like a hawk, his posture protective and tense.

"Is that all, Officers?" Aiden asks, hurrying them along.

"One more question," Evans says, flipping a page in his notebook. "Where were you on the night of May 24?"

"Um…" I have the answer, but the weight of their stares flusters me, and I stumble over my words. "I was at my graduation. At UNLV."

"Thanks for your cooperation," the younger officer nods and says.

Officer Evans hands me his card. "If you can think of anything else that happened the night of the wedding, please contact me."

That won't be happening. My memory is slim pickings as it is. I keep my lips pressed together and nod. Aiden doesn't move, so I follow his lead as we watch the officers step onto the elevator.

Once the doors close and they're out of earshot, Aiden twists toward me. "Does Brooks need to call his lawyer?"

I shake my head.

At least I don't think so.

CHAPTER 29

BROOKS

Someone give me a butter knife so I can cut off my balls. It has to feel better than this.

How long does it take for an update? A lifetime has passed since they promised to keep me informed. My gaze keeps flickering to the bustling streets below, scanning the crowd like I might somehow spot her down there. It's irrational, but the hope of her appearing, that this is all some horrible mistake, is the only thread keeping me from losing it.

Aiden, Max, and Stone left to follow up on a tip the FBI received around the location of where the car stopped being tracked. Hours ago. Where the fuck are they?

The picture of the woman in the car was blurry, but I didn't recognize her. If Jessie is behind this, she's working with someone. But how did Presley know her? When did that happen? That's what's eating me alive. Presley knew someone that I didn't. Someone Judith didn't. And she trusted this stranger enough to get into the car with her. None of this makes sense.

If only there was something stronger than bourbon. Something that could keep me both grounded and aware during this agonizing wait. Inside, I can barely contain my fury, my mind racing with worst-case scenarios, each darker than the last. Addison and Gracyn watch me. Not sure what they think I'm going to do, but they couldn't stop me from taking matters into my own hands if I wanted to.

I'm desperate, not stupid.

If anyone can find Presley, it's Max and his team. Also, if Jessie was looking for help, it'd be people who weren't on the up and up. The ones who operate in the shadows. Which is why I called Travis. When Aiden finds out, he might lose his shit, but there's nothing I wouldn't do to find Presley. *Nothing.* Had it been one of his kids, I'm damn sure Addison would've called him too.

Pacing the entire length of the living room like a caged animal, I glance at my watch every few minutes. "Have you heard from Aiden?" I bark, stopping in my tracks just long enough to glare at Addison. I've asked the same damn question a dozen times, and it's always the same answer. Hell, I'm even annoying myself.

She opens her mouth to say no again, but her phone rings, cutting her off. I freeze in place. She nods, confirming it's them. I double back over to her, and she answers it. "You're on speaker."

"We found the car. But that's it. She might have had another car to switch into. Stone's already searching."

My gut twists with the realization that this wasn't random. Whoever this woman is, she's planned the whole thing. Every detail, every step. My scowl deepens, my jaw tight with rage as the weight of the situation sinks in.

Ransom. That has to be it. If they knew me, they'd understand I'd give every single damn cent to my name to get her back.

So call already.

More minutes crawl by, morphing into endless, excruciating hours with no new information. Max, Stone, and Aiden are again at the kitchen table, hunched over, speaking in low, clipped tones. Judith stares out the window, wrapped in a blanket. Addison and Gracyn sit on the living room floor, with a deck of cards they found on the coffee table. I stare from the barstool, watching their mindless game of war, the repetitive flip, swipe, flip, swipe gnawing on my frayed patience. They're barely paying attention to the game, the cards nothing more than a distraction. My eyes drift close for a moment, my mind locking on Presley's toothless grin. *Snarky, I'm coming for you. Just hold on.*

Flip, swipe, flip—

Addison freezes mid-swipe when there's a knock at the door. My heart jolts, and I'm off the stool in seconds, striding toward the door with Max and Aiden right behind me. When I open the door, I'm surprised to see who's here. I didn't think he'd come around with all the law enforcement here. But I'm glad Travis sent his right-hand man.

He nods once and pulls me in for a quick shoulder bump. "Sorry, man," he says, his voice low but firm. "We'll find her."

"Frankie," Addison says, getting up off the floor. She walks over and gives him a hug. I catch the subtle shift in the air as Aiden steps beside me, his body tensing.

"You called him?" Aiden sneers.

"Don't start," I snap, not in the mood for a debate. "If this were your kid, you'd do whatever it took to find them."

He curses under his breath but nods and extends his hand out, and Frankie shakes it. Frankie's eyes sweep the room before saying anything. He's not careless enough to talk without assessing who's around. Especially the police. They are worlds apart, the good guys versus the bad guys. But I don't give a fuck. He's here to help. Aiden might be FBI, and he might hate Frankie because he's a jealous ass, but in the end it was Frankie who saved Addison, so he earned a debt Aiden could never repay.

Frankie's eyes land on Gracyn, and he looks at her with a hint of curiosity. She stands up and walks over to where we're standing.

"You must be Gray? I'm Frankie," he says, holding out his hand.

She reads the intense vibe between the guys when she hesitates a beat to shake his outreached hand.

"He works for Travis," I explain.

Nodding in understanding, she slips her hand into his. "It's nice to meet you."

"Do you have anything to update?" Max clips, cutting straight to the point.

Frankie shakes his head. "Not yet," he says, his tone a little too calm for the situation. "But we're digging. And when we find something, trust me, you'll want to hear it from us first, not them." He jerks his head slightly in Aiden's direction, the subtle jab unmistakable. The bad guys don't play nice with people who kidnap kids.

Max lets out a dry chuckle and pats Aiden on the back as he walks away. "He doesn't know you at all," he murmurs under his breath.

Addison squeezes Frankie's arm and flashes him a grateful smile before she and Gracyn return to their card game.

Frankie watches her for a moment before locking eyes with me. His chin jerks toward the hallway, and he says, "We need to talk."

Without a word, I follow him out of sight, far enough away to ensure no one can overhear.

I narrow my eyes, confused. "I thought you didn't have any updates?"

"I don't," he replies, rubbing the top of his bald head. "But I need you and Gray to meet me at Kao's tonight," he says.

The fuck I am. It's the restaurant I used to meet Travis when he was in town. The place reeks of dirty deals and shady alliances. "No way. I'm not taking Gracyn anywhere near Travis." Considering our fathers' backgrounds, this shouldn't come as a surprise.

He hikes a shoulder. "I'm just the messenger."

I take a step forward, my jaw tightening. "What is this, Frankie? I'm not dragging her on some sort of ambush. I don't have time for Travis's petty bullshit."

"It's not like that. Trust me, you want to go."

"Stop with the messenger crap. What. Is. Going. On?"

He exhales and rubs his head again. "I was told not to say."

I relent with an aggravated sigh, knowing if Travis told him to keep his mouth shut, there's no way he'll tell me. "What time?"

"You'll get a text tonight."

I stroke my beard, still unsure. On one hand, Travis wouldn't summon us without a damn good reason. On the other hand, Gracyn should stay as far away from my father as possible.

Gracyn's warm hand settles on my shoulder, surprising me. She parks herself next to me, her curious gaze shifting between me and Frankie. "Everything okay? I thought I overheard my name."

I grumble, avoiding her eyes. "Yeah," I finally mutter. "I'll explain later."

"We hear anything," Frankie says, "you'll be the first we call." He then gives Gracyn a single nod before walking out the front door.

The soft click of the door echoes in the room, and when I turn around, all eyes are on me, expecting an explanation I don't have. I shrug, not having the energy to string together a bullshit excuse.

By the time everyone leaves, the silence in the place is deafening, like it's holding its breath, waiting for the heart of our world to walk through those doors. My chest twists that we're at the end of day two and nothing. No leads. Nothing but the hollow ticking of the clock to remind me she's still missing.

Max and Stone checked into a hotel nearby, prepared to come over if I need them. Aiden and Addison reluctantly headed home. Judith didn't want to leave either, but I told her she needed a break. It's hard not to glance her way and feel the sharp sting of blame. I'm trying to push it down, trying not to hold it against her, but it lingers. I have to dig deep to remember that she loves her like her own, and she's living in hell, too.

Now, it's just me and Gracyn. With my eyes closed, I lean my head back against the couch, exhausted. And it's only seven o'clock. The couch dips beside me, and I loll my head to the side, meeting Gracyn's worried expression. She runs her fingers through my hair. I've never been so powerless.

"I'm so sorry," she whispers.

My phone buzzes in my pocket. Pulling it out, I sigh at the text.

Unknown: 8:00

"What is it?"

I shake my head and drop the phone on the couch beside me. "It's time to go."

"Go where?"

"It's why Frankie was here earlier. I really don't have any idea."

"Do you want me to go with you?"

Fuck, no. But it didn't sound like I had a choice. Rather than tell her we were both summoned, I nod, thankful she gave me an out.

We stop in front of the restaurant doors, and I hesitate, debating whether we should turn around and leave. The only reason I'm here is the hope that Travis found something out about Presley. But why not tell me earlier?

Gracyn tilts her head up, expressing skepticism. If she's thinking this place looks sketchy, she's right. Blacked-out windows in a deserted strip mall don't exactly scream *come on in*. Rather, this is the place you avoid at all costs.

That's why Travis likes it here.

Quiet, hidden, and full of people just like him.

I take Gracyn's hand, the pang of guilt twisting deeper in my gut. I should've told her where we were going. "I promise I won't let anyone hurt you."

Her eyes widen. "That's not a promise I want to test. What am I walking into?"

"Travis requested we meet him here."

"We?"

I sigh. "I wasn't going to ask you, but then you offered. It better be about Presley," I add.

She pulls in a deep inhale, exhales, then squares her shoulders, standing tall. She's calm, composed—*everything I'm not.* Most women would've turned around by now and left me here on the sidewalk without a second thought. But as I've learned, Gracyn is definitely not most women.

"Then let's go," she says, grabbing the door handle. "Stop stalling and worrying about me. I'll be fine."

She swings the door open, and we step inside the dimly lit room with empty tables, save for one in the far corner. Two men stand off to the side, tracking our every move. Travis and another man watch us walk toward them. I give Gracyn a reassuring squeeze, but she's not looking at Travis. She's glaring at the man sitting across from him.

Both men stand as we approach, and Gracyn marches straight up to the second guy. "A heads-up would have been nice," she murmurs, and then surprises me by giving the man a hug. I'm too surprised that I forget to say hi to Travis.

"Brooks, this is Raymond Knight," Travis says, pulling me out of my stupor.

I scratch my head and wonder if this is what they brought us here for. To prove to us they aren't at war. But their war is so far off my radar, it only angers me.

"Please tell me this isn't what I think it is. I could be missing information about finding my daughter because I'm fucking here placating your relationship."

"Son, that's not what this is about."

I'm not a total asshole, so I extend my hand to Raymond and introduce Travis to Gracyn before we sit down.

Travis leans forward, resting his elbows on the table. "Jessie doesn't have Presley."

I scoot to the edge of my seat. "You sure? Because that bitch is up to something."

Gracyn clears her throat, clearly unhappy with my choice of words. If she only knew the real Jessie. I held back. I was going to call her a cunt.

Raymond moves his tented fingers from his lips and leans back. "We are. She's here if you want to talk to her."

My chair screeches as I jump up and slap my palms against the table. "Where?"

"She's in the office," Travis says, but he grabs my arm before I have time to dart off. "Take Gray with you."

"What?" she protests, holding up her hands. "I … I don't need to get involved."

I agree.

"Jessie said she won't talk to Brooks without you being there," Raymond adds.

I swallow my anger, my fists balling at my sides. "What right does she have to make demands?"

"You're angry, and she knows that," Travis says, meeting my gaze, unblinking.

"Damn right I am! And I don't think she's innocent. Why is it that my daughter goes missing not long after she surfaces? After she tries to worm her way into Gracyn's life?"

It's been five years since I've seen her. Five years of silence, five years of staying the hell away from us. After they released her from the facility, I flew to California to find out what her plans were. What she thought was going to happen versus reality. I didn't want her crazy anywhere near Presley. What I wanted her to say was that she'd stay away forever. As Addison pointed out, that wasn't realistic, so I was prepared to give her visitation rights. Joint custody of Presley was not an option. I had the resources to fight it, and I'd spend any amount necessary to make sure it didn't happen.

End of story.

But in typical Jessie fashion, she surprised me. Giving me everything I wanted. Full custody. She said Presley was better off without her in her life. *Her exact words.*

It seems her crazy is showing again.

"Let's go talk to her," Gracyn says, her voice steady and way more composed than mine.

I lift a brow, side-eyeing her. Why isn't she mad? Gracyn doesn't put up with bullshit, so how is she so calm?

"She has answers, so let's hear her out," she says, reading me. "And this isn't about what she did to me. It's about finding Presley."

We make our way to the office. Gracyn pauses at the door, her hand resting on the knob. She glances over her shoulder at me. "You good? Storming in there, all fire and brimstone will not get answers."

I grunt with a sharp nod, sounding like a caveman who got put in his place by his wife.

I guess it's not far off base.

As we step into the office, my body tenses like a live wire, every muscle coiled and ready to strike. Gracyn reads me well, stepping in front of me, creating a barrier between us.

Jessie stares at us from a worn leather couch, clutching a crumpled tissue in her hand. She pats her swollen eyes and stands up. "Thank you for coming," she chokes out. After clearing her throat, she continues, "I know this looks bad."

"You have no idea," I snap, lunging forward.

Gracyn squeezes my bicep, stopping me. "Is it true you don't have Presley?" she asks.

Jessie's red-rimmed eyes lock onto mine. "I don't. I swear. I'm just as devastated about this as you are."

"You don't have a right to feel devastated!" I roar, my words echoing off the walls. "You gave her up!"

She takes a step forward, her voice rising to match mine. "I gave her to you to keep safe, and you failed!"

The unexpected jab freezes me in my spot, stealing the air from my lungs.

"Okay, enough," Gracyn chimes in, stepping in between us, holding her arms out like a referee calling a foul. "This isn't helping. Both of you need to take a breath and calm down."

The ice-cold stare down between Jessie and me lingers a few more tense beats, the air thick with anger and accusations. I pull in a harsh breath and take a step back.

"That's better," she says in a teacher's voice, calm and commanding. "Let's start with how we met. Why did you use a fake name?"

Jessie scratches her temple, and when she looks at Gracyn, she releases some of the anger. It's as if she thinks of Gracyn as a friend. "I found out that you were married to Brooks. I wanted to meet the woman who might be my daughter's mom."

You've got to be kidding me.

I squeeze the bridge of my nose. "You are so fucking psycho, woman."

"Brooks." Gracyn's eyes bore into me. "Not helping," she mouths.

Can't she see that she's a few screws short? That is the most asinine reason I've ever heard.

She turns to Jessie. "That's a little extreme."

See! She agrees.

Jessie throws her hands up. "I'm an extreme person, okay? I can't help it. When I saw that you and Brooks had gotten married, all the better judgment in my head flew out the door. My baby was going to have a new mom."

"It's not like that at all. We got drunk one night, made a mistake, and got married in Vegas," Gracyn says.

The mistake part is debatable.

"It's more than that," Jessie says, her gaze ping-ponging between us. "I've seen pictures. Brooks hasn't ever looked at someone like he does you. In every picture he's in with a woman, she's just a prop. With you, you're like the center of his universe."

Not that she's wrong, but what the hell? "You haven't even been around me. How the hell do you know what's going on in my personal life?"

"Presley told my parents about her," she deadpans.

I sigh, rubbing my jaw. I can't argue with that. Yesterday, I was begging Gracyn for a chance to make this work. She is different, and anyone with a pair of eyes could see it.

Jessie continues, "I didn't plan on working at the hotel. But then you were so nice, and I needed a job, so I took it as a sign of being in the right place."

Gracyn's brow arches high. She casts a glance at me, wide-eyed, and I give her a single nod. Yep, like I said, psycho.

When neither of us replies, Jessie fidgets, shifting on her feet, before adding with a tinge of remorse, "I wanted to see if my little girl was getting a good person as a mom."

This visit was pointless. They could have told me they'd found her or handed her over to the police to be questioned. Anything other than dragging me down here. I blow out a ragged breath as I stare at Jessie, shaking my head. Without another word, I storm out of the office, hoping it's the last time I'll ever see her again.

"Son," Travis calls after me, following me out the exit. "Hold on."

I spin around. "She didn't do it would have sufficed. I didn't need to see her," I snap. "Instead, you make me waste my time with her pointless explanation and whatever the hell that was!"

He slides his hands in his slacks and leans against the brick wall. "Yes, you did. You needed to hear her side of the story to believe her. Whether or not you like it, she is Presley's mom, and she's terrified for her daughter, as well."

I bark out a bitter laugh. *Why are they on her side?*

"She's back to her antics. Who knows what she had planned for Gracyn? Because I can promise you, she had a plan."

The door swings open, and Gracyn steps out, pausing when she sees us. "I can go back in…"

"No. We're done. Let's go."

Travis straightens and pulls me in for a firm hug. "Whoever has her can't stay hidden for long."

I nod, knowing he's doing everything in his power to help find Presley.

After sliding in my car, I grip the steering wheel, my knuckles white as I stare blankly at the dashboard. The weight of everything with Presley disappearing, Jessie's bullshit, and the unknown, crashes down all at once. A headache throbs at the base of my neck. I close my eyes and rub the back of my head, trying to ease the tension.

I can feel Gracyn's eyes on me. "She's going to her parents' house," she whispers.

That didn't help the throbbing. "I don't fucking care where she goes."

She hesitates for a second, weighing her words, but then she adds, "And I told her I would call her if anything happens."

Well, if Jessie has any more questions about Gracyn's integrity, that should answer it all. Because she's a better person than I am.

CHAPTER 30

BROOKS

"Okay, so it's not Jessie," Gracyn says as we walk through the front door.

I want to believe that. *I really do.* But I'm having a hard time thinking that despicable woman knows nothing.

"Then who?" she whispers to herself.

If I knew the answer to that, my daughter would be home with me right now. In her bed. Dreaming of dancing on a stage on Broadway.

"Who the hell has my daughter!" I roar, chucking my keys across the dark living room in a fit of rage. "How could she have just disappeared?"

Rage boils over as I storm over to the whiteboard, ripping Jessie's picture off and shredding it to pieces. I can't stand to look at the woman a second more. The pieces fall to the ground like confetti at my feet.

I continue on to my bedroom, Gracyn's soft footsteps trailing behind me.

"Addison said your parents and Jessie's parents will be here tomorrow."

Just what I fucking need. More people hovering over me.

She continues. "I just don't want to be in the way or a distraction. Addison didn't mention Judith's mom. Will she be here, also?"

I freeze mid-step, spinning around so fast, she nearly walks into me. "Did you say Judith's mom?"

Gracyn blinks, startled by my reaction. "Oh, does she not see her very often?"

God, I hope not.

"Judith's mom died three years ago."

She tilts her head. "Are you sure?"

"Of course, I'm sure," I snap, though my anger isn't directed at her. "She took off for two weeks to go out west for the funeral. I even sent flowers to the funeral home."

She hums, her gaze shifting to the bedroom windows. I blink twice, trying to keep my irritation in check. *Calm down. She's only trying to help.* I'm about to turn to head into the bathroom when she finally looks back, her expression curious but cautious.

"When Presley called to tell me she was excited that I was her new mom," she starts, and I cringe. The reminder is a slap in the face that my daughter has not been my priority for the last few weeks. "I overheard Judith tell Presley that her mom was waiting for them."

She must have misheard her.

"Since that's not possible, they must've been going with someone else," I reply, but the idea doesn't sit well with me.

That isn't supposed to happen. Judith can do whatever she wants in her free time, but when she's with Presley, she's working. Not going on dates with friends. And if she was meeting someone with Presley, she should've had it approved.

"I remember it distinctly because it occurred to me that even though Presley didn't have a mom, she has a lot of female influences in her life."

I shake my head and shrug, not sure what to tell her.

"Call her and ask who she was with that day," she says, her stubborn streak showing.

I rub my temple. "I'll ask her tomorrow. It's late."

She stares at me, not satisfied with my answer. And now she's planted a seed. It wasn't her mom, so who was it? With a slight irritation, I swipe the phone off the nightstand and sit on the edge of the bed. Sitting beside me, she leans her head to listen.

Judith answers on the fourth ring. "Brooks, did they find her?"

"No," I mutter in disappointment. "Sorry to call so late. Where are you? Why do you sound out of breath?"

"At home. I just got off the treadmill," she says, her breathing slightly labored. "What's going on?"

I could use a long run at the moment. "A couple weeks ago, did you take Pres out with you and a friend?"

There's a pause and shuffling on the other end. "Uh … are you talking about the weekend you flew to Vegas?" After a sharp yes, she replies, "We did. We met my friend, Tom."

I sit up straighter, her reply sending a flash of heat down my spine. "Tom who? And why the hell is this the first time I'm hearing about this?"

"I told you. It wasn't a secret," she replies confidently, making me second-guess my memory. "We already had plans, but you needed me to take Presley last minute so you could go to Vegas. I asked you if it was all right."

I was so distracted, so consumed by the thought of Gracyn using me. Is it possible that I forgot?

"Right," I murmur. "I must've missed that. Sorry for calling so late."

"Brooks, don't apologize. I'm trying to go over everything with a fine-tooth comb as well. This was under my watch. I was responsible for her."

Her voice trembles, and a wave of guilt hits me for questioning her.

"It's not your fault, Judith. I know how much you love Presley."

She's sniffling when I end the call. I stare at the phone in my hand. Why the hell did I do that? That was like me questioning Addison.

"Fuck!" I belt out, throwing the phone across the bed. When Gracyn doesn't say anything, I take a deep breath, exhale through my nose, and turn toward her. "I didn't mean to make her feel bad."

When she twists her lips but continues to stay quiet, I wonder if I pissed her off, too.

"What?" I quip.

She crosses her legs under her with a serious face. When she puts her palm on my arm and hesitates, I lift a brow.

"I'm saying this from an outsider, so don't get mad."

It's a little late for that. She pauses and waits for me to agree. I do a single frustrated nod.

"I get that she's been in your life for five years but..." she says, scrunching her nose.

Six, but who's counting?

"Spit it out, Gracyn."

"Does Judith usually meet men when she has Presley?"

"Hell no. It's in her contract. All men have to be approved of by me if Presley is around them."

She points her finger as if she's made her point. I look up at the ceiling and groan, the headache growing under pressure. *Tom.* Who the fuck is Tom? Why have I never heard of him? Why didn't I question *that*?

Because I hurt her feelings.

Fuck feelings.

My daughter is missing.

Realization hits me. That was the night Presley got sick. Why didn't she mention him after I got home? Why didn't Presley ever say anything about him? I crawl across the bed to grab my phone and dial Aiden.

"What's up?" he answers on the first ring, sounding wide awake.

"The day Pres got sick and I was in Vegas, did Judith mention having dinner with a guy named Tom?"

"Who's Tom?"

Exactly my thoughts.

"No. Did she say something to you about him?" he asks.

I repeat everything that's happened tonight, including Jessie. He voices his anger about being left out of that meeting. Jessie, surprisingly, isn't the topic of this discussion, so I revert to *Tom*.

"You know damn well Addison would've run a background check on any guy that Judith brought around Presley. What did Judith say?"

"She said she had my approval, and I had so much on my mind."

He hums, knowingly.

"I could've forgotten, but I have a hard time believing that. Her telling me what she ate for dinner, I would've forgotten. Her meeting with a man and taking my kid? Highly unlikely."

"Okay," he says, thinking out loud.

Before he continues his train of thought, I'm already shoving my feet into a pair of shoes.

"Where are you going?" Gracyn says, jumping off the bed after me.

"Brooks, don't go over there," Aiden warns.

As if you can stop me. "I need to find out who Tom is."

"I'm on my way," I hear him say right before I hang up.

I dig through the junk drawer, searching for Judith's spare key. If it weren't for the bright orange tag attached to it, I might've been taking ten keys to try.

Gracyn meets me at the door with her shoes on. We descend the one flight of stairs without a word.

When I reach the door, I knock twice, but there's no answer. *Nothing.* I pound harder, but still nothing. I slide the key into the doorknob and draw in a harsh breath, afraid that the one person I trusted the most with my daughter betrayed me.

Betrayed us.

Presley loved her.

"Please let me be wrong," I murmur to myself. The door clicks open with a quiet turn of the key. The room is pitch black and quiet. "Judith?" I call out and then listen.

Silence.

The faint glow from the hallway spills into the apartment, just enough for me to search for the switch. I've only been inside her apartment a handful of times. The room lights up, and the scene stops me cold.

Presley's toys are neatly stacked in the corner. Pictures

painted by Presley line the walls. I blink back the tears threatening to fall. I never let Presley hang her pictures in the living room. Her artwork stayed confined to the fridge, her room, or tucked away in drawers, hidden in a way I told myself was acceptable.

A knot of guilt tightens in my stomach seeing the artwork displayed with pride. My finger outlines a stick figure on one of the papers. I sniff. "This is ridiculous," I mutter, more angry with myself. "This woman"—I throw my arms out, gesturing to the room—"would never harm my daughter."

Gracyn walks back to Judith's bedroom, flips the light on, and disappears into the room. I hate that I'm here. Questioning things. I fall back on the couch. She can look, but I'm done.

"Brooks," she calls out. "You'll want to come see this."

I push off the couch and rush to the room to find Gracyn staring into an empty closet.

"All her clothes are gone," she whispers.

Maybe she likes to fold everything. I pull out every drawer, only to find it the same—empty. My worst fear becomes reality. "Where is she? We talked fifteen minutes ago!" I scream, panic choking me.

A chill wraps around my spine, paralyzing me with the horror of it all. Has she had my daughter this whole time? Sat in my living room, acting like she was living in the same hell I was? She might have been in hell, but she was on her fucking throne, enjoying the show. I look to Gracyn for answers she can't give me. She didn't hire her. She doesn't even know her.

"What did I do?" I stare at the walls, lost. My mistakes, my choices, all pile up so high I can barely see over them. I don't trust myself anymore. I collapse onto the bed, my head hangs low as tears sting my eyes. I pinch them together. "How is she going to get through this?" The words strangle me as they escape. "Is she frightened? Is she crying for me? Will she hate me for not protecting her?" All my fears tumble out. The strength I was holding onto as a lifesaver crumbles to my feet in a pile of rubble. I brought her into our world.

This is all my fault.

Gracyn drops to her knees in front of me. "Brooks, that little girl could never hate you. You're her everything."

"I broke my promise. I told her I'd never let the monsters get her." I'm the worst dad ever. "I'm no hero. Because I'm the one who let the monsters in."

CHAPTER 31

GRACYN

The worst monsters are the ones that go after your heart.
After what matters most to you.
Until your heart is blind to their evil.
That's when they strike.

My mom's words surface. A hard lesson I learned in high school. My best friend, Jack, whom I loved like a brother, had been in my life ten years before he was arrested for raping and killing a teacher. I couldn't believe it. He was my sweet, soft-talking Jack. Someone I didn't think could hurt a fly. At first, I was more confused than angry. I still have a hard time accepting that underneath his faux sweet exterior lived a horrible human being. It was my mom's only explanation. And an enormous eye-opening experience. You really don't know someone.

And now, Judith.

Betrayal always cuts deeper when it comes from someone you trust. It leaves a sharp wound in its wake. And for Brooks, it's not just the betrayal, it's everything. It's the crushing weight of failure bearing down on him, the relentless ache of his bleeding heart now fueled by a firestone of rage. Anyone who crosses in his path is bound to feel its searing heat.

But everyone takes it.

Nobody knows the hell he's in, but they can see the torture in his eyes.

The morning erupted with chaos. New information. New suspect. Addison and I sit side by side on the couch, listening. Around us, the room buzzes with activity, five phone calls happening simultaneously, where we catch snippets of each conversation.

"She got spooked and ran when Brooks started questioning a man she was with," someone says.

"We got her leaving the building at 11:15. After she talked to Brooks, she ran," comes another voice.

My brows furrow. "That's not right," I whisper to myself.

"What was that?" Addison asks, glancing over.

I shake my head, a nagging doubt swirling in my mind. Something doesn't add up. Goose bumps prick up and down my arm when an unsettling thought pops into my head. I swallow hard, hesitating, knowing I'm wading into territory I have no business being in, especially with a room of official law enforcement.

"I think she has Brooks's room tapped," I whisper.

Her head tilts in confusion, and I second-guess myself. Did I use the wrong term?

"Or bugged?"

She lets out a soft chuckle. "No, I know what you mean. But, why do you think that?"

"Judith left at 11:15. That's before Brooks called her."

"You sure?"

"Positive. I remember looking when he called because he

mentioned it was late. It was 11:23 p.m.. It doesn't make sense. She was here all day, so what happened at that exact moment to make her run? It's when we were talking about her mom. When she answered, she sounded out of breath. Brooks asked her about it, and she said she just got off the treadmill."

Addison twists her lips with a hum, then jerks her head toward Brooks's room, gesturing for me to go there. I nod and wait for her to get up first before following her in. As soon as she shuts the door, cutting off the noise from the others, she holds up a finger to her lips. She pulls out a blue pair of gloves from her bag, puts them on, and begins touching surfaces around the room.

I watch her closely, anticipation building that her fingers will connect with something foreign. Every time she pauses, my heart stops. But then she keeps going with a head shake. She moves swiftly through the room, and when she's made it completely around, I twist my lips in defeat.

Well, it was worth a try.

"I would've sworn—"

I stop mid-sentence when she holds her finger to her lips again. She spins in place, staring at the walls. She walks over to a wall socket, bends down, and runs her finger around the small white rectangle.

"Screwdriver," she mouths.

We both jump when the door swings open. "What are you two doing?" Aiden asks, looking at Addison crouching on the floor, to me, stiff and rigid, as if I was doing something I shouldn't be doing.

Addison stands up, yanking off her gloves and tossing them back into her bag. She growls in frustration. "Do you have equipment to sweep the room?" she asks, giving up trying to be quiet. I mean, what's the point now?

Judith will still be a monster.

He nods and walks out without any questions. Considering she investigates crime scenes every day, I wouldn't question her either.

A half hour later, we're all staring at three devices on the kitchen table that were hardwired into various wall sockets throughout the penthouse.

"She knew everything about our life. When she wasn't here, she was listening." Brooks pounds his fist on the table, and everyone watches in silence. There's nothing anyone can say to help him not feel violated. "Why the hell was she spying on me?"

One of the police officers that's processing Judith's place walks in. She's holding a bottle of something in her hand.

"We found this in her trash. Has anyone been sick lately?" she asks.

"Yes. Why?" Brooks grinds out.

Her lips press together as she drops the bottle in an evidence bag. Max looks at Addison with an uneasy expression, and she nods. Brooks doesn't miss it either.

"What's going on? What is that?"

Addison hesitates, her expression pained. "Ipecac syrup," she finally says. "It's used to induce vomiting. It could mimic symptoms of a stomach bug."

"She poisoned us!" he roars.

Oh my god. This keeps getting worse. She made them sick? Deliberately? For what? To keep Brooks away from me? Did jealousy really drive her to this twisted extreme?

Oh, Brooks. My mind reels as I steal a glance at him. His

face is a mask of cold fury, his jaw clenched tight as he stares blankly off. His hands ball at his sides, his knuckles bone white. He looks like he's barely holding it together, and I'm afraid he might break at any moment.

I think about walking over to him, but something inside tells me not to. Instead, I tuck my legs up underneath me in the chair, watching him with a mix of guilt and worry.

Stone's voice slices through the suffocating silence. "Okay, here's what I've found so far," he announces. All eyes snap to him as his fingers pound on the keyboard, his screen flashing with different windows, navigating through them as if he's in a maze.

Brooks stomps over, his fury radiating like a heatwave.

"Her real name is Sawyer Judith Jackson."

Stone glances up at Brooks, and he nods once, confirming this isn't new information. "She told me her dad's middle name was Sawyer, and she always thought it sounded masculine, so she went by Judith," Brooks says in a matter-of-fact tone.

Stone switches to another screen. "She was born in 1984 to a Janie Jackson in Circleville, Ohio. Her dad and twin sister, Sydney, died in 1989." Stone again looks over his shoulder. "Did you know she had a twin?"

"No," Brooks hammers out. "But I ran a background check on her, and everything checked out."

"It wouldn't have uncovered anything. She's clean. You did your due diligence, Brooks."

"A lot of good that did," he mutters under his breath.

I catch Aiden shift his gaze Addison's way, his expression tight as he shakes his head ever so slightly. He knows more, and it's not good. I quickly glance at Brooks, afraid whatever is next might be what pulls him over the edge.

Aiden clears his throat. "When I was undercover with Travis, I ran across Willie Jackson's name. He worked for Travis. Janie Jackson was his wife," he explains. The room stills, and Addison curses under her breath. "Judith's twin sister and dad were found dead from gunshot wounds in a vehicle during the time of the bloodbath between Knight and Travis back in the late eighties. There were rumors of each side's fault, but the fighting stopped right after. Officially, it's a cold case."

I gasp, covering my mouth in horror. A little girl died at the hands of our fathers. My heart pounds, and for a moment, I can't breathe. When Brooks looks at me, his hazel eyes fill with ice. Regret. And utter hatred.

Toward me.

Specifically, toward me.

CHAPTER 32

GRACYN

F our days.

Fifty-seven hundred agonizing minutes.

With each passing second without Presley, Brooks's anger grows sharper and more volatile. Everyone's frustrated. Exhausted. Presley could be anywhere by now. Our only hope is that Judith loves her enough that she's safe.

Brooks is shutting me out. At first, he welcomed my comfort, leaned on me in his moments of weakness. But now, he's so consumed by his own anguish, he's throwing blame like daggers. And those daggers? They're aimed squarely at me.

Everything was fine before I came into his world.

The guilt of enjoying a weekend with me while someone took his daughter is eating him alive. And it doesn't help that it's *my* dad who is the root cause.

I've tried to give him space, tried to step back while staying available for the team if they need anything. But it's taking a toll on my mental health.

Staying here is breaking me. It would be better if I just …

left. At least then, he wouldn't have to see me. Be reminded every minute of how everything went wrong the moment I stole his coffee.

Me being here is doing more harm than good. But how do I walk away?

I open my eyes after another sleepless night, rolling over to find the other half of the bed empty. When I step into the living room, Brooks is folding up a blanket on the couch. He can't even bring himself to sleep next to me.

I hold my breath as he walks past me. His beard has grown out, and I'm certain he hasn't taken a shower since day one, considering he's still wearing the same clothes he wore the night we found out about Presley. He won't meet my eyes as he trudges to the kitchen to turn on the coffeemaker. It's the early mornings that are the worst. Where it's just the two of us. Gone is the carefree guy from the Grand Canyon days ago, the one who was begging me to try. That guy is gone.

"Can I make you some breakfast?" I whisper.

I see it immediately. The way his hands clench into fists, his shoulders tense, his entire body reacting to the sound of my voice as if it pains him.

It breaks my heart.

"Do you want me to leave, Brooks?" My voice cracks as I blink back the tears I'm desperately trying to hold in. The last thing he needs to deal with is my emotions.

With his back to me, his shoulders rise and fall as he stands still and quiet. Moments later he replies, "Yes. Us thinking we could be something was a mistake. You were never meant to be a part of my world."

It's the way he says it—cold, detached, and final—that

causes my breath to catch in my throat. I nod once, turn and walk back into the bedroom.

Stay strong. This isn't about you. I repeat over and over to myself as I shove my clothes into my bag, trying to hold myself together. He's hurting, drowning, and lashing out. But it doesn't help the sting. The tiny shards of glass slicing me apart from his words.

When I walk back out, bag in hand, he storms by me, slamming the bedroom door behind him.

The sound of shattering glass echoes from his room, followed by a string of curse words. My hands freeze, clutching the handle of the bag as I stare at the door. Every inch of me wants to run in there and comfort him. I wait. Hope. Desperate for him to open the door.

Tell me you made a mistake.

Tell me you're sorry.

Tell me to stay.

Instead, it's unnerving silence. More deafening than hearing his emotions spew out. He's made it clear. It's time for me to leave. I've overstayed my welcome.

I glance around the room one last time. Humming computers and whiteboards have shoved aside all the remnants of a little girl living here. It's a war room rather than a warm family room with laughter, dancing, and *life.*

I let out a shaky sigh, looking up to the ceiling. *Please, God, bring that little girl home.*

The soft click of the front door breaks me. The hallway is quiet, and I make it halfway to the elevator before my legs give out. I lean against the wall, cold and unforgiving, and slide down to the floor. My fingers fumble for my phone, shaking so badly it almost slips from my grasp. I press my mom's number.

With my back to the wall, I pull my knees to my chest and sob, soft, guttural cries that tear me apart from the inside out.

"Tell me you have good news," she answers on the first ring.

I wish. My throat tightens, and the words catch before I can get them out. "Mom, I don't know what to do. He's so angry."

"Oh, sweetheart. There's nothing you can do. If something happens to that little girl, it's going to break Brooks. Even your love won't help mend his shattered heart."

I lick the salty tears off my lips. "I know that. I do. But I can't stay here anymore. He hates me. But how do I leave him like this?"

"I promise, he doesn't hate you. All you can do is tell him you're there for him. Other than that, this is his fight."

I don't think he'll ever need me. More gut-wrenching tears fall as emptiness fills me. "This is horrible."

"It is. I can't even imagine what he's going through." Mom's gentle voice does nothing to soothe the pain.

I hang up and dig a receipt from my purse and a pen. I don't want to leave like this. He needs to know I'll always be on his side. A tear falls, landing on the thin piece of paper and blurring the ink.

What do I even say?

I sniffle, swipe my tears, and try to focus. Staring at the receipt, I grip the pen tighter, willing the words to come. But they don't. Every time I write something, I stop. Nothing feels right. Nothing feels *enough*. Everything I want to say only risks making it worse. He doesn't need that.

He hates me.

Until she's back in his arms, that won't change.

The thought crushes me. My fingers curl around the paper,

crumbling it until it's nothing but a ball of regret. I shove it back in my purse. With my knees drawn up, my forehead resting against them, I give myself a moment to pull my emotions in.

One more breath. Just one more.

I push off the hard floor. My legs are unsteady, but I square my shoulders and force myself to walk to the elevator.

Each step feels like I'm walking away from something I'll never get back.

This is the end of our story.

CHAPTER 33

BROOKS

Everyone needs to leave me the fuck alone.

I don't want to eat.

I don't need to shower.

I don't need to sleep.

What I need is for them to find my daughter.

I'm ready to explode. If one more person asks how I'm doing, they might get a fist to the nose. How the hell do they think I'm doing? I'm in hell, and there's no way out until Presley is home.

Addison's face flashes in my mind—disappointment, questioning—when she asked where Gracyn went. I told her she had left. Of course, she knew why. But she didn't say a word. She didn't have to. Her eyes said it all.

Gracyn was distracting.

Every moment with her came with guilt trailing close behind, curling up beside me at night and sinking its claws into my chest. Those moments of peace I found with her tore me apart later. Dreams of Presley screaming for me, her little voice calling out in fear, while I was making love to Gracyn, burned into my subconscious. They left me waking up in a cold sweat, hating myself. Hating *her*.

Then I'd throw up.

That's my life at the moment. Irrational thoughts and nightmares.

I'm not allowed outside anymore. Yesterday, I made the mistake of stepping out of the building and talking to the press. The news and media swarmed, hungry for information. So, I stood there, facing a sea of cameras, and begged. Pleaded with Judith to bring her home.

And then someone shouted, "It's been six days. Do you think she's still alive?"

His words hit me like a freight train. He was too close, and my control snapped. At least I only have to pay for a new video recorder and not worry about charges for attempted murder. That guy was lucky Aiden was within reach of stopping me.

Today is Monday. Dance night.

I go to Presley's room, as much as it pains me to see it empty, and pull out a black leotard with pink tights and stuff them in her dance bag, the ritual as familiar as breathing. Her ballet slippers lie tossed in a corner. I grab those, too.

Then sit on her unmade bed, clutching the bag like it's the last piece of her I have left.

I can smell her. If I close my eyes, her laugh echoes in my head, high energy and full of joy. A ghost of a smile flickers on my face, but it doesn't last. The ache is too strong.

I fall back against the tiny bed, the mattress creaking underneath me. My arms curl tighter around the bag. Tears slip out of my closed eyes.

Baby girl, I'm so sorry. I'm so sorry I wasn't here for you.

"Brooks, we got something," Max says from the doorway.

I'm on my feet before he can say another word. That's the first I've heard those words in seven days. *Optimistic words.*

"We've been helping the FBI sort through all the tips," Max says, walking with me to the kitchen.

My heart lurches at the possibility of another false lead. People mean well, but calling in every time they see a blond six-year-old doesn't help.

"This one is worth looking into," he adds, reading my apprehension. "A woman called in. She says she saw a woman with a child at a gas station. She swears the woman called her Presley and then quickly corrected herself and called her Annie. We pulled the security footage from the station."

I'm right on his heels, hope filling my chest. My pulse thunders in my ears as I crowd behind Stone, staring over his shoulder at the computer screen.

"It's her," Stone says.

He points to the image so clear it almost steals the breath from my lungs. Presley. My baby girl. She's holding hands with Judith, exiting the store. My knees weaken as my eyes lock onto her. Her blond hair is gone. That bitch dyed it brown and hacked it short.

I can't breathe. A relieved sob escapes my lips as I stare at the frozen screenshot.

"When was this?" I choke out.

"Yesterday." Max places a firm hand on my shoulder. "We found her, brother. Now, let's bring her home."

The words hit with a shot of adrenaline, enough to keep me standing when my legs threaten to give out. Max squeezes my shoulder once before moving to make some phone calls.

With the make, model, and license plate of the car, Stone does what he does best. Scanning through security footage, hacking into databases, piecing together fragments of a trail like a master craftsman.

"We've got her," Stone mutters, pulling up a new image on the screen. It's grainy, but clear enough. A car stopped at a red light. Two women sit in the front seats, Judith driving, but I've never seen the other one.

By early afternoon, Stone has tracked their path since they left the gas station. His focus is unshakable. I haven't left his side all day as he pulls up footage after footage.

"She's headed for Canada," he says.

Canada.

With every clip of her vehicle Stone pulls up, my nerves fray a little further. The idea of her crossing the border, disappearing into another country, never to be seen again, tightens in my chest. Another irrational thought. I have to push the thought that I'm this close to losing her forever out of my head. The FBI has already contacted the Canadian authorities, and the Mounties are watching for their car.

Max and Kase, another one of Max's guys, start packing their bags. The sound of zippers and shuffling gear fills the room.

"I'm going," I snap.

They both stop and look up, apprehension written across their features. Max steps toward me, and I already know he's going to stop me.

"I don't care what the fuck you're about to say. I'm going."

"I can't let you go."

"The hell you can't."

Max doesn't have to abide by the FBI rules. He doesn't have to play by their handbook. He can do whatever he wants. And that includes letting me go.

"I won't get in the way. I just want to be there for Presley when you get her. She'll be scared as hell when everyone rushes in with guns drawn." When he doesn't look like he's going to change his mind, I try begging. "Please?"

Max sighs and looks over to Kase, who stands silent but contemplative. After a moment, he gives a slight nod. "We've all been there," he says.

He's right. Every single one of these guys has stepped into the fire to save their woman at some point, and none of them stayed behind. It is even more crucial that I'm there because she's a child. My child. She needs me.

Max turns to me, his jaw tight but his resolve cracking. "Get your things. But you're staying in the vehicle until we have Presley safe."

I nod, jogging to my room to toss a few things in a bag.

When I come out, Max stands there, arms crossed, scrutinizing me like a hawk. "You better not have grabbed a gun," he warns with narrowed eyes.

I hold up a small, pink stuffed dog and shake my head. I've been sleeping with the damn thing every night because it smells like Presley. Her favorite stuffed animal. One that she misses probably as much as she misses me. When I found it under her bed, I couldn't believe Judith didn't take it with her. What a heartless bitch.

The plane's engine roars to life as we board, the hum vibrating underneath my feet. There's no time to settle in before the aircraft is already taxiing. Aiden and another agent met us on the tarmac, both of them looking tense and worn as the rest of us.

While in the air, I take a corner seat in the rear of the plane, trying to keep out of the way. My ears tune in as the team lays out the game plan, their voices sharp and focused. I soak in every word, making mental notes. *Just in case they need my help.*

The flight is quick. Too short for me to process anything but my nerves and anger. When the wheels touch down, I'm vibrating with restless energy. I can feel it. I'm steps away from rescuing my daughter.

Local FBI agents are there to pick us up. As we speed through the streets of Theresa, New York, Stone's updates the filled car. He and the local FBI identified where Judith's been staying—in a dingy, run-down motel on the outskirts of town.

It's the kind of place that reeks of desperation and shadows. It's a known haven for prostitutes, drug dealers, and worse. Imagining my daughter sleeping on a bed in a place like that sends my anger spiraling into an inferno. It's another way for Judith to get her revenge. Twist the knife.

As if I had anything to do with her sister's death.

She's looking for revenge.

I clench my fists as the car pulls to a stop in front of a small satellite office. My orders are clear—stay put while the rest of the team moves in. Theresa, New York. A speck on the map, a city I'd never heard of, but right now, it feels like the most important place in the world.

A couple of agents work at a desk, ignoring me as I pace the length of the cramped room. Every ring of the phone sends my heart into overdrive wondering if it's news, good or bad. The anticipation makes it impossible for me to stay still.

I think of all the things I'll never do again, like getting frustrated with Presley for taking too long to get ready or snapping at her for talking when I'm on a work call during the weekend.

But most of all, I'll never, ever leave her again.

The phone rings again, and I freeze. I hold my breath as the officer answers, his eyes flickering to mine before he listens. He nods, then says, "Got it." A tick of a smile pulls at the corner of his mouth, and he adds, "I'll tell him."

He smiled.

Smiled.

He hangs up, and I wait for confirmation. Wait for the words that will put me together again. He stands up and nods. "She's safe. They got her."

I stare at him, the words not yet solidified. "Say it again," I murmur out of desperation.

He nods again, taking a step toward me. "She's safe, Brooks."

My heart explodes with relief as my knees buckle, and I sink to the floor, tears blurring my vision. My chest is tight with the force of all of it, the overwhelming surge of emotion.

"She's safe," I repeat through broken breaths, still working through the process that's it's true.

The officer kneels beside me and puts his hand on my shoulder.

"Thank you. Thank you. Thank you," I whisper, not able to form any other words.

"They're on their way," he says, standing back up and giving me space, allowing the moment to settle. A part of me won't accept it until I see her with my own eyes.

I push myself up from the floor and walk over to my bag,

my hands shaking as I pull out Presley's stuffed animal. The officer stands at the door. Wiping the tears from my cheeks, I tap my heart, a silent gesture of gratitude before walking outside.

"Daddy!" Presley screams out of the SUV window, waving her arms wildly.

Her smile is so bright it almost knocks the wind out of me. It's been one week since I've heard her voice, but it seems like a lifetime. I sprint to the car as the car door opens. She pops out and flies into my arms. I scoop her up, burying my face in her neck. Her giggle bursts in my ear like a song I thought I'd forgotten.

"Snarky. I missed you so much."

"I missed you too," she says, pulling back. She tilts her head from side to side. "Do you like my new hair?" She turns her head to show off the short, uneven cut.

I hate it. I force a smile and nod. "It's beautiful."

"It's part of our trip. Judith said that while we were on vacation, we should pretend to be someone else. So, I'm Annie." She says it like it's the most fun thing in the world, her eyes sparkling with excitement. "It was hard sometimes to remember our pretend names. But then Uncle Aiden showed up at the hotel room and said I had to go home. Did something happen?"

She thinks she was on a vacation.

She doesn't know Judith kidnapped her.

How am I going to explain to my little girl that the woman she loves so much just caused me gut-wrenching pain and that she'll never see her again? I glance up at Aiden and Max, confused.

"Hey, Pres," Aiden says, crouching down to her level. "Can

you go into the office with me and tell me all about your trip? I saw some cookies in there."

Her eyes light up. "Cookies?"

"Yep." He nods. "I want you to tell me about all the fun things you did. I bet you had some pretty cool adventures."

She takes a deep breath, puffing out her cheeks as she lets it out dramatically. "There's a lot of stuff. I'll try to remember."

I squeeze her hand one last time before Aiden leads her into the building. I can't take my eyes off her. She disappears behind the door, and the weight of everything Judith did crashes down on me.

I run a hand over my face. "She thinks they were on a fucking trip."

Max steps closer, his typically unreadable expression in place. "Judith didn't cause a scene. When she saw it was us, she let Aiden take her without saying anything. Janie Jackson was the other woman with her. Of course, Judith denied saying her mom ever died."

It's not like I thought she'd be forthcoming *now*. She's lied the entire time she's been in our life. My shoulders fall, and he puts his hand on one, squeezing.

"It's the best outcome. There'll be a few bumps in the road, but you have your daughter. That's all that matters. It's over."

My body shakes from adrenaline as I nod. Max pulls me in for a hug, his grip strong and steady, anchoring me as my emotions overwhelm me.

"Take a second," he says quietly. "Then go get your baby girl." He walks into the building.

I bend at the knees, crouched low as I squeeze the bridge of my nose, willing the tears to stop. She can't see me like this. She'll know something is wrong.

I blow out a ragged breath and look up at the sky. "Thank you," I whisper.

For the first time in seven days, I can breathe. I stand tall and swallow the lump of relief in my throat, pull the stuffy from my back pocket, and head toward the door.

Let's go home, Snarky.

CHAPTER 34

GRACYN

> Me: Thank God she's okay!! Thinking of you.

T he last text I sent Brooks three weeks ago. No response. I'm not surprised, but it still hurts. Every morning, the headlines scream with new articles about Judith and her mom, their lives dissected and dragged through the mud by relentless journalists. Those who knew them recall Judith as a sweet and shy child and her mother as a reserved woman who kept to herself. They lived in an affluent part of Tennessee where Judith went to private schools, and her mom worked part-time as a receptionist at a local dentist's office.

Ray filled in the blanks. The part that no matter how deep they look, nobody will uncover. Judith's father used to work for Travis. He confirmed it was her twin sister's death that ended the war between them. Her dad had been out doing a delivery for Travis when it happened. On the way there, someone ran him off the road, riddling his van with bullets before stealing the shipment of drugs. No one knew that he had just picked up his daughter from school sick, and she was sleeping in the back. Ray and Travis figured out it was a rival who had orchestrated the entire thing to escalate the war. But none of that changes anything. In the end, they're both to blame.

It was too late.

The war they started left behind irreparable scars and anger that festered into revenge. I asked Ray how much they paid the mom for her silence. It was obvious they received money from somewhere. A single mom working part-time wasn't going to afford them the luxuries that they were living. They each paid her a million and a half. It wasn't enough. There isn't enough money in the world that could ever make me forget the loss of my child.

Judith is pleading not guilty. Her attorney claims their trip was a pre-approved vacation and insists this is all a misunderstanding.

Misunderstanding my ass.

Here's what I'll always wonder, and I'd ask her if I had a chance. She clearly set out to get revenge on Travis by taking the nanny job with Brooks. But did plans change after all the years with them? Did she realize Brooks was a better man than his father? Did I trigger her plan again when I came into the picture?

Was I her breaking point?

Guess I'll never know.

I set the phone down and grab the paintbrush, staring at the freshly painted bright green bookcase. One more coat should do it. When I spotted the bookcase on the side of the road, discarded like some piece of trash, I couldn't leave it. I had to stop and rescue it.

Mom thinks I only picked it up because I see myself in this

beat-up piece of furniture. As if fixing it up somehow will fix me, too. She's wrong. I picked it up because it felt like a crime leaving it there. What kind of monster abandons a perfectly good bookcase?

And it'll fit perfectly in my classroom. If I can just get this stupid paint to go on smooth. Turns out, restoration is way harder than they make it look on TV.

Just as I dip the brush into the paint, a knock at the door stops me. Ignoring it, I keep working, letting the bristles glide across the raw wood. I haven't been in the mood to see people since I've been home, and this bookcase won't paint itself. I swipe the brush down the side when another knock comes.

Jesus, people. Take a hint.

My head jerks toward the door when someone sticks a key into the door. I watch as the deadbolt clicks unlocked. There are only two people who have keys, and I know it's not my mom since she has court today.

Sure enough, the door creaks open, and Charli walks in like she lives here. She glances at the bookcase and then at me with a smirk. "Now I see why you didn't answer. It's not that you've been ignoring me, right?" she asks sarcastically.

I dip the brush again. "Sure," I mutter, brushing the paint on, double-checking that my lines are smooth.

"Gray, c'mon," she whines. "You can't hole up in here forever. The fumes are going to kill you." She scrunches her nose and walks over to the window, cracking it open a bit.

"They're not bad," I murmur, taking a sniff.

She lifts a brow. "That's because you're used to the smell. But they're awful. I'm surprised your neighbors aren't complaining."

When she plops down on my couch, I lift a brow as she makes herself comfortable. "They must not be *that* bad."

She laughs, sticking out her tongue. "Did you hear the recent news story on Judith?"

My hand freezes mid-swipe. "Don't tell me they let her out."

"Oh, god, no. But this will help keep her behind bars. Remember good ol' Cooper?"

I sigh, painting the last section on the side. "I already know. An NYPD officer called me yesterday and told me that it was Judith who hired the guy to rough 'em up. *His words.*" At this point, nothing that woman does surprises me.

"I can't believe she told the guy she would pay his family an extra ten thousand if he was caught and told the cops it was you who hired him. She tried to frame you!"

"In the end, she kept me away from Brooks, so I guess she wins." I shrug, bitterness lacing my voice.

Setting the brush down, I stand and walk over to her, snatching the phone to read the article for myself. At least the media isn't focusing on our failed marriage at the moment. I hand the phone back and flop down beside her on the couch, exhaling hard.

She puts her head on my shoulder. "I miss you."

I miss me, too. Focusing on reviving this damn bookcase was only a distraction, something to keep my attention off my real life. I was working on giving it life, but I should've been working on mine.

I pick a speck of green paint off my nail. "It looks like shit, doesn't it?"

Charli glances over at the bookcase, assessing my restoration attempt, and then winces. "Well … you tried."

We both dissolve into laughter, the kind that feels like exhaling after holding your breath for too long. It feels so good to laugh.

"Let's grab dinner," she says, looping her arm through mine. "Nowhere fancy, just somewhere to get you away from these paint fumes before we both start seeing unicorns in the walls."

"Okay."

"THANK YOU, I'll call you back in a couple of days with my answer," I say into the phone before hanging up.

Why didn't I say no?

Charli's eyes bore into me from across the table, a smug grin growing larger by the second as I slide my phone into my back pocket, pretending the call didn't just knock the ground out from under me. I shrug, feigning indifference, even as my insides buzz like I've swallowed a hive of bees.

"Of course I applied to many schools," I blurt out, reaching for my glass of wine, taking a slow sip.

"Of course," she echoes flatly, raising an unimpressed brow.

I drop my head into my hands. I should've let the call go to voicemail. Like the last time they called, and I was afraid to answer. But they might not have called a third time.

"Where is this school that you'd..." She pauses, tilting her head in mock thought before tapping her finger against her lips. "What were your words? *'I'd need time to move and find a place to live.'*"

I drain the rest of my drink, my mouth suddenly parched. "I'm not taking it," I mutter.

She laughs at me. "Where, Gray?"

I hate her. She's going to make me say it out loud. Say out loud that I contemplated chasing a man cross-country.

"I'm not—"

"Where?"

"New York City!" I yell, throwing my arms out. There. I said it. Yes, there was a fleeting moment of weakness when I thought there might be something between us worth fighting for. Granted, that was before the kidnapping and before I knew we would never work. I never imagined I'd get a job offer.

I should've said no.

She grabs a piece of bread, tears off a chunk, and pops it into her mouth. "You should take it."

My eyes widen. She's insane. "No, I shouldn't. The only reason I was going was because of Brooks. And that's over."

A flash of a *liar, liar, pants on fire* expression crosses her features. She's not wrong. It's been almost a month, and I still think about him every day. Every night. The dreaded what-ifs hit me like a game of darts, one after another. Hitting the intended bullseye, my heart.

It's still broken and hasn't healed completely.

He still doesn't want me.

I need to say no.

"We should move," she says out of nowhere.

I jerk my head up. "What are you talking about, we? Since when do you want to move to New York?"

She leans forward on her elbows. "There are a lot of opportunities with the networks there. A few headhunters contacted me after seeing my social media post about the football player that married the president's daughter. They loved the piece. And two of them are looking to fill jobs in New York City."

"That's awesome!" I say, excited for her. She worked hard

to grow her following and make a name for herself. Forget about me and my emotional conundrum. This is big news. There aren't many job openings here in Vegas right now, so she was trying to wait it out. "What are you going to do?"

"That depends on you."

"Noooo," I say, pointing my finger right in her face. "This is *your* future. Why didn't you tell me?"

She picks up her drink and takes a sip, staring at me over the rim of her glass. When she puts it down, she shrugs. "Because I hadn't decided yet. And you've been shutting me out for weeks."

Ouch. Instant guilt slams into me. I've been a horrible best friend.

"But I understand," she adds, reaching over the table to grab my hand, giving it a squeeze. "Now that you got an offer, though, it's like it's meant to be. We should move!"

"I don't know." I grimace. "I've already accepted the job here."

"So un-accept it. You haven't even started yet."

I stare at her, blinking. School starts in three weeks.

She leans back, crossing arms and legs. I don't like the knowing smile she's sporting. "Why not decline it, then? Why do you need a *couple of days*?"

Before I can answer, the server shows up with our salads, saving me from having to admit the truth. Or lie. Because I don't want to move. *Right?*

New York sounds like a fun adventure, especially if Charli is there with me, but then again so does Florida.

"Why don't we move to Miami?" I say. "Beach and sun year-round. Sounds perfect."

She laughs out loud, shaking her head. "Did you get an offer in Miami?"

"No," I admit, fiddling with the edge of my napkin. "But I could apply."

Her gaze pins mine with amusement. "Or," she says pointedly, "you could accept the offer you already have. New York would be so much fun. And I'd be there with you. You wouldn't be alone."

If Brooks ever found out I moved there, he'd lose his shit. I chuckle to myself. Who cares? He doesn't own New York City, despite what he might think.

For the first time in weeks, a flicker of spite sparks in my chest. Warm and alive, cutting through the haze of heartbreak. It feels like my old self.

"If I go, it's not because of Brooks."

"Uh-huh." The corner of her mouth twitches.

"I mean it," I reply, giving her my teacher stare that I've practiced many times in front of a mirror. "I have to make this about me."

She nods, her expression shifting to mock seriousness. "Of course. Totally about you."

"I'm serious! If we go…" I pause, emphasizing the uncertainty. "And I mean if, because I'm still not sure, you better not tell Brooks I'm there."

There's so much to figure out. Ugh. I never in a million years thought they'd offer me a job. They're so desperate for teachers that they offered me a probationary certification for a year. There's moving to a new state, finding a place, and all within a month. The thought alone twists my stomach into knots.

She raises her right hand, repeating what I always do. "I swear I won't."

I pick up my fork and stab at my salad. My mind drifts to the money my mom gave me, sitting untouched in my bank account. It'd be a nice safety net to have while I build my life in one of the most expensive cities in the world. Plus, schools don't start in New York for another six weeks, so I'd have a little breathing room to settle in. But could I move without thinking of him? Can I separate the city from the man?

Or is the tiny voice in the back of my mind, screaming at me to do it, not just chasing a fresh start, but rather holding out hope?

"Ticktock," Charli says, tapping her watch as she tries to contain her excitement. "We have a lot to do if we're headed east in a couple of weeks."

I draw in a breath and hold it, afraid to exhale. Because my next breath will flip my entire world upside down. It will change everything.

And I'll be living in the same city as my husband.

CHAPTER 35

BROOKS

Her laugh.

My head snaps toward the line of customers at the counter.

Am I imagining her laugh now?

"Dammit, Brooks, stay with me," Jared snaps, yanking my attention back to him. He points at a graph on the papers spread across the table between us, his tone sharp and frustrated. "We need to get these forecasts done for quarter four."

I blink at him, trying to pull my head back into the game. He pinches the bridge of his nose. He's annoyed. And it's well deserved. If I were in his place, I'd throw my phone at me. I can't get my shit together these days. As if he already knows this meeting isn't going anywhere, he throws down the papers on the table and sits back with a heavy sigh. It's the first time I've seen him in person since our last meeting here, two weeks ago.

"Okay," he says, staring at me with the kind of exasperation you reserve for someone who's completely lost their way. "How can we fix this? How can we get you to return to work? Do we need to start a daycare? So Presley's steps away from you?"

He means well, but anger simmers beneath my skin. I press my lips together so I don't snap at him and tell him he's an asshole for not understanding. I'm not able to leave Presley. It's almost been two months since I thought I lost her forever. Two months of nightmares that when I wake up, she won't be there. School starts next week, and I'm contemplating homeschooling. Pay teachers to come to our home if it means keeping her close.

"You should talk to a therapist."

He thinks I'm crazy. At least I'm a crazy person with a daughter who is safe.

"This isn't healthy for you. Or Presley," he adds.

The moment the words leave his lips, my anger ignites like a match to gasoline. "Don't you dare talk about my daughter like that," I snap. "How could having her own father around be unhealthy for her?"

I expect him to back down. Instead, he meets my glare, his jaw clenched in frustration. "I'm not questioning you being around her, but this ... obsession, Brooks, it's not healthy. For either of you."

I grit my teeth. "You don't understand."

"I'm trying to," he says, his voice softening. "But you're suffocating yourself. You need to give her room to breathe. Let yourself breathe."

The only thing keeping me sane right now is being with my daughter, regardless of her being sick of me. We finally told her what happened because we couldn't hide it anymore. Not with the news covering Judith on a daily basis. Then there was why she would never see her again. She took it harder than I expected. For fuck's sakes, the woman stole her from me, and Pres was sad about her not being in our lives now.

Judith should be thanking the asshole who jumped Cooper for admitting that she hired him. Before that, my attorney warned me that the judge could grant her bail. I wasn't worried. *I was ready.* Now, she's sitting exactly where she belongs—in a cage. Alongside her mom, who is very much alive.

Jared holds his hands up and sighs. "Sorry. I just wonder if talking it out with someone will help."

I drop my head, nodding, exhaling as my muscles loosen because he's right.

He slides a business card in front of me. "She's a good friend of Anabel's. Make an appointment. You know I love you like a brother and Presley like my own daughter. Fuck the business. This isn't about that. I'll run the show for as long as you need. But it's time to do something. You can't keep living like a hermit and hoarding your daughter."

His words are laced with genuine concern, but they do little to quell the fire inside me. I take a deep breath, trying to calm down.

"I'm not hoarding her. She still has a life."

He lifts a brow, calling bullshit. "A life with you Velcroed to her side. When's the last time you got a haircut? You're looking like a grizzly bear."

I want to argue, but I can't. It's been weeks, *maybe months*, since I did anything for myself. Even during the short hour-long meetings I've scheduled here and there, when Presley stays with Addison or my mom, it's impossible for me to shake the feeling something bad is going to happen. I'm emotionally drained because I'm unable to relax until I have eyes on her. My mind can't focus.

Except when I hear Gracyn's laugh.

Or I thought I did.

"Can she hypnotize me to forget about Gracyn?" I ask, picking up the card.

"You haven't talked to her at all?"

I shake my head, a bitter laugh slipping from my lips. "Why? What's the point? Whatever we had, I messed up, and still, it just won't work."

Before, I was willing to meet her halfway. I'd go there. She'd come here. It was a give and take. But now? It'd be one-sided because I'm not leaving Presley here for anyone.

I'd only take, and I wouldn't feel one ounce of regret. Gracyn deserves a man who can give as much as they take. Someone who can show up when it matters, not someone who's drowning in their own mess.

And I'm drowning.

THAT NIGHT, lying in bed, Presley on the other side sound asleep with her pink dog covering her eyes, I pick up my phone. *"What are you doing, Handley?"* I whisper to myself as I pull up Gracyn's number, my fingers taking on a mind of their own.

Dammit, Jared. Why'd you have to bring her up?

I stare at her last text. The one I never responded to. What a dick move. After I was the biggest asshole to her, she still reached out, and I couldn't even muster up the decency to say thank you. I let out a deep sigh and type, wondering if she's blocked me. I wouldn't blame her if she had.

> Me: I thought I heard you in the coffee shop yesterday.

I don't expect a reply. Not after what I did. What I said. I've yet to say sorry even though every time I think about how I treated her, I want to hurl. I'm afraid if I say sorry, it'll open a door that needs to stay cemented shut. So why did I text her?

When the three dots pop up, showing she's writing, my heart pounds against my chest.

She didn't block me.

> Gracyn: Did your coffee disappear?

I chuckle softly, then peek at Presley, hoping I didn't wake her. I can't help the smile plastered on my face.

> Me: Not this time.

> Gracyn: Then I definitely wasn't there.

You definitely weren't, *my coffee thief.*

> Me: Thank you for thinking of us.

I wait for her next response, wondering if I'll ever be able to fix the damage between us. But I glance over at Presley, watching her chest rise and fall with her tiny breaths, I realize maybe it's not about fixing what's broken. Maybe it's about accepting that we're at two different places in life and letting go. When she doesn't respond, I'm okay.

Not the ideal closure, but better than we left it.

Bye, beautiful Gracyn, you were the best mistake I ever made.

CHAPTER 36

GRACYN

Don't mind me if I break out in a dance. I twirl around the bright classroom, adding the last finishing touches while I belt out, "Too legit, too legit to quit, hey heeyyy," as MC Hammer plays in the background. If it hadn't been for Charli's help, I'd never have finished in time. But we did it. The classroom is perfect.

Posters of smiling cartoon animals line the walls, and the smell of fresh crayons lingers in the air. Charli helped me arrange the desks into a cute horseshoe with a bright blue reading rug in the middle, ready to welcome tiny feet.

It's *meet the teacher* night. My first one ever, not counting when I was student teaching.

Sheryl, the seasoned teacher from next door, peeks her head in, her laughter cutting through my off-key singing. "I can promise you that high won't last for long."

I scoff, waving her off. "Hush. Don't drown my sunshine." I march over, grab her by the arms, and pull her into my impromptu dance party. "This is going to be an amazing year."

"That's what every newbie says. Two weeks. That's how much time I give you before you come crying to me, saying the devil's spawn is in your class."

I roll my eyes and playfully nudge her toward the door. "This is an optimistic zone, and you, my friend, are being kicked out."

She chuckles, waving her hand in mock defeat, disappearing to her room. Despite her grumpy exterior, she's become my work wife, or maybe more like a grandma with warm hugs and a stern voice. She's been my go-to for questions, advice, or just when I need to talk. It sucks she's retiring at the end of the year.

I glance at my watch to see it's almost go time. I switch the playlist to be more kid-friendly and wait. My heart skips when my first student bursts in. I almost let out a squeal, but I swallow it down, fighting to contain my excitement. She skips across the room, her eyes lighting up when she sees everything.

Yes! She loves it!

I blink back my happy tears and introduce myself to the incoming parents as they filter in. One by one, they greet me with warm smiles and comments about the classroom. Most make a note about me not being from here. What gave it away? The color in the room or my non-New-Yorker accent?

Just as I turn to organize the stack of papers parents have filled out, a small hand taps me on my arm and says, "Hi, I'm Jett."

I smile and lean down to meet his gaze. "I love that na—"

"Gracyn?"

My heart lurches in my chest as I raise my head to the woman's voice. I've lived here almost a month, managing not to bump into Brooks. I knew his daughter didn't go to this school, so I wasn't concerned about that. Instead, his sister stands tall, staring at me with a mixture of surprise and confusion.

Awkwardly, I raise a hand and wave with a lopsided grin. "Hi."

"You are not Ms. Jenkins," she says as a matter-of-fact.

Definitely not. She was the teacher who was supposed to teach this class but quit this week, and they moved me here instead of to a second-grade class. They told me an email was sent to parents.

She shakes her head, still processing the situation. "Wow. You live here now?"

I nod, opening my mouth to explain, but a kid darts between us and asks, "Can I have my assigned seat on the beanbag?"

"It's the reading corner. So, if you'd like to read all day, we can discuss it."

His eyes widen to saucers, his expression comical as he overemphasizes, "I can't read that much," before turning on his heels and running away.

I shift my focus back to Addison.

"Mom, you know my teacher?" Jett says, standing next to her hip, his eyes curious.

She looks down at him, her hand resting on his shoulder. "I do." She meets my eyes with a raised brow. "Does Brooks know you're here?"

"You know my uncle, too?"

Oh. This is so awkward. Glancing down at Jett, I give him a soft smile and instruct him to go find his seat and write his name on the construction paper that's waiting for him. He nods and scampers off.

I wring my fingers in front of me. "He doesn't. Please don't tell him." How do I explain that I'm not ready for him to reject me and then still be okay with living here? I'm not there yet. "I will eventually. I have to find myself here before I can think about Brooks."

Woman to woman, I see in her expression she understands. "I can appreciate that." She pulls her phone out of her crossbody bag, handing it over to me. "Here. Text yourself, so I have your number. I hate thinking you're here by yourself."

While I text myself, I say, "My best friend moved out here with me, but thank you for thinking of me."

"Well, call me, anyway. I'll take you two to the best brunch in town. I'm all for leaving the kids with Aiden to remind him he wanted ten of them." She laughs, slipping her phone back into her bag, before scanning the room for Jett. She calls out for him, and he rolls his eyes in response, already huddled in a group of boys. "That didn't take long," she jokes.

By the end of my first day, my feet are sore, and my voice is raw. I'm already excited about tomorrow. As I tidy up the room, I can't help but laugh, remembering what Jordan told all his friends at lunch, right before popping a Twinkie in his mouth.

"Eat dessert first. You never know when the world is going to end."

He got a round of applause, even from me, despite the morbid ending. The other teachers, however, didn't find it as amusing as they hurried over and shushed everyone, throwing me a disapproving glare. I didn't care. They're seven. They need a chance to laugh and goof off. The things that come out of these kids' mouths are hilarious.

An idea to journal all the priceless comments they say has

me searching my bag for a notebook. I title it *Chalkboard Chronicles* and jot a couple funny quotes from today and toss it back in the bag before heading home.

Ten blocks to the apartment. Ten blocks too many. Rounding up twenty-two six-year-olds feels like I just did eight hours of cardio. Thankfully, the subway is located across the street. It's one of the coolest concepts in the city. It comes with daily entertainment and a few questionable people, but I love it. It's weird, though, to realize I haven't driven in over a month.

"How were the rugrats?" Charli asks as soon as I walk through the door. She's not a fan of kids, and I'm not even sure she wants them. Which is fine, but we couldn't be any more different in that regard.

"Exhausting," I croak, dropping my bags. My vocal cords are shot. "But they are so eager to learn. They're like little sponges right now, desperate to know how the world works. I love it!"

I collapse onto the couch, kicking my flats off and propping my feet up on the ottoman. I wiggle my toes. Why did I think standing in those for eight hours was a good idea? It's no wonder a lot of teachers wear tennis shoes.

My phone dings from my bag that I dropped on the kitchen table. I stare at it. Why did I drop it way over there? My legs feel like Jell-O. I give Charli my best puppy dog look. "Any way you can grab that for me?"

"You need to run with me to build your endurance," she says, picking up my bag, then dropping it next to me.

She's talking to the wrong person. I don't run. Not unless it's away from something terrifying like clowns, fire, or freaking geese.

"Don't you remember the last time you tried to convince me

to run?" I ask, raising an eyebrow. "We both got bit in the ass by two mean geese."

She laughs, tossing herself into the chair across from me. "Oh yeah! And you had the nerve to tell me I wasn't running fast enough."

"Because you weren't! If I was going to be chased down by psycho birds, you better believe I was running like Usain Bolt."

She shakes her head, laughing harder, and I grab my phone, grinning at the memory. That feathered asshole left a bruise and a forever fear of geese. After reading the text, I send a quick reply and glance up at Charli with an irresistible smile. This is a bad idea. A terrible idea, especially since I'm trying to stay off Brooks's radar for as long as humanly possible.

But...

"We're going to brunch with Addison and Sydney next Saturday."

Charli's eyes widen, and she leaps to her feet, her water bottle flying out of her hand and rolling across the floor. "Sydney as in *Sky Owen*?"

"The one and only."

"Oh my god!" she squeals. "We need to go shopping. We need to have our nails done. My highlights need a refresh." She freezes mid-panic. "Saturday? There's not enough time to get ready. I need more time!"

I snort as she spirals further, grabbing the nearest pillow and launching it at her. "Calm down, fangirl. She's just a person."

She catches it, glaring at me. "*You're* just a person. Sky Owen is a goddess. A mythical creature sent to bless us with her heavenly vocal cords." She drops back down on the chair, lifting a brow. "And let's not forget how excited you were when you first met her."

She's not wrong. I had to restrain myself from screaming when Addison introduced me. But the circumstances were different. I had a chance to meet her—*the real her*—the woman behind the spotlight. She's shockingly down-to-earth and one of the sweetest people I've ever met.

But being around her, comes fanfare, cameras, and a lot of attention.

"Shit. What if this isn't a good idea?" I mumble, second-guessing saying yes.

Charli throws the pillow back at me. "No. No. NO! You can NOT take this back from me. You should've decided that ten minutes ago before you told me!"

"But what if—"

She rushes over to me and tackles me, making me giggle. "I will buy you a wig, dammit. But we are going," she declares, pinning me down with a playful glare.

"A wig? Really?"

"Yes, a wig. And sunglasses. Whatever it takes," she says, grinning ear to ear. "But *nothing*. Nothing is stopping us from having brunch with Sky freaking Owen."

"Fine." I snicker. "If my life blows up, it'll be all your fault."

"Totally worth meeting Sky," she teases.

CHAPTER 37

BROOKS

"*I need the competitive analysis for Xavier by the end of the day.*"

When I hang up the phone, Addison stares at me like I have two heads.

"What's that look for?"

"It's Saturday."

"And?"

"Well, you seem to be back to normal," she says in jest.

A new normal, but yes, normal.

"I heard Jessie's living with her parents now."

I hope someday I can hear the name and not immediately cringe. Just another issue to add to my therapy list.

"Yep," I say, smacking the last letter, then sigh. "Presley met her mom for the first time last week."

"Oh. Wow. How'd it go?"

"Well, I was hoping Pres would scream at her for abandoning her and hate her as much as I do." I pause, shaking my head with a bitter laugh. "But no, Pres has a heart of gold. And she wants to get to know her mom."

"You okay with that?"

She knows the answer. Hell no. "I want what's best for Pres. This isn't going to be an instant relationship. Jessie's not a horrible person, she just makes the dumbest decisions. She's going to have to prove herself. All visits will be monitored, but if Pres wants to get to know her mom, she's old enough to tell me if something is wrong."

Addison coos. "My big brother is growing up."

I flip her off, and she laughs, quickly grabbing my finger so no one else can see.

Presley waves at me from on top of the play structure. My eyes zero in on her wrist to make sure the GPS watch is still there. I wave back.

"Why do we even come to the zoo if all they want to do is play on the jungle gym?" she mutters, leaning over to pull a tumbler out of her bag before taking a sip.

I nod in agreement. If it were up to me, I would've opted for something in the air conditioning. At least we scored a shaded spot. I almost bribed some women to move, but luckily for us, they were done.

"We could've taken them to a park and saved a lot of money," she says as Jett comes barreling over, his chunky cheeks rosy and glistening with sweat. He grabs his water bottle and starts guzzling down his drink like he's been lost in the desert for days, barely pausing to breathe.

"How's school, little man?"

Jett gives me a wicked grin and nods. "My teacher's hot."

I can't help my burst of laughter. That's my nephew. Little baller already.

"Jett, we've talked about this before," Addison says, play-fully kicking him.

"Hot for the teacher, huh?" I tease.

"Yep. She's my girlfriend."

I hold my hand up for him to give me a high-five.

Addison shakes her head and gestures for him to go play. "Go. Find a girlfriend your own age."

He spins on his toes and takes off, running to the slide, yelling for Presley.

"Please tell me she's not a crotchety old lady," I joke, settling back against the bench.

"Nope, she's young."

"She hot?"

Addison smirks. "Why? You interested?"

I sip my iced coffee and shrug, keeping my gaze on the kids. "*Maybe*. Maybe teachers are my thing."

Right now, I don't know what I'm interested in. Gracyn messed me up. I let one of the best things slip through my fingers.

Our court date is next week. *Finally*. The missed opportunity of what might have been hangs over me like a storm cloud. I'm ready for it so I can move on.

Addison zips up Jett's Spiderman lunch box. "Syd and I went to lunch last week, and I invited Jett's teacher. Of course, someone recognized Syd and snapped a picture. It's on Insta-gram. Look at it. If you're intrigued, let me know."

I chuckle, shaking my head. "I was kidding."

"Whatever. Look. Don't look. That's up to you."

As much as I'd like to say I'm willing to search for someone to fill the void Gracyn left, I'm not. Not even close. I can hardly wrap my mind around moving forward, let alone meeting someone new. Hell, I just hired a new nanny, and that was hard enough. You can bet your ass I made Stone handle the background process. Thoroughly. Down to her blood type.

With my outstretched arm resting on the back of the bench, I nudge her shoulder. "I've mastered the reverse psychology trick. Why are you trying to get me to look?"

She laughs out loud, stuffing her tumbler in her bag. "You're reading way too into this. But..." She nudges me back in the arm. "You're not getting any younger."

I smirk, raising a brow. "True, but at least I'm aging like fine wine."

"Definitely back to normal." She laughs.

IT'S ALWAYS night when my thoughts drift to her. The midnight hour, when it's silent and still, is what lures me back to our short time together. A couple of glasses of wine later, and I wonder if being a single dad is all I'll ever be.

I was fine being alone before that day in the coffee shop, but now there's this ache, this knot tightening in my chest every time she creeps into my head.

I miss the feeling of being with Gracyn.

The way she made me laugh. Or how I stared at the cute freckles on her nose and thought they were the sexiest thing on her. Fuck! I shake her memory out of my head, realizing that I need to date other people to move on. I need someone else to focus on.

My therapist agrees. Apparently, letting go takes work. Also, they don't hypnotize people for that, because I damn sure asked. I think about Jett's smile—the way it lit up when he was talking about his teacher.

Curiosity gets the best of me, and I grab my phone.

Nothing else.

I just want to see the woman my nephew is so enamored with. That's all. I pull up Instagram, scrolling through countless tagged photos of Sydney. I find one with Addison in it, taken recently at a restaurant, and my heart slams into my chest wall.

It can't be.

My pulse races as I pinch and zoom in on the image, making sure that my eyes aren't playing tricks on me.

Immediately, I fire off a text to Addison.

> Me: What the actual fuck?

> Addison: Guess you're interested?

CHAPTER 38

GRACYN

"So ... you're *still* married."

It's my new life's slogan.

I drop my head on the table with a moan. "Don't remind me. It's like the universe is playing some cruel joke on me. It's like the mistake that won't ever go away." I lift my head back up. "The judge is determined to make me stay married to him."

"It's just for another week," Charli says, trying to ease my torment.

"Yeah, but I thought I'd be a single woman today. I would've never made plans for tonight, knowing I could still be *technically* married. Ugh!"

When my mom called me yesterday morning with the news, I could've cried. She was certain it was a credible reason, given Brooks's attorney was there as well. Apparently, the judge had a legitimate conflict and rescheduled it. Just another seven days. Seven more days of being tied to him.

Charli let me wallow for a bit longer, then began to tell me about her new job she started this week working for FOX Sports as a freelance reporter. I welcomed the change of subject.

"Gray. Charli."

We slide off the barstools and make our way toward the counter. The packed coffeehouse on the corner of our street continues to get busier with each passing day now that school's started. Even on weekends. Why did I ever allow myself to get addicted? A few months ago, I didn't need a caffeine fix. In fact, I didn't even like coffee. Having to get up at five each morning and Charli introducing me to lattes, I've changed my tune. *And my budget.*

Charli continues her story about her first day on the field, animated as ever. "So, then, the quarterback runs over and has the nerve to question my understanding of football, all the while smiling at me. As if he was trying to flirt with me in some back-ward-ass kind of way. I bet he gets all the girls," she says, shaking her head in disbelief.

"What a presumptuous ass."

She shrugs, acting like it doesn't bother her, but it did. In her male-dominated field, where she's constantly fighting to prove herself while her counterparts waltz right into their position, yeah, it irks her. "I threw out some stats about the quarterback at Crimson who's been killing it and asked him how the team plans to beat him next week. I've heard rumors about how much he hates the guy. His smile turned sour real quick."

We have to squeeze in between people waiting for their order to make it to the counter. Charli grabs her coffee as I scan the names on all the cups.

"Excuse me. You called out 'Gray,' but I don't see my drink."

The barista glances at me from behind the espresso machine, an eye roll barely contained. "If it's not there, it'll be out soon."

"If it's not done, why would you call my name?" I respond, matching her tone. *There's no need to be rude, lady.* Her eyes flitter with irritation before asking me what I ordered. I rattle it off without hesitation because it's the same one every day. "Grande iced blond vanilla latte, almond milk, vanilla sweet cream cold foam."

"I definitely made that," the guy beside her responds, busy pulling shots for another drink. But neither of them makes a move to help me, both turning their backs as if I'm invisible.

"O-kay," I say, frustrated, gesturing to the ten other orders out. "It's not here."

"Someone took it," a woman who's standing close to the bar mentions as she's waiting. "I wanted to see who Gray was, you *know, the name and all,* and he did not disappoint." She places a hand on her heart and blows out a breath.

Someone took my drink?

No. *They stole it.*

Goose bumps trail down my legs as I turn around, my stomach flipping when my gaze locks with the one man I've been doing everything to avoid. He's leaning casually against the wall near the exit, a cocky smirk on his face as he holds up *my drink.* He looks a million times better than the last time I saw him. He looks good. It throws me back in time to the day we met. My chest tightens, and my heart hammers like I sprinted a mile. Hard and heavy.

Damn it. I hate that he still has this effect on me.

But I don't know what to do.

Time stands still, the noise fades, and we're the only two people around. I knew this moment would come since I see his sister all the time, but being five feet from him brings a rush of emotions I'm not ready to confront. Anger. Hurt. *Hope*?

Do I run to him? Or run *away* from him?

I once threw in his face that he needed to pull his big boy pants up and deal with the situation, so I tell myself the same thing. Sucking in a deep breath, I gather every ounce of courage I have and close the gap between us. I stop in front of him, and there's an awkward silence between us, neither of us sure what to say.

I force out a simple, "Hey."

"Hey."

I swallow hard. I've dreamed about the sound of his voice for months. But I started to push those thoughts aside. It's been three months. I was moving on. I even have a date tonight.

A date not with him.

Not that I want to go on it, but I was trying to prove to myself I was over Brooks. He's a friend from work who asked me out for drinks. A casual meeting between two friends. That's it.

Does he know about it? Is that why he's here right now, standing in front of me with that maddening smirk? He doesn't want me but can't stand the thought of me going on a date? That'd be typical of him. Possessive, yet distant. The thought pisses me off.

I lift a brow, pointing to the cup in his hand. "You stole my drink."

"And you *stole* my heart."

His words catch me off guard, and before I can react, he cups my cheek and pulls me to his lips. For a fleeting, electric second, I lose control. My body betrays me, melting into his touch. It craves his warmth, his taste, the intoxicating feel of him I've tried so hard to forget.

But my mind snaps to attention, throwing his words back in my face. *You were a mistake. You were never meant to be a part of my world.* The sting drowns the moment in cold, harsh reality.

I pull back, stepping away from him as I wipe the taste of him off my lips. My eyes water, and I blink the tears back. "Well, you shattered mine." I snatch the coffee from his hands, refusing to break eye contact so he hears me loud and clear. "Bye, Brooks."

I'm damn near close to swearing off coffee shops for the rest of my life as I rush out. This was a mistake. Moving here, thinking I could pick up the pieces of my heart and live this close to the man who broke it and be able to move on was nothing short of insane.

"Wait up!" Charli calls out, hurrying after me.

I duck between two buildings, my chest heaving, and spin around to face her. The anger boiling inside me erupts. "How dare he say I stole *his* heart! That jackass doesn't have a heart."

She nods silently, her expression cautious. Her lack of response only makes me more mad.

"You don't agree with me?" I challenge.

"I agree that he broke your heart."

I narrow my eyes at her. Whose side is she on? Because it's not mine at the moment. If it were, she'd be all up in arms with me, not nodding.

"*Annnddd*, I hate what he did to you. But, there were so many extenuating circumstances."

My mouth drops open. "Are you saying he had a right to treat me that way?"

"No. No." Charli shakes her head, holding up her hands in defense. "That is not what I'm saying. Well, shit, maybe I am." She winces, knowing she's stepped onto thin ice. "But you can't deny the attraction you two have. I just witnessed it." She points a finger at me like she's driving the point home. "I saw how you let go for a moment. You still have feelings for him."

I let out a groan, leaning against the red brick wall, and release a long, frustrated sigh. "How am I supposed to forget the hateful things he said to me?"

"It came from a place of desperation. He didn't mean it."

I shake my head, bitter laughter bubbling up inside my chest. "He also didn't apologize. Ever."

A voice cuts through the air behind us. "Then let me do it now."

CHAPTER 39

BROOKS

She stares at me with those wide, beautiful, uncertain green eyes that have haunted me every night for months. My chest heaves as I give her a moment to catch her breath, to process. Maybe I shouldn't have grabbed her and kissed her, but I couldn't stop myself. Not when she was standing right in front of me, so close the pull of her gravity took hold of my heart.

And then she pushed me away. *And left.*

Why is it that everyone wants something from me, except the one person who I'd give everything to?

Charli takes her drink from her hands and offers a small smile as she brushes past me, leaving us to ourselves. I stand at the entrance of the alleyway, not to intimidate her, but to stop myself from reaching out for her again. And, if I'm being honest, to make sure she doesn't run. Not that I want her to feel trapped, but dammit, we need to talk. Right here. Right now.

Addison gave me her address, and I parked outside her apartment building at 6 a.m. this morning, waiting. It bordered on being stalkerish, but desperate times call for desperate measures. Sure, I could've called her—*probably should have*—but I needed to see her face. Her eyes. I needed proof she lived here.

I followed Gracyn and Charli into the coffee shop, and when she ordered a drink, I took it as a sign. I knew what I needed to do. But now, standing here, face-to-face with her after she walked away from me, the words I'd rehearsed a million times catch in my throat.

I clear my throat. "I'm sorry. I should've done a lot of things differently." I drag my hand across my beard. "But I wasn't in the headspace to fix everything I messed up. Especially not with you. I was scared, but that doesn't excuse the way I treated you."

She blinks her long, endless lashes, staring at me, her expression unreadable. The tension between us is killing me.

Just say something.

She crosses her arms defensively over her chest and murmurs, "I'm not here for you."

Well, that fucking hurt.

I thought she'd be happy to see me. At the very least, *interested.* I figured she was afraid to reach out because of how things left off between us.

Not because she hated me.

What on earth possessed Addison to give me her info, knowing how she felt?

I crack my neck, nerves getting the best of me. My immediate reaction is anger, hot and sharp. The only woman that I've ever imagined myself with now lives a few miles away. The thousand-mile barrier isn't there anymore, and all she has for me is she's not here for me.

Why is she here then?

I draw in a calming breath, square my shoulders, and step to the side, giving her an exit. "Okay."

Her eyes widen, surprised by my callous reply. Not as much as I am by her dismissal, though. What the hell does she want me to say?

I throw my hands up. "Jesus Christ, Gracyn. Help me out a little here. I'm trying." Raw emotions I haven't mastered spill over. "So, if not for me, why are you here? You said you hated New York."

She stands her ground, stubborn as ever. "I never said I *hated it*. I received a job offer and thought it would be a great opportunity to get out of Vegas."

I narrow my eyes. "You already had a job. But you could have gone anywhere. Why *here*, Gracyn?"

She doesn't answer. Her gaze darts to the ground as she paces the narrow length of the alley. I watch her, knowing there's more than what she's saying. She can lie to herself all she wants, but she's here for me.

Finally, she stops and drops her arms to her sides. "I ... I don't know. Brooks, your life is a circus, and I question whether I belong in the ring."

A circus? Is that how she sees me? "It's not really."

She gives me an incredulous stare. "Oh, come on, Brooks," she snaps. "Reporters, cameras, the constant attention. Being with you means signing up for all that chaos. It means giving up my privacy, my peace, my normal life." She pauses and looks past me. "I'm surprised there's not a camera here right now."

I release a sigh, guilt heavy on my chest. The hell the reporters put her through wasn't fair. They never are. I wanted to protect her from them, to shield her from the storm, but once the story was out there, the narrative spiraled out of control. And it was not in her favor.

"I know it can seem that way," I admit, having become numb to it. "But it dies down when there isn't a story. They move on."

"It's not only that, Brooks. Well, it's *mainly* that because we'll always be in the public eye. I'm afraid you'll regret choosing me when I fail at being your wife. There's so many expectations that come with that job. I'm a first-grade teacher. I enjoy cutting and pasting things. Doing fun projects with crayons and paint and scrapbooking."

She's so much more than that.

"Stripped bare, I'm just a man who's in love with a woman who stole his coffee," I say softly, trying to express myself in the most vulnerable way. "Everything else is background noise. The only expectation I have is that you'll be you. Because you, Gracyn, are perfect."

The tension in her shoulders releases. She blinks, trying to hold back tears. "Geez, when you say things like that." She hiccups, pressing a trembling hand over her mouth.

I close the gap between us and wrap my arms around her waist and pull her close. Her warmth, her scent—it's everything I've missed and more. Her wide, tear-brimmed eyes meet mine, and I hold her gaze, refusing to let her look away.

"I've never been so certain about anything in my life," I tell her, my voice as certain as today is Saturday. "You are the one for me. Let me prove it to you. Let me prove to *my wife* that I will do anything to make this work."

She shakes her head slightly, a soft, disbelieving laugh escaping. "You had something to do with our postponement, didn't you?"

I let out a chuckle. "Like I said … *anything*."

"I can't believe you."

I wink down at her, biting my bottom lip. "He only gave me a week."

"Your confidence might actually be bigger than your ego," she teases, but then her expression softens as she studies me. "We're going to take this slow, Brooks."

"We'll take it as slow as you need." I stare at her, excitement and hope building in my chest. This is it. *Don't screw it up this time, Handley.* "Will you go on a date with me?"

"Date?"

"Isn't that the normal thing two people do when they first meet?"

She snorts. "We're way past the point." She takes a quiet moment, mulling it over. "What if I say we should get the annulment?"

I swallow hard, her words hitting me square in my ego. If that's what she needs to start over, I'll push my pride aside and give it to her. "If that's what you want. But it's not going to change the fact that I love you."

Her eyes search my face for sincerity. I hope she can hear my heart because it's drumming right now. *For her.*

I don't need her to say it back. She's here. That's proof enough for me. "But let's take the week, and we'll swing back to this then."

Her green eyes widen with a faint smile on her lips. "You think you'll win me over in a week, huh?"

Now that there aren't any barriers, I have no doubts this woman is mine. "It only took me a night to get you to marry me."

CHAPTER 40

GRACYN

Six months later

"How many times do you masturbate each week?"

Did he really just ask me that? I poke my head out the bathroom door, my jaw dropping when I find him lounging on my bed.

"Excuse me, sir, but that is personal."

He chuckles, waving a bullet vibrator in the air. "Just wondering how often this little thing gets a workout."

"You are so invasive." I rush over and take a leap over him to grab the toy.

He pulls it away, holding it out of reach. "I just want to know how often *my wife* is pleasing herself," he teases, his tone smug as hell.

"Wife?" I snort, planting my hands on his chest as I straddle him, giving up the tug-of-war. I choose my next words carefully, knowing how he'll react. "We fixed that problem months ago."

His eyes widen, and the toy slips from his fingers, landing with a soft thud on the ground. In one smooth movement, he flips me on my back and pins me beneath him. "Woman," he warns, tickling my side. "We don't make jokes like that."

I squirm under him, laughter spilling from my lips as I grab his hands, trying to fend him off. "Stop! You're horrible!"

He hates that I went ahead with the annulment. He understood, but nevertheless, he'd rather have kept me legally bound to him. But that marriage meant nothing to me. A year later, I still don't remember saying I do.

My actual wedding day will be one of the most important days of my life. *Remembering is most important.* I want to breathe in every second. All the excitement, the nerves, the overwhelming love when I see him for the first time, waiting for me. If we stayed married, the day wouldn't be the same. It'd only be a show.

"Well, we don't ask those types of questions either," I fire back, pushing him off me with a laugh. I roll over, snatching the toy off the floor and tucking it into the drawer he shouldn't have been snooping through in the first place.

He lies on the bed, sprawled out, arms tucked lazily behind his head, staring at me. His gaze trails me, heated and playful. "It's sexy," he says with a slow smirk, wagging his brows like a fool. "I kind of want to try it out now."

I snort, shaking my head as I cross the room. "Not going to happen. Your ex-wife needs to get ready for tonight."

He growls, pushing up on his elbows. "You love torturing me, don't you?"

I grab the curling iron out of the bathroom and wrap the

cord before tossing it in my overnight bag. "It's become my favorite hobby."

He scoots off the bed and saunters toward me with that lazy, confident stride that drives me crazy. God, I love him in a T-shirt and jeans. The fabric clings to his broad shoulders, and the dark denim sits low on his hips. My heart stutters as he closes the distance, stopping just short of touching me.

"You're playing with fire, sweetheart."

I lift my chin, licking my lips. His gaze flickers downward for a beat. "Maybe I like the heat."

"Maybe," he murmurs, as he runs his thumb over my wet bottom lip. "We skip tonight. And celebrate our year anniversary properly. I'll give you *all* the heat you want."

He steps closer, every sense I have on high alert.

Tonight marks a year since Vegas.

A year since my life flipped upside down.

"We can't," I exhale.

This is his event. *His charity*. There is no way he'd miss this. And I'd never ask him to.

His thumb lingers on my lip for a moment longer before he drops his arm.

"Who picked this night for the event?" he grumbles, wrapping his arm around my waist and pulling me into him.

I gasp, feigning shock. "What? The fortune teller you hired for your Christmas party last year didn't predict your *wedding night*?"

The fact that they had one is hilarious to me. Anabel told me about her over drinks one night, laughing so hard she had wine coming out of her nose. Apparently, the woman made the party very interesting. Predicting soulmates, dropping ominous warnings about death, and telling Jared he'd end up with two sets of twins. Anabel told me he fainted.

Brooks's low chuckle vibrates against my chest. "I'll have to file a complaint. She's not as psychic as advertised."

I lift a brow. "You never told me what she said to you."

"She was full of shit."

"Come on, tell me!"

With a slight shake of the head and a hint of amusement, he replies, "She told me I was going home with someone that night." He rolls his eyes. "*Her*, specifically."

I snort, biting back a laugh. "And? Did you?"

"Hell no! She was a nutjob."

I wrap my arms around his neck. "Glad to hear you have standards," I tease.

"Oh, they're sky-high. If only she could really predict the future, she would've tried stealing my drink. Apparently, that's the secret to persuade me to marry someone."

"If only I knew…"

"Gracyn," he growls again, his lips dropping, eyes narrowing. "Your next words better not be that you wouldn't have done it."

My expression softens, staring at the man who is my forever. I might joke with him, but there's not an ounce of regret.

I lift on my toes and give him a chaste kiss. "Never."

Brooks: Is my wife ready?

Me: Girlfriend

Brooks: Tomato, tomato.

I CHUCKLE, knowing what he's trying to say, but it looks funny because it's the same word.

Me: That's the same thing.

Brooks: Exactly.

I walked into that one. "Your brother is relentless," I say over to Addison, getting the finishing touches on her hair.

"I don't take responsibility for anything that man says or does." She tucks her hair behind her ear, much to the annoyance of the hairdresser. "But I've learned he gives one hundred percent to get his way."

I've learned.

I send him a text back.

Me: Almost.

I put the phone down on the makeshift vanity and walk over to where our dresses hang, running my fingers over the silky fabric, remembering the last time I wore a red dress. The day I served annulment papers. It seems like forever ago.

Charli pushes off the couch, tightens her robe, and strolls over. We were the first ones finished with hair and makeup.

"I *love* your hair up," she says. "It's so sophisticated."

Sydney's people are absolute magicians. When she told us her glam team would do our hair and makeup, I might have squealed. I usually keep my hair down, but she convinced me to sweep it into a low, loose bun with a few strands framing my face. There's a reason she's the professional and I'm not.

"And look at yours! It's never out of a ponytail." Her long blond hair flows free with soft curls. She bends down and glances in the mirror again.

"I feel so girly," she adds, running her fingers through the curls.

"Same," Addison calls out with a playful grunt, sending Sydney a scowl.

Sydney rented the penthouse suite at the hotel for us to get ready. There are certainly days I have to pinch myself that this is my life now. This bedroom could fit four king-size beds, with floor-to-ceiling windows that offer an awe-inspiring view of the city below.

The event is being held across the street, at the children's museum, which makes things easy. No traffic, no long drives. But there's still a red carpet with a million cameras ready to go off.

"Wait," Sydney calls out, blowing Zoe, her makeup artist, a kiss before jumping out of her chair. She rushes over to the table, pours six glasses of champagne, then hands one to everyone. "We have to make a toast before everyone gets dressed."

She pretends to throw a croissant at Addison when she sees her and the hairdresser fighting over a piece of hair. When she clears her throat, Addison looks over, amusement lighting her face. I'm thinking she's making her mad on purpose. Addison clearly isn't the pampered type.

"Cheers to new friends," she begins, raising her glass and flashing a warm smile at Charli and me. Her expression sharpens, and she turns to Addison. "Cheers to annoying ones." Her pointed stare makes Addison laugh. "Cheers to a wonderful night of raising money for some beautiful kids in need," she says, holding a hand to her heart. It's still surreal being in the same room as her. She's singing tonight at the gala, a night where people paid twenty thousand dollars per chair to attend. Of course, Brooks paid for mine and Charli's tickets. "And cheers to a night to never forget."

She winks at me, but before I have a chance to question what that was for, everyone lifts their glass and echoes, "Cheers." I follow suit, raising my glass.

"Um," Addison says, waving her phone in her hand. "Brooks texted and said he's on his way up."

"What?" I panic, looking down at my robe. Why is he rushing me? I pull the dress off the hanger and step into it. Charli helps me zip it up. I take a deep breath as the silky fabric settles against me. The one-sleeve, burgundy red gown is elegant yet sexy, hugging every curve.

"Wow," Charli murmurs, stepping backward, her eyes wide with approval. "Your man has fantastic taste."

I bite my lower lip, glancing at myself in the mirror. I'd asked Brooks to pick out my dress, and he absolutely did not disappoint. When he invited me to the gala, my insecurities got the best of me. I'd worried I wouldn't live up to the picture-perfect image expected in his world. I'd been a fool because that wasn't me at all, but I had already asked. The last six months, he's eased me into his world, but this is the first extravagant event I'll be attending. His event. So all eyes will be on us all evening.

Yay, me.

I spin, running my hands down the sleek sides of the dress.

Sydney whistles and then breaks out into a song, "Something about the way you're smiling..." Her voice lifts with a teasing grin as she continues to sing Jason Aldean's "Tonight Looks Good On You."

"…I just gotta tell you, baby, tonight looks good on you."

Caught between awe and surprise, I can't believe Sydney sang to me. I want to tell her to keep going, but a knock at the door stops me.

The door opens, and Graham, Sydney's manager, peeks his head in. "Hey, multiple sweet cheeks," he announces, then finds me. "Your date is here." He turns to Sydney and points sternly. "And *you* … stop singing. You've got a concert in an hour. Save your voice."

She salutes him and flops in her chair with an exaggerated flair, mumbling "bossy."

I grab my clutch and double-check I have everything I need. Lipstick? Phone? Nerves? Check. Check. Check.

Turning to the mirror one last time, the thought of Brooks in the other room sends a flutter through me that I can't quite calm.

"Love you guys," I say, blowing kisses toward the room. "See y'all soon."

Brooks turns at the soft click of the door behind me, his posture straightening as our eyes meet. He was mid-conversation with Max by the windows, but his words died on his lips. His gaze travels at a slow pace, taking every inch of me in from head to toe. I catch a hitch in his breath, making my heart skip a beat. He looks drop-dead gorgeous in his tailored tux, the epitome of power and elegance, his presence commanding, yet effortless.

Graham sneaks a quick peek from the couch but continues tapping away on his laptop with extreme focus, as though nothing short of an earthquake, or *Sydney singing*, could pull him away.

Max clears his throat, tapping Graham on the shoulder.

"We're just gonna, uh, check on security. Make sure everyone's ready."

"Right," Graham says, snapping his laptop shut and standing. They head for the door, leaving Brooks and me in the charged silence of the room.

"Wow," Brooks mouths, closing the space between us. "You look exquisite. Breathtaking."

"Thank you," I say, running my fingers down his silk lapel. "I like this tux. Especially on you."

His eyes darken, the intensity of them sending a wave of heat through me. His hands settle on my waist, his fingers pressing in just enough to make my pulse quicken. "Are you sure we have to go to this thing?"

"Considering you're one of the hosts, that would be a yes. Are your parents and Presley on their way?"

"Mm-hmm," he hums, ignoring my attempt to cool things down. He leans in and pulls in a whiff of my perfume, and his lips graze my bare neck, leaving a featherlight kiss that sends a shiver down my spine. "Damn," he murmurs, pulling back enough to meet my eyes. "You're going to hypnotize me all night."

I bite my lip, the blush deepening. "You're impossible."

"Impossibly lost without you."

My eyes soften at his words. "God, I love you," I say, pressing my palm against the scruff of his beard.

He captures my fingers, his thumb brushing over my knuckles as he steps back. My brows knit together, wondering what he's doing. Until he slips his hand into his pocket, then drops to one knee.

Is he...? My heart races. My free hand flies to my mouth as my eyes widen in shock.

"Brooks..." I manage a whisper, my voice barely audible.

He looks up at me, his expression certain with unwavering love, and holds up a large sparkling diamond ring that catches the light just right. Tears prickle my eyes as I stare down at him.

This is really happening.

"There's not a day goes by that I didn't think about this moment," he begins, his voice thick with emotion. "I know I'm far from perfect, but you make me a better man. With you by my side, my world feels complete."

His gaze locks on mine, unguarded and raw, and my breath catches in my throat.

"When you thought I wanted to own the woman I married, I want you to always remember this. *This very moment.* When I'm here, on bended knee, in front of you, asking, *no, begging,* you to marry me. To choose me. I could never own you, Gracyn. You have it backward. You own me. You have since the second you turned around in that coffee shop."

My heart's about to burst as his words wrap around me like a warm blanket. I sniff, smiling obnoxiously at the man in front of me.

"Gracyn," he says, holding my trembling left hand, "will you marry me? Will you be my wife forever?"

My heart screams the answer before I can say it aloud. My lips part, a soft gasp escaping as I nod my head. "Yes," I murmur. "Yes, I'll marry you."

His eyes light up, and his grin spreads wide as he slides the ring onto my finger, and I can't stop staring at it. It's stunning, delicate but bold. A perfect fit in every way.

He jumps up and lifts me in his arms, twirling me around, laughter bubbling out of me.

"She said yes!" he yells.

Doors swing open from both directions, and cheers and applause fill the room. I'd forgotten we weren't alone. The girls swarm me to check out the ring. The guys pat Brooks on the back, congratulating him. Before I can catch my breath and let my head catch up to my heart, Presley bursts into the room.

"Am I late?" she exclaims, tackling me with a hug. She picks up my left hand and lets out a high-pitched squeal, jumping up and down. "You said yes!"

"Of course I did, sweet girl." I hit the jackpot for a step-daughter. You always hear those horror stories about raising kids that aren't your own, but Presley already feels like she's mine. I spend as much time with her as I do with Brooks, and we've even created our own special date nights. They're always filled with fun mommy-daughter adventures.

Brooks's parents come through the open door, and right behind them are … my parents.

"Mom? Dad?" I gasp, my voice filled with shock and delight.

My mom rushes over and gives me a big hug, followed by my dad. "Brooks sent us tickets," my mom explains, a knowing smile spreading across her face. "And we couldn't miss this." Her eyes drop to my hand.

I adoringly look at Brooks. My heart is so full, it's hard to breathe. He stands there, looking calm, unbothered by all the chaos, and winks at me with easy confidence.

Why is he so damn sexy?

"Well, it's about time," Addison says, breaking the moment as she gives Brooks a quick hug.

"Right?" he replies. "Now she can stop arguing with me about calling her *my wife*."

I arch a brow, unable to resist teasing. "It's *fiancée*, now," I correct, adding a playful lilt to my voice.

He drops his head, letting out a low laugh. "Stop making up names," he huffs, still grinning, wrapping his arms around me. He lowers his mouth, placing a soft kiss on my lips. He lets it linger until my dad clears his throat.

"Sorry," Brooks says, pulling back, his hazel eyes flaring with affection. "I can't resist the taste of forever."

"Eww," Presley moans, slapping a hand over her eyes. "Is this what I have to deal with the rest of my life?"

The room erupts in laughter.

I have found my forever in this room.

And who knew all I had to do was steal a cup of coffee?

Epilogue

Gracyn

THE LETTERS

"Is this thing on?" Charli wags her brows at me as she clutches the mic in one hand and a champagne flute in the other.

I lean over to Brooks, stifling a laugh. "Ignore her. Nothing she says is true."

"As the maid of honor, I have a duty to say, *you're welcome.* But we'll circle back to that later. First, let's start with the obvious. How y'all met. Has everyone heard this story?"

My face heats as I drop my head, silently pleading for her to stop. Nobody's heard this, and she knows it.

"So," she continues, flashing a mischievous grin, "there we are, grabbing my afternoon coffee fix, and this one over there" —she tilts her glass toward me—"let's just say, she thought she was part of Ocean's 8. If you've seen the movie, you understand. If not, it's worth a watch." Everyone chuckles. "But in a bold move, she decides to steal his coffee right off the counter."

Gasps, laughs, and cheers ripple through the room as I bury my face into Brooks's arm. I'm going to kill her later.

Brooks leans down and whispers, "You were the sexiest thief ever."

"Right?" she exclaims, throwing her hands in the air dramatically as the crowd roars in laughter. "For a second there, I was afraid I was going to jail for being an accomplice." She pauses, waiting for the room to settle before continuing, "But then he told her 'Gray was his favorite color,' and she didn't throw his drink in his own face. That's when it became clear he was a keeper."

The cheers shift to a chorus of "aww."

"And apparently, she thought so too, because next thing I know, my girl decides she doesn't just want his coffee, she wants his last name."

I gasp, swatting at her leg as I burst out into laughter. "That was his idea," I protest, my cheeks flaming as the room erupts.

"But people … don't try this at home. Because *I did*. Yep, I tried to steal a hot guy's coffee. I thought maybe this was the new way to meet a man, you know, like Tinder, but with caffeine." She shakes her head dramatically. "Nope. All it got me was banned from the coffee shop for a year."

I tilt my head. Huh? Is that why she always says no when I mention Brewed Awakening? I giggle just imagining her trying it.

"But with love, sometimes you can't see what's in front of you. You need a little help." She picks up an envelope that I didn't notice was there earlier. "Jump ahead to the first court date, and the judge told Gray that he received two letters, pleading with him not to grant the annulment. Let's just say they worked."

I had totally forgotten about those.

"Um? What is she talking about?" Brooks asks, glancing at me with a raised brow.

Oh, guess I forgot to tell him, too.

"Gray's mom thought this would be a great time to share them." She pulls out two letters from the envelope and waves them in the air. "We'll let the person who wrote this do the honors." Flashing a wide grin, she holds it up in the air. The DJ plays a drumroll as Brooks and I exchange a puzzled glance, scanning the room.

Suddenly, Presley jumps up in her chair beside Brooks. He reaches for her to steady her. Wait. *Presley wrote a letter*? How? I glance at Brooks, and he looks equally stunned as he stares at his daughter. She giggles. Charli, grinning from ear to ear, strides over and hands her the letter and mic.

"It was me," she squeals into the mic. Claps and cheers ring out.

Charli gestures to the crowd to quiet as she stands behind Presley, placing a steady hand on her hip. "Remember, keep it close to your mouth," she whispers to her.

Presley nods excitedly as she opens the letter. Tears already gather in the corner of my eyes, watching her. I lean my head on Brooks's shoulder.

"I want to thank Aunt Jade for helping me," she starts and points to Jade at the front table. Jade blows her a kiss back. "Dear Judge, thank you for taking my letter. You will see my daddy soon. His name is Brooks Handley. He's pretend married to Gracyn. Sorry, I don't know her last name." Her voice lowers at the last part, getting a laugh from the crowd.

She straightens the paper and continues. "But you don't know this, I have always wanted a mommy. A mommy to do fun things with me, or a mommy to hug me when she picks me up from school, or a mommy to lie with me when I don't feel good."

Brooks sniffles beside me, quickly wiping a tear running down his cheek. It's useless to fight my own tears as they stream down.

"I want a mommy like Gracyn. She helped me find my doggy, and she's really nice, and she likes to dance. I really like her, and so does my dad. He gets this weird smile when he talks about her. That's how I know. Please don't let them get an—" She hesitates and looks back at Charli over her shoulder.

"A-nul-ment," Charlie pronounces in her ear.

"Annulment," she repeats slowly. "You can even tell Santa, because I'm sure you know him, he doesn't need to get me any presents this year if you let me have Gracyn as a mommy. Love, your new best friend, Presley."

The room erupts in soft laughter, sniffles, and applause, but all I can focus on is Brooks pulling Presley into his arms, holding her tight. She turns and throws her arm around my neck, drawing me into a tight hug.

"I love you, sweet girl," I cry, my voice cracking. "Thank you for accepting me into your family."

"I love you, Gray," she cries with us. She started calling me Gray because that's what all my friends called me, and I love it.

"I should've let the other person go first." Charli chuckles, dabbing under her eyes. She hands me a tissue, and I blot my tear-streaked face.

We let go of Presley and sit back down. She nestles in between Brooks's legs as we watch Charli wave the next letter in the air. "I'd hate to be the person to follow that," she teases. "But, I guess I'll have to."

My eyes widen, and I slap her legs again. "Charli!" She acted so surprised in court when the judge announced he wouldn't grant us an annulment. And she was partly to blame.

"Yeah, yeah, it was me. Unfortunately, mine is not as good as Presley's, but here it goes." She clears her throat. "Dear Sexy Judge, do you really wear nothing under your robe?"

Oh. My. God. I put a hand over my mouth to stifle my loud laugh.

"I'm kidding. I did not write that, but you all know damn well we've all wondered." She takes a breath, controlling her laughter. "All right. For real this time. Dear Judge. This is probably one of the weirdest letters you've ever received for an annulment case. But please hang in there with me. This is about our friends Gracyn and Brooks Handley.

"You know the moments when you make impulsive choices like eating gas station sushi or, I don't know, getting married to a guy after a few shots of tequila? Yeah, we've all been there. At first, I thought this was one of those moments. But then something unexpected happened.

"Gracyn's smile got brighter like she was suddenly living in a toothpaste commercial. And despite her extensive lists of reasons why it wouldn't work (some valid, some questionable), you could tell her heart and head were in an epic tug-of-war. She can deny it all she wants, but she's falling for him.

"I know what you're thinking, why can't they keep dating after the annulment? Sigh. Because Gracyn is stubborn. You're familiar with her! She'll see the annulment as this cosmic sign that they weren't meant to be. Meanwhile, Brooks's ego will take a big hit, and the next thing, they'll both be miserable, second-guessing everything, and stuck wondering, 'What if the judge hadn't given us an annulment?' for the rest of their lives.

"So please, Judge, give them the time they need to see what the rest of us already figured out. That this isn't just a drunken mistake, it's the first chapter of their love story.

"And if it doesn't work out, then we did the best that we could. But honestly?"

She pauses, glancing down at me with a soft smile as tears spill freely from both our eyes.

"I'm betting on these two," she says, folding the letter.

I jump up and pull her into my arms. "I love you! Thank you. You are the bestest friend on this earth."

Brooks gives her a hug next and whispers something in her ear that I didn't catch over all the applause. She blots her tears again and holds the mic to her mouth.

"And here we are, full circle. You're welcome to the best two people here." She holds her flute up high. "Here's to years of happiness and endless cups of coffee."

When I look at Brooks, an overwhelming wave of love hits me. I was stupid to not see what was right in front of me. He winks at me, and in a heartbeat, his hand wraps around my neck, pulling me into a kiss that's all fire and feeling—raw and passionate.

As someone shouts, "Get a room," we break apart, laughing and breathless.

He rests his forehead against mine. "*My wife.* I love you," he whispers. "Are you ready for chapter two of our wedded chaos?"

I smile, rubbing my thumb across his bottom lip, wiping off the gloss. "I'm ready for forever."

Also by Tina Saxon

TWIST OF FATE Trilogy

Aiden and Addison

Fate Hates

Fate Heals

Fate Loves

Twisted Wings

Max and Sydney

Blinding Echo

Kase and Ellie

Wild Distortion

Ryker and Aspen

Wedded Chaos

Brooks and Gracyn

Deadly Ruse

Paxton and Kali

Join my reader group to get to know me and get early access to what
I'm working on! Saxon's Sirens on Facebook

FOLLOW ME!

Facebook

Instagram

Website

TIK TOK

ACKNOWLEDGMENTS

Who do I want to thank? YOU! If you're reading this, you are the reason I write! Whether you've been with me since the beginning, or you took a chance on me now, you are a kick ass human being and I appreciate you more than words can say!

The other day, someone asked me how long it takes me to write a book. My answer? It depends what year it is. Because, holy shit, these last five years have been crazy! And peri-menopause hasn't helped at all! But no matter how long it has taken me, it's the people cheering from the sidelines that have kept me going. I hear you!

Writing this book has been a roller coaster ride. It took me four years to get it right, but the end result is one of my favorite couples. I hope you loved Brooks and Gracyn as much as I did writing them!

And behind every writer, is an incredible team. To my sister and best friends—Lori, Tiffany & Traci—thank you will never be enough. You ladies are always there for me and I love y'all!

Ellie and Imogen, thank you for polishing my words, and taking out a few (or a ton) misplaced comma's. Hang, thank you for creating the perfect cover again and patiently waiting four years for me to release this beauty!! It's been hard to keep this under wraps that long! Kate, my special edition cover queen, thank you for listening to all my requests (quirks and all) and giving me exactly what I want. I know you love me!!

Bloggers, ARC readers & influencers, thank you for spreading the word about Wedded Chaos. Time is invaluable these days, and the fact that you chose to spend yours reading, reviewing, and sharing this book means the world to me. I'm endlessly grateful that you're a part of this journey with me!

Last, but definitely not least, my husband—who's an absolute badass at his job, making it possible for me to do what I love and bring you all the words. I couldn't do this without you, babe! I love you!

See y'all in the next book!!

Xo
    Tina

www.ingramcontent.com/pod-product-compliance
Lightning Source LLC
Chambersburg PA
CBHW072119250626
47159CB00007B/2497